Guntl

Book 1

Lynn Donovan

Copyright

All rights reserved
Gunther City Mail-Order Brides Series© Lynn Donovan 2017, 2023
The Blacksmith's Daughter© Lynn Donovan 2017, 2023

All rights reserved under the International and Pan-American copyright Conventions. No part of this book may be reproduced or transmitted in any form or by any means, electronic or mechanical, including photocopying, recording, or by any information storage and retrieval system, without permission in writing from the publisher.

This is a work of fiction. Names, places, characters, and incidents are either the product of the author's imagination or are used fictitiously, and any resemblance to any actual persons, living or dead, organizations, events, or locales is entirely coincidental.

Warning; the unauthorized reproduction or distribution of this copyrighted work is illegal. Criminal copyright infringement, including infringement without monetary gain, is investigated by the FBI and is punishable by up to 5 years in prison and a fine of $250,000.

This book was written by a human and not Artificial Intelligence (A.I.).
This book cannot be used to train Artificial Intelligence (A.I.).

Cover Copyright © 2023 Atlantis Book Design
Editing by Cyndi Rule
Continuity Editor: Amy Petrowich
Special Beta Read: Sandy Sorola

Series Introduction

August 1889, four months after the initial land run in Gunther City, Oklahoma, six men are ready to take a wife. Acting in conjunction with an affiliated church in Portland, Maine, they write a letter describing what they want in a wife.

Six women in Portland, Maine select the letter that suits them the best. Their church arranges their travels, thanks to a generous donation by a mysterious man named Nugget Nate who visited the town after a "calling" brought him to Maine. The girls board a train going to Oklahoma as mail order brides.

The six men anxiously meet the train and their new brides, except seven brides step off the train. A last-minute addition muddies the waters a bit, but the boarding house has room. Will the matches line up to be right for the couples? Can Widow Drummond keep order with so much amore in the air? Who will marry first? Only time will tell.

These are their stories.

Introduction

The Blacksmith's Daughter

An experienced Blacksmith's daughter desperate to escape the men who murdered her father, a blacksmith wounded by an act of kindness and cannot fulfill his obligations.

Minnie Smith's father was murdered, leaving her desperate and alone in Portland, Maine. Traveling with a group of mail order brides who have always disliked her is challenging enough, but with no groom at the end of her journey, will she find happiness or hopelessness? Samuel Knight came to Gunther City, Oklahoma to build a life in the town that was established with a Land Run. As the town's only blacksmith, he's done very well until one heroic act puts his career in jeopardy and him in a wheelchair. What will he do when he discovers his shop has been broken into and the intruder turns out to be the lovely mail-order bride who came here without a groom to meet her?
This Blacksmith's Daughter knows what she's doing at the forge, will he let her save his business and follow his heart to make her his wife?

DEDICATION

In memory of GW Canning, the coolest cousin a girl could ever have.

LYNN DONOVAN

Chapter One

"Whatsat?" Minnie sat straight up in bed. Something woke her, but what? She called out quietly, "Poppa?" Eerie silence crept through the house.
She pulled a dressing gown over her nightgown and rushed to her father's room. "Poppa?"
Empty! His bed had not been slept in. Where could he be?
She hurried down the stairs at an angle, like always, to be sure her large feet landed on each step without her tripping, and ducked her head so she didn't knock herself out as she passed the upstairs header beam. Quickly she scanned the open room.
The hearth was grey and cold. The enamelware coffee pot sat on the stove. A burned smell filled the room. His hand-thrown coffee mug sat on the cupboard. Poppa was nowhere.
Despair filled her heart. He had stayed up after she went to bed, but why? Where was he now?
She ran out on the stoop, searching the yard. It was a new moon. She could hardly see to the street. The stars were beautiful with the moonless night, but she

paid it no never mind. A rattle and a thud from the rock blacksmith shop caught her attention. Did Poppa fall into the metal tools and crash to the dirt floor? She leapt from the stoop and ran toward the shop.

The chickens squawked and flapped in their coop as she ran around to the back of their clapboard house. It startled the wits out of her, but then she kept running to the shop doors. They stood slightly ajar.

"Give me the gold!" an unfamiliar voice growled.

"Never. It ain't your's," her father snarled in his heavy New England sing-song accent.

"Look Smithy, we're calling in your debts, donchaknow? You're gonna pay us in full with that gold." Another man's voice.

Who could that be with her poppa?

"Over my dead body, right there."

She knew that tone. Poppa was angry and hell-bent stubborn. He wasn't going to give them a plug nickel, let alone any gold. What gold did he have anyway?

Minnie shoved through the doors. A flash blinded her and a loud pop deafened her ears. She closed her eyes and turned her head to recover from the blast, blinking and blinking again, trying to regain her sight.

"Graves! Dammit!" one of the men shouted, but it sounded like it was down the street, inside another building. "I told you not to kill 'em 'til we got what we came for! You idiot! Now we gotta find it ourselves, donchaknow?"

The smithy shop slowly came out of the darkness as her eyes adjusted. Large boots stuck out beyond the forge.

"Poppa!" She ran forward but something slammed into her gut. She bent over with the pain and fell to her knees, gasping for air that would not come.

A man stood before her. Blazing, angry eyes met Minnie's. The devil was behind those bloodshot eyes.

Her heart pounded against her chest.

"Well, what have we here" —he strolled closer to her — "the blacksmith's daughter. I'll bet you know where your pappy hid my gold, Ayah?" He too bore the New England sing-song accent she knew so well.

Minnie mustered every ounce of strength she possessed. She closed her eyes and willed her lungs to function. Air seeped in and she let it ebb and flow. She forced her trembling legs to hold her as she crawled to stand to her full height. Her chin jutted out with dignity. "I have… no idea… what you're… talkin' 'bout."

A man to her right, moved toward her. With all her might, she plowed her shoulder into his gut. He went down. She turned and rammed her elbow into the man behind her. Air escaped his lungs. She turned to find the third man. Something hard slammed into the back of her head.

The room swooned away into a darkening tunnel. Everything went black.

BAM! Preacher William Gunther slammed his gavel on the table. "I hereby call the Gunther City Town Council meeting to order!"

Mary Etta winced. "William, my love, do you have to be so loud?"

William laid his gavel down gently and patted her age-spotted hand. "I'm sorry, wife. I rather like my gavel." He turned a jovial grin back to his council members. "Now" —he cleared his throat— "the first order of business is Old Business."

He reached for the gavel, but Mary Etta laid a gentle hand across his. "I second that."

"Mary Etta, you don't second my calling the first order of business."

"Oh, sorry dear." She waved a dismissive hand at him. "Go on then."

Sheriff George Wilson Gunther, known to everyone as GW, smirked. "Mom, please."

Samuel Knight, the town blacksmith, clenched his jaw and raised exasperated eyebrows.

Mary Etta lifted stern eyes to him.

His silence spoke volumes of his irritation.

She dipped her pen, prepared to take minutes.

"Now, we got six mail order brides arrivin' soon, Lord willin', and I believe the correspondence between the brides-to-be and our bachelors has been going well?"

"Oh! That reminds me!" Mary Etta dropped her pen. "Mrs. Forrest, I got the Rocking F Ranch's mail." She reached into her apron pocket and pulled a bundle of envelopes. She leaned across the table to hand them to Gladys. "Looks like your boys each got a letter from their betrotheds. How excitin' to be gettin' three daughters-in-law."

William glared at her. "Wife, just because you're the Post Mistress, does not mean you can conduct your business durin' mine."

"Sorry, dear." She dipped her pen, poised to continue dictations.

Sam fidgeted in his seat and audibly sighed. William raised his eyebrows but didn't say anything to him. William dipped his head toward Widow Francine Drummond, and then slid his gaze to his daughter-in-law, Wilma. "Ladies, how are the preparations going for our brides?"

Wilma tugged at her ear lobe. "Um, yeah, well, Mrs. Cambridge and I have been fixin' up six of Widow Drummond's twelve boarding rooms, three on the second floor and three on the third, so the ladies have a choice."

Wilma smiled at Dahlia Cambridge sweetly. She returned her gaze to the chairman. "Mother Gunther generously donated her quilting scraps, with which Franny" —she tilted her head toward the widow, who visibly cringed— "and Angie Drummond have braided rag rugs for each room."

Mayor Jack Drummond huffed. "That's all she's been doing these last two weeks. Braidin' rugs. A man could starve to death."

The widow yanked her ever present wooden spoon from her apron pocket and shook it at the mayor. "Mayor Drummond, these brides are important to our town… besides, you could stand to skip a meal… or two."

The blacksmith sighed heavily. "Can we get on with this?"

Preacher Gunther glared at Sam and then tapped his gavel. "Now, ladies, let's get back to the business at hand."

Widow Drummond swallowed and lifted her chin. "I been learnin' them boys table manners, no offense Gladys, and discussing the proper ways to court a lady."

Gladys lifted cool eyes to meet the widow's. "None taken, Franny. I'm certain my three boys know how to sit a table proper. You must be referring to the other three bachelors needing *learning*."

Widow Drummond puckered her mouth and lifted one eyebrow.

Dahlia Cambridge cleared her throat. "When Newt order those bolts of gingham, I thought of you, Franny, and our new brides."

Widow Drummond closed her eyes and cringed. "Don't. Call. Me. Franny!"

Dahlia shrugged. "I'm sorry, Gladys calls you Franny, I just thought—"

The widow gritted her teeth. "That's 'cause she's knowed me since our Nebraska days and" —her voice deteriorated into tear clotted emotion— "refuses to respect an old widow woman's dignity."
Dahlia continued, "Oh, you're not that old. Besides, you-know-who left a generous fund in the bank to ease the burden of getting the boarding house fixed up for a Bride House."
Mary Etta Gunther bowed her head as if in prayer. "Yes, God Bless Nugget Nate and his beautiful bride."
Gladys's eyes widened. "Mary Etta! He's supposed to be an *anonymous* benefactor!"
"Who cares!" Sam re-crossed his legs.
Dahlia glared at Sam. "And… Newt has ordered an assortment of the latest bolts of fabrics for the brides to make themselves new dresses."
Doc Savage raised his hand. "I would like to examine all the girls before they" —he glanced at the council members— "get too settled."
Widow Drummond yanked out her spoon and shook it at the doc. "You mean before they meet their intended? How you gonna do that? Every one of those boys are gonna meet that train. You gonna

jump on board and give them a look see, afore they come out on the platform?"

"Oh, good God!" Sam shifted and sighed as heavily as he could. "Can we get this over with?"

Doc flustered. "No, Mrs. Drummond. I'm just saying, we should err on the side of cautious."

"Fine." Widow Drummond pointed her wooden spoon at him. "But I won't have you strippin' 'em down neked like they were going up on an auction block. They's proper girls. Sister Robertson has assured me personally."

"I'm sure they are" —Doc swallowed with difficulty— "and that wasn't what I was implying. They will have travelled in less than perfect conditions. I just want to make sure they are healthy and our men aren't going to end up widowers." His smile was warm and calming.

She glared at him a moment, and then gingerly she put her spoon back in her apron pocket.

Gladys glared at her husband. They exchanged a look and Pete turned to the council. "We got the hands workin' on the big barn for the First Dance. Homer and his son has agreed to play the fiddle and that bass thing." A strained smile drew his face taut.

Sam crossed his legs and hung an elbow across the back of his chair. "Oh wonderful. Hate to have a dance without a fiddler."

Wilma pursed her lips. "Now, Sam."

"Well!" He shrugged. "What do I care? How does any of this help me? I won't be attendin', don't got no bride comin', don't want one. Can't be gone from my forge for an entire evenin' no how. These meetin's are bad enough on my business. I'll never get caught up!"

William cocked his head back. Thirty years of being a preacher had prepared him for hostility such as this. He spoke softly. "The council is your voice in important decisions for our new little town."

"I know that, Preacher Gunther, but six homely, desperate women comin' here to catch a man, ain't gonna affect my business one way or 'nother."

Chapter Two

A shiver racked over Minnie's limbs, bringing her to consciousness. A high-pitched whining sound filled her ears. Gradually, muffled voices and heavy boots clomping around surfaced out of the buzz.

She turned her head to hone in on what she was hearing, but a white-hot stab of pain slammed into the base of her head, causing her stomach to reel. Her shoulders hurt and her wrists burned. She blinked her eyes open.

She was in her poppa's house, tied to a table leg. Those three men were pacing the wooden planked floor. She looked down and gasped. Her dressing gown gaped open, revealing her thin cotton nightgown and bare legs. Modesty flooded her mind.

"Poppa!" She looked around, frantic to find him. "What did you do to my poppa?"

She held back tears, not wanting to give them the satisfaction.

One of the men stopped abruptly, bending down to look into her face. "Jet, she's awake."

It was Alford Graves. A flash of memory sparked in her mind. *Graves!* Another man had cursed at him in her poppa's shop. Right after the blast.

She shook her head slowly, wincing with the nauseating pain. Then his words came back to her. "I told you not to kill 'im 'til we got what we came for!"

"You killed my poppa!" she growled through gritted teeth, her voice deep, unfeminine. The morning light pouring through the tatted curtains her mother had made, stoking the pain in her head. She squinted in an effort to bring Graves into focus, then rolled her eyes to the other man. Hayden Gray. The third man they called Jet, must be Jet Butterfield. Together they ran the Portland Gambling Parlor and Pool Hall on the other end of town. Jet was the boss, but they each had a stake in the business.

What did they want with her Poppa… or her?

The Gunther City Council adjourned with Preacher Gunther giving the gavel a final slam, and Mary Etta fussing at him for it. Mayor Jack Drummond stood at the Town Hall entrance and shook each member's hand as they exited as if he were campaigning. The townsfolk were no longer bothered by his absent little finger. Rumors had run its tide that Widow Drummond had smashed his pinky with that wooden spoon, when he was a boy, for some infraction, but the truth was, he had been playing with her wash tub wringer and crushed his little finger between the wooden rollers. It was no wonder people called them a mangler! The only thing their Doc back home could do was amputate to save his hand.

He thanked the members for serving on the committee and contributing in their own way to make this first arrival of Mail Order Brides a successful experience for everybody.

The smithy shook the mayor's hand with a bone-crushing handshake and hurried out the door. His shop was across Broad Street and to the south three store bays. It was the last building before the open prairie. Katherine Turner walked briskly beside him and bid him good day as she turned to enter her saloon.

The embers had died down while he served his duties on the town council, and his charcoal bin was low. He stoked the embers with what he had.

The only permanent black couple in Gunther City, Sampson and Emma Cherry, made their living by cutting down dead trees, chopping them down to size, and then splitting it for fuel-size logs. The townsfolk bought or bartered a daily supply from the couple who lived a mile east of Broad Street on the prairie in a sod dugout near a dry creek.

They had just passed the cross street everyone called Division Street, although it was no more than a gap between the north and south buildings. Mr. Cherry always started on the west side of Broad Street at the stables and made his way up that side of the town, turning at the train depot, then back down the east side, reaching Sam's shop last.

Samuel waited for the Cherry's to reach his back doors. He'd load up on some hardwoods and spend the rest of the afternoon making more charcoal. He paid Mr. Cherry with farrier services for their mule and wagon iron work as needed.

A snake slithered between the mule's hooves and spooked the usually subdued equine. The mule's dark eyes were framed by huge whites, and she reared against her yoke, breaking the leads. Emma tried to control the beast's outburst by holding taut on the reins, but Bessy's fear of snakes overrode her training and she lunged forward. Mr. Cherry dropped his armful of firewood he had been carrying into the Drummond Trading Company: Hardware, Guns, Pistols, and Ammunition store, and ran after the wagon. Mrs. Cherry screamed as the runaway wagon careened down the back street with her hanging onto the bench for dear life.

Samuel saw the out-of-control mule and stood with a broad stance, determined to stop her. The hysterical mule rammed into the smithy, dragging him with her. He lost his grip on her harness and heard the bones in his legs snap just the jenny plowed over his body. The wagon passed over him, leaving him lying in its dusty wake, unable to move. Nausea lapped at the back of his throat as he realized the pain coursing from his legs and hips. The mule's hooves trampled the broad man as if he were a sapling.

He closed his eyes and willed the agony to leave his body. Instead, his stomach heaved and vomit spewed into the dirt. The involuntary movement intensified the torture in his legs and hip, engulfing him in a ring of darkness. Mr. Cherry's voice, deep and muffled, faded into the darkness that took over his body.

Chapter Three

"I need water." Minnie swallowed against an arid throat.

"Sure, Sweetheart." Jet grinned. A gold tooth sparkled, which made him look even more evil. "Get the lady a drink of water, Graves."

Butterfield's breath sickened her already upset stomach. She closed her eyes and swallowed the bile. Her heart filled with hate for this man. Slowly, she opened her eyes and glared with as much disgust as possible. Under no circumstances did she want him to misconstrue her feelings at that very moment. A tin cup touched her lips and she drew the cool liquid into her parched mouth. Her dry throat refused to accept it causing her to cough and spew the water into Jet's face.

"You bitch!" He slapped her, hard. "You done that on purpose."

Tears stung her eyes, but she refused to allow them to spill. Her glare hardened into steel as she clenched her teeth. Then she touched her tongue to the cut on her lip and drew it into her mouth. "What do you want, you… murderer?"

Jet leaned back. The anger slipped from his face like wax runs down a candle. His mouth twitched and then curved up into a smile. A belly deep laugh barreled out of his gut. The other two chuckled but didn't seem to know why they were amused.

Minnie maintained her death-wish stare which she hoped penetrated Jet's soul. She wanted him to dream about the hate in her heart right now and wake up in a cold sweat. She hoped, when he killed her, she could haunt him to the point that he would go insane. She visualized him lying in bed with boils covering his body, hands, and feet. She wanted him to suffer miserably and pray for death to give him relief. Then she'd watch him burn in hell for eternity.

His laughter waned, fading back into a frown. A flicker of something, fear, she hoped, flashed in his washed-out blue eyes. He sobered as her rage penetrated his jocular abandon. He turned his head, but couldn't take his eyes off of hers. She held a power over him he couldn't pull away from. At last he growled, "There's gold hidden 'round here somewhere. Lots a gold. And me and my boys aim to take it."

It sickened her to hear the New England accent she loved be used to tear her heart to shreds.

Her eyes never moved, never blinked. "Why?"

"Cause your pappy owes us a debt and we're calling in the note."

She was losing her soul-wrenching hold on him. "You're lying!"

"Am I?" Jet snapped his fingers and motioned for Alford to come closer. "Show little Miss" —he paused to look her over. She was anything but little — "her pappy's debt, signed, sealed, and held by the Portland Gambling Parlor."

She gasped. "My poppa never—"

Jet tore his eyes from hers. "No, Sweetheart, he never gambled in our fine establishment." He turned a chuckling glance to Hayden, then Alford. "But he sure 'nough borrowed against this Smithy building when times got down to slim pickin's."

Confusion creased her brow. Her eyes dropped to the floor. Was that what Poppa meant when he told her, "Don't judge, you never know what a person's circumstances might be."

Had Poppa's circumstances been such that he had to borrow money from these scalawags?

When her momma died, Poppa gave the gravedigger a lot of money to build her a better casket than a plain pine box. He paid Mrs. Tucker to make a beautiful silk lining, and he'd given money to the preacher to allow Momma's service to be held in the church. They buried her in the Waterfront Cemetery attached to the church grounds. Had Poppa paid to have that done, too?

Had he borrowed all that money? She couldn't think of a single time they had suffered from slim pickin's.

"When?" She gulped back the tears. "When did he sign that note?"

"Never you mind. Womenfolk don't got the mind for finances. Besides, if your pappy didn't think it war important 'nough to tell you then, it ain't important 'nough to tell you now." Jet smiled that evil, devil's smile.

She wanted to raise her over-sized foot and kick his teeth in, gold bicuspid and all.

"But, why'd you kill him?" She loathed the whimper in her voice.

"That?" Jet turned a steely glance to Alford. "Wasn't s'pose to happen. Not 'till Smith gave us the gold."

Minnie sat up straighter. "Wait. What gold? Poppa don't got no gold."

"Aint you paid no kinda attention to the ladies' gossip?" Delight twinkled in his eyes.

Minnie fought the urge to spit in one of those eyes. She could do it, too. Her aim was better than her Poppa's, or any boy from school. She could ring the school bell with a watermelon seed on a windless day. She suppressed the notion and focused on what Jet was saying.

"Some rawhide mountain man came through here back around the time your pappy was lookin' ta hitch himself up with a bride, donchaknow? He had your pappy make some fancy smithy work outta pure gold and silver for a swanky Pullman train car for his new bride. In gratitude, he set your pappy up with some wayward gal from over the Mason Dixon line."

Minnie gasped and then glared hard at him.

"Now, don't get your bloomers in a twist, I've not got no prejudices against such women. We make a hefty bundle having 'em in our establishment."

Minnie fought against her bindings. "Let me go!" She twisted and pulled the table, scraping the legs against the log planks.

Jet chuckled but kept his distance. "Seems she was a might bit in a family way, too."

"YOU'RE LYING!" Minnie pushed to her feet, lifting the table with her. Tin cups and a bowl crashed to the floor. Her eyes darted around the room. How could she get untied and strangle those fibbing lies out of his mouth?

Startled fear flashed in all three men's eyes, but it was Jet who swallowed hard and stepped toward her. He flipped out a pocket knife and paused. She lunged at him, but he gestured his intent to cut her ropes. She stilled and let him come closer. He leaned around her and sawed the rough bindings. She yanked her hands forward and rubbed her bloody, raw wrists.

She heard the click. When had he drawn the gun?

"Now, don't do nothin' stupid." Jet growled.

She stilled and sat down in the wooden chair she always sat in when her and Poppa ate. Sadness weighed her down to the seat. She had a thought. "I can prove you're lying."

He cocked his head back as if he challenged her to do so.

A smirky smile crossed her lips. "I'm the spittin' image of my poppa. I'm no bastard child." Satisfied she'd proved her point she leaned back in the chair, crossed her arms and legs and stared out the kitchen window.

Slowly, Jet smiled. His mocking gold tooth shone with the ever rising sun. "I never said your maw was carrying you."

His words hung in the air, like stale, skunky water. Minnie dropped her eyes to the floor. Poppa defended them girls Minnie had been bad mouthing about leaving town to find a husband and a new start. Had her own mother done the same thing? Was that why Poppa had such a kind opinion about her friends? There was a small grave next to her momma, but she'd never thought it might have been her sibling. Had it been a boy or a girl? How did Momma lose the baby? The answers would be forever laid to rest in that beautiful box Poppa had made for Momma. Tears broke loose from her resolve, like a prisoner set free. She hated it, but couldn't hold them back any longer.

"So, why do you think Poppa's got gold hidden?" She hated the weakness in her voice. She sounded like the little girl Dixie Levine had told Minnie about who begged for more bread from the cruel orphanage mistress.

Jet sat down in her poppa's chair. "Legend has it known for a long time that the mysterious mountain man gave a dowry to your pappy. Why else would a self respectin' man accept a woman into his bed what was carrying another man's child?"

His words stabbed Minnie in the heart like a red hot iron rod. They were her own words when she had placed such unworthy judgement on her friends who were leaving tomorrow.

She didn't have an answer for Butterfield. She loved her momma, and missed her with every fiber of her being.

And… now Poppa—

The tears fell, soaking her cheeks and dripping from her square jaw. She slumped over the table, but then another thought came to her. "What makes you think Poppa kept the gold?"

Jet smiled. "Little Missy, look around. You see any signs a your pappy spending a lot of money?" His eyes darted around the modest home. "He's still got that gold. It's hidden somewhere and you know where it is!" His voice morphed into an angry growl and his eyes narrowed into a loathsome glare. "I feels it in my bones."

Fear rose in Minnie's chest, strangling her voice. All she could do was shake her head. Her hand touched her throat. She couldn't breathe. Never, in her life had she heard these tales about her Momma or this mountain man. She'd never heard about any gold or a baby before her. At last she found her voice. "I don't know nuthin' about it." She collapsed against the table and sobbed.

Jet sat beside her. The heat from him glaring at her with loathing contempt burned into the back of her head. She cried all the more. What on earth could she do? She had no idea where her poppa might have hidden any gold or if he really had it at all. What could she do?

"I swear on my momma's grave, Mr. Butterfield. I don't know about any gold." She dissolved into a bawling mess. She'd never been so weak or vulnerable in her life. Poppa had always kept her safe. Momma, too. Who would save her from this?

Butterfield paced the floor. His two partners stared at him but remained silent. He obviously called the shots.

At last he turned to her. "I tell you what. Your pappy owes my establishment a debt. If you honestly do not know where your pappy hid that gold, then you're gonna find another way to repay his debt."

Her eyes widened. "I-I don't got no money." She looked around the room. "All I got is this house and my poppa's business. That's all I got, Mr. Butterfield."

"Fine." He pressed into her face. His breath nauseated her. "I'll take it."

"What?" She stood. "Your taking my home? My poppa's business? What am I s'posed to do? I got no where else to go?"

"Not my problem." Jet turned and made long strides toward the door. "Be outta here by dark, or I'll throw you out."

"But!"

"Oh, and don't concern yourself with burying your pappy. We took care a that for ya. And if ya tell a living soul 'bout this, we'll make sure ya meet your pappy real quick like, donchaknow?"

"What?" She flinched as the door slammed shut. "Where? Where'd you bury my poppa?" she shouted at the closed door and collapsed in a heap on the floor?

"I have nowhere to go," she said meekly to no one. "What am I supposed to do?"

Sunlight poured through the window. Sam started. He'd overslept!

Intending to leap out of bed and get up, he moved, but pain slammed him back and his body was stiff as a ramrod. He gasped as the torturous agony washed over his limbs, shot up his back, and into his neck. His head felt like he'd been hit with his hammer.

A voice came from his right. "Whoa, there. You're pretty banged up, Mr. Knight. Take it easy." It was Doc Savage.

Sam opened his eyes. This wasn't his bedroom. It was the doc's back room and his body was bound in hard white plaster from the waist down. "What happened?" Sam grumbled.

"Mr. Cherry's mule spooked and you thought you were big enough to stop her. You were wrong on that account. I'm afraid you got trampled."

"What's this stuff you got me bound up in?" Sam swallowed against a dry mouth.

Doc Savage tipped a glass of water against Sam's lips before continuing to explain. "This is Plaster of

Paris and linen. It's fairly new in the American medical practices. It was either this or amputate both your legs. One at the knee and the other at the hip. Mr. Knight, you broke both legs and your pelvis." He set the glass down. "I've got some medicines that will help you handle the pain, opiates and laudanum, but I have started you on some morphine and I'll adjust as you get better. The morphine will let you sleep, too."

The doc stood. "I suggest you do that as much as possible until you are healed enough for us to remove this cast, and then your gonna need time to recover your strength and muscle mass."

Sam closed his eyes, absorbing what the doc told him. Finally he said, "Why? What's wrong with my-my muscle mass?"

"Look," Doc Savage tilted his head in an empathetic way and sat back down. "There's a medical explanation as long as my arm, but let's just say, when your immobile like this for several weeks, your muscles quickly weaken, a lot. You'll need to exercise after the casts come off to get back to where you were before the accident."

"What about my work?" Samuel clenched his teeth.

Doc sat back down. He laid a gentle hand on Sam's shoulder. "Mr. Knight, it's going to take a while for you to heal completely. Your work's gonna have to wait."

"How long?"

Doc paused. Sam waited as the man rubbed his hand down his face with a heavy sigh. "We're talking several months."

"Several months!" Sam tried to sit but the pain and the cast nailed him back to the mattress. "I can't be gone from my forge for several months! The people need iron work done. Horses need shoeing. What'll they do?"

Doc Savage patted his shoulder and then filled a syringe with a clear liquid. "I don't know, but we'll just have to manage until you can work again."

He punctured Sam's arm with a tube that had a needle at the end. The liquid burned as the doc suppressed a plunger. A buzz started far away and gradually became louder. Sam fought the drifting sensation but eventually had to give in. He floated into a black suspended sleep where people yelled at him because they needed iron work done.

His forge flared behind them. Sweat poured down his face.

"My horses are going lame because of you!" one screamed.

He reached for the iron in the embers, but the forge had gone cold and the charcoal bin was empty. Panic consumed him.

"But I got hurt!" He looked down at his body. His legs were bloody stumps wrapped in white plaster bandages.

"Your always gone for town council meetings!" another man yelled.

"It's my voice in important decisions. The town needs my opinions."

"My wheel's busted, Knight! *I need you* at your forge!"

Six homely women with bridal veils covering their faces shrieked at him. "We need a man! Get back to your forge!"

His body was heavy and he couldn't move. Yet the people screamed, "We need work done!"

Chapter Four

Minnie cried herself completely dry of tears. Her fists were sore from pounding the planked floor. Finally she lifted her head and stared at the door. What on earth could she do? Jet Butterfield would be back at dark. She had no money or anywhere to go. Mrs. Broomhouser's Boarding House might have a room, but she couldn't pay for it. The woman wouldn't rent her a room without any payment. She wished she did know where her poppa hid that gold, then she'd have something to pay Butterfield… or make a new start. Like Poppa said.
She sat straight up. "A new start!"
Maybe Pastor Robertson could help her get on that train to Oklahoma and start a new life. She didn't want to marry nobody, but—
Why not? She could cook or clean for the Bride House. Her momma taught her a melt-in-your-mouth dumpling recipe. She could win the girls over with a chicken dumpling dinner that would endear them to her for the rest of their lives.
Or she could work. She had skills, good skills.

First, she needed to talk to Pastor Robertson. He *had* to agree to this! Lou Lou Lee, Dixie Levine, neither of them had any money. They were helping them. Lou Lou got four chickens. Minnie didn't need no chickens. She had chickens out back. She could crate some up and take them with her.

Dixie came from nothing. She grew up in an orphanage. Minnie wasn't any worse off than Lou Lou or Dixie.

Surely they'd help Minnie.

She looked around the room, panic-stricken. What to do? The root cellar! She had food down there. She'd boil a mess of potatoes and... she had cheese out there, too. Mrs. Baird baked the girls two loaves of bread, she could bake her own. She yanked out the flour tin and pulled down the kneading tray.

Frantically, she began mixing bread. She looked out the window. There wasn't time. She ran down into the root cellar and brought out as much as she could carry. She put a large stew pot on the table and dumped all the root vegetables in. Then she ran out to the pump and filled a bucket with water. She put it all on to boil.

She hurried back to the table. There wasn't time for bread, but she could make some biscuits. Quickly, she began mixing baking soda and flour, salt, and lard. She dumped in some buttermilk and squished it all between her fingers. Soon it was ready to turn out on the table. She punched out circles with a tin cup and placed them on a lard-smeared tray.

At least she wouldn't be begging for help without bringing her own food. Once the vegetables were boiling and the biscuits were baking, she had twenty minutes to run to the church and beg for help.

But she had to get dressed. She couldn't run through the street in her dressing gown. She ran upstairs and stared at her wardrobe. She'd need her dresses. Lord, how could she get all this done by dark. She pulled her dresses from the wardrobe and slung them onto her bed. She'd tie them up in the sheet, that way, she'd have a set of sheets to bring, too.

Satisfied with that idea, she tossed her boots on top, pulled the sheet off the mattress and tied it snug across the top. Lifting it, she moaned. All those dresses were heavier than she expected. She needed to pack them proper, but there wasn't time. She heaved the bundle and shoved it down the stairs, then pulled it across the floor and left it by the door. The biscuits were done and the vegetables were done enough, but what to put it in. A picnic basket!

Momma's was hanging in the root cellar. She flew out the door and slammed into Jet Butterfield.

"I'm almost done. Just two minutes."

He held her fast. "Hold up, Missy. I said dark and I meant dark."

"It's still light. Let go. I'm nearly ready!" She squirmed. Her strength was greater than his. She pulled loose from his grasp and dashed down the cellar stairs, grabbed her momma's basket and darted back to the porch.

Jet blocked her. "Where you going? This is my property now."

"No, please. I've almost got everything." Her eyes darted from his to inside the door. Her food, her clothes, they were all right there. All she needed was two seconds. "Please."

Jet glanced to his right at the bundle on the floor. He bent to inspect its content. "You thinking you'll be needing these purdy dresses where you're going?" Then he stood and grinned that devil's smile.

Her heart sunk into her stomach. What did he have in mind? She swallowed.

He nodded, as if the thought was settling right nicely in his mind. "I know what you can do. I've got the perfect solution. We can bill you as some amazon giant woman with skills beyond a man's wildest imaginations." He wiped his hand across the air as if he were revealing a banner.

"NO!" She stepped back. She'd never work for him. Surely the church would help her. She just needed her food… and clothes. "Please just let me get my things."

"Your things? Miss Smith, everything in this house is now mine. Unless you got a way ta pay your pappy's debt, *this* is all mine."

He held his hands out wide. "Now, why don't you walk on down to the Portland Parlor and I'll meet you there in a few minutes. We'll get you squared away real quick."

He looked her up and down. "On second thought, Madame Rosemont won't have anything your size. Maybe I do need to let you have a few of these dresses." He bent again and flipped the sheet back.

He tossed a boot at her.

She fumbled to catch it.

He tossed another, but it wasn't the match.

She looked at the mismatched boots. "I—wait! I could just lift the whole bundle, save you going through it all."

"You think so, do ya?" He tossed another boot and then lifted a dress.

"Here." He threw the dress and it landed over her head. "Oh, you'll definitely need this." He tossed a corset and camisole, a pair of bloomers and some stockings, another boot, then two petticoats.

She scrambled to pull the dress off her head and bent to pick the other unmentionable up from the stoop, wadding it all in her arms. He tossed another dress and she dropped what she had to try to catch it. She bent to scoop it all back into her arms.

Butterfield kicked her behind, sending her stumbling forward and then tumbling off the porch. Her clothes were strewn on the ground and she landed on her hands and knees.

"There. That ought to tide you over until we can get Mrs. Tucker to make you some proper attire. Won't take nearly as much yardage for your new line of work neither."

She glanced up at the street. People were stopping to see what all the commotion was about. The humiliation was almost more than she could bear. She bit her lip to stay the tears.

He leaned back and laughed from his belly, then slammed the door.

She climbed to her feet, gathered her things, and found the matching pair of boots. She grabbed the other one with no match just because it was there and it was hers.

She stared at the closed door. Her food was inside, but Butterfield wouldn't let her in. She could run back into the root cellar, but where would she put her clothes.

Tears soaked the fabric under her chin. She staggered back and spied the washing stand next to her poppa's shop. She ran to it. She grabbed a set of clean clothes from under the wash bowl. He'd wash up and change into these before coming into their home.

Desperation drove Minnie to have them. She flopped his shirt and britches on top of the pile of her own wadded up clothes and paused. What to do now?

The front door slammed and Minnie started. Boots stamped across the stoop. She grabbed her poppa's wool hat, then ran up the alley toward the only refuge she knew.

The church was on the hill, four blocks away. She ran with her wadded clothes as fast as possible. Suddenly, the ground slammed into her chin and her clothes and boots went flying. Despair pinned her to the ground. She laid her head on her arm and sobbed.

Why get up? Butterfield was going to throw her into the brothel anyway. Once he caught up to her. Footsteps coming toward her from the direction she had ran caused fear to replace hopelessness. She inhaled deeply, shoved away tears with the back of her hand, which held one lone boot, crawled to her feet, and hurried across the street to the church. More people stopped their activities, entering and exiting shops, to stare. But no one offered to help or asked if she was all right. Butterfield's influence on the town kept decent folks from doing right by people. She didn't care! She wouldn't have accepted any help even if they had offered. It was time she left this hateful town.
She needed a new start.

At last, Minnie reached the five steps to the veranda of the pristine whitewashed church. She'd always loved the walk to church on Sunday. This time she had scurried like a rat up the alleys to get here. The veranda held such wonderful, treasured memories of playing as a child. Now she stood here in desperation for her very life.

Stone cold silence greeted her as she shoved through the doors. Where was Jesus now?

She had dropped the lone boot she had clung to so vehemently. Her dresses were filthy from having been dropped in the dirt several times and probably ruined. She'd stepped on a petticoat, ripped the lace, and dragged it in the muddy street.

She had lost everything, her Poppa, her home, her pretty dresses, everything, and now there was nothing she could do to seek justice for her father's murder. Jet made that very clear. He had all the power and she had nothing.

Her meager belongings slid from her arms. Her knees gave out and she collapsed on top of them. Sobs raked her body as she cried into the heap of fabrics. Footsteps rushed toward her, but she didn't even bother to lift her head or explain. A tender voice cooed over her and gentle hands lifted her by the shoulders.

"There, there dear." Mrs. Robertson gathered Minnie into her motherly arms. "What's all this?"

Minnie tried to speak, but her words came out in garbled nonsense. "He won't… let me… in… I

have… no food… Momma's biscuits… no gold… Poppa… can't pay… start over… tore my lace—"
With that she collapsed to her knees and Mrs. Robertson knelt beside her and rocked her against her bosom.
The Pastor's wife sang as she rocked as if Minnie were a child.
"Safe in the arms of Jesus, Safe on His gentle breast; There by His love o'ershaded, Sweetly my soul shall rest."
Minnie listened against the woman's ribcage, like she used to in Momma's lap. She drifted to sleep in the woman's arms.
A firmer hand shook her awake. She lifted her head and wiped drool from her mouth. Mrs. Robertson struggled to stand. She had knelt so long, she had stiffened. Her husband helped her to her feet, then pulled Minnie to hers.
"My child," Pastor Robertson spoke softly. His eyes perusing her disheveled appearance and the bloody rope burns on her wrists. "What has brought you here in this state?"
Tears poured from her soul. The Pastor tilted his head and tenderly guided her to sit in the pew. He waited patiently for her to gather her words.

She told him everything, including her father being murdered, and why she had the few clothes with her. Mrs. Robertson and he exchanged a look the way married people do. Momma and Poppa used to do that. It made her smile and yet, she was terrified. "Please, you can't tell the Constable! Butterfield'll kill me in my sleep!" She held her hands up in prayer, begging him to listen to her.

She had until three tomorrow to board that train and get away from him. New tears sprang from what she thought had to be a dry well. "Please, please don't tell anybody."

"My child, you're always safe here in the house of God."

She stared at Pastor Robertson. Could God truly protect her? He hadn't protected her Poppa. "I need to get away. But I have no where to go and no money. I don't even have any... f-food."

She sobbed yet again. Would these tears ever dry up? "May I please go to Oklahoma with the other girls?" Mrs. Robertson rose from the pew and left the sanctuary. Minnie watched her leave. "I could clean... or cook. I could help the girls with anything they need help with. I'm strong! I could carry their trunks, serve as their handmaid. I'll do anything, Pastor. Please help me get on that train tomorrow!" Mrs. Robertson returned with a sweet smile on her face and nodded to her husband.

"So, you're thinking you want to go with our mail order brides?" Pastor patted her hand.

Minnie nodded and lifted pleading eyes to meet Mrs. Robertson's. "I've gotta go."

"But you don't have a betrothed waiting for you."

"I know…" She slumped over in the pew and began to sob, again.

"Dear one." Mrs. Robertson wrapped a loving arm around Minnie. "You certainly can go to Gunther City, with the other girls. You'll be safe there and we'll sponsor you. We'll send a letter with you explainin' why you're coming unannounced and Widow Drummond will take you into her bosom and love on you." Her sing-song voice sounded so convincing Minnie found herself believing it, too.

"But Mrs. Robertson, my clothes are ruined, I only have one pair of boots besides these here I got on" —Minnie held her large foot up to show the Robertson's. Mr. Robertson diverted his eyes— "and I-I don't have… any… food." The tears rolled down her cheeks.

"Oh, now listen here." Mrs. Robertson gently pushed her foot down and tugged at Minnie's skirt, to cover her ankle. She subtly pushed her elbow into her husband to signal him it was safe to look. "You don't need to worry about none of that. You got more than some brides when they go out west. Let me take a look at your dresses. I'll bet we can brush them clean or set an iron to 'em. We'll polish your boots and have you looking good as a shiny new penny in no time."

"I tore my" —she glanced at Pastor Robertson and covered her mouth to whisper to his wife— "my petticoat and dragged it in the mud, donchaknow?"

"Well, I got an extra sewing needle and some thread. I'll fix you a small sewing box you can take with you in case any other repairin' is needed along the way."

"But, what about food? I'm gonna starve to death."

"No honey, I wouldn't let you go on that train without a basket of food and some means. You'll be just fine."

Chapter Five

Seven women knelt in front of the dais. On the altar above them were their sole possessions: a leather pouch, a food basket, and one to two trunks. These were everything they were taking to start a new life in Oklahoma.

Minnie had even less. Mrs. Robertson had looked through the left-behinds from a recent rummage sale and found Minnie a black hat and handbag to match, some red gloves, and a tattered, but functional, suitcase. She had cleaned and pressed Minnie's dresses, polished her boots and placed it all in the humble case. Minnie's name had been written on an attached leather tag. It wasn't much, but it was hers. Among them, one held a carpet bag, two held a stack of books bound with a leather belt, and the others held a handbag. Pastor Robertson stood behind the pulpit, reading from Exodus.

The women remained kneeling as the pastor stepped down with a small bottle of sacred oil. He blessed each in turn. One by one they stood and joined Mrs.

Robertson on the first pew. Minnie prayed extra hard that God would keep her safe from Jet Butterfield. Mrs. Robertson moved to the piano and played a hymn. She touched the ivory keys and laid out the introduction. Minnie let the music wash over her worried mind. She joined them in song, although she did not have her mother's voice.

"Listen to the heav'nly music, Made by those who never tire, Wondrous song that has no ending, Sung by all the angel choir…," they sang.

Mrs. Robertson distributed the baskets. "Now, ladies, these baskets are not enough to sustain you for the entire trip to Oklahoma."

Minnie winced. Perhaps if she rationed the food carefully, she wouldn't starve. Not completely.

"But!" Mr. Robertson handed each of them the leather pouch that had been set in front of her belongings. "A generous benefactor who has asked to remain anonymous has given each of you these leather pouches. This is your purse. They hold enough coins to allow you to buy three meals a day from the dining car—"

"Yes." Mrs. Robertson interrupted. "And the baskets are for snacks, to tide you over between meals or late at night." She smiled sweetly.

The pastor continued unflustered by his wife's interruption. "And, ladies, there are enough coins to provide you personal spending money when you arrive in Gunther City. This benefactor wanted you to be able to purchase clothing, property, or whatever you find will help you establish yourself and to be independent, allowing you to take your time before you commit to the gentlemen with whom you have been corresponding."

His eyes met each woman individually. Minnie lowered her eyes when Pastor Robertson met her gaze. Mrs. Robertson handed each of the ladies an envelope with their names written in a calligraphy style pen and ink, and a second envelope with their names in various handwritings.

Minnie's eyes dropped to the floor. She wouldn't be getting a letter, but then Mrs. Robertson handed her an envelope. Her eyes widened in surprise. Mrs. Robertson simply smiled.

"Now ladies, the lovely handwritten letter is from the Widow Drummond. You will meet her at the train depot in Gunther City. It is her boarding house where you will be living until you marry. The second letter is the last one we have received from your betrothed."

Minnie couldn't imagine what her envelope contained. Perhaps it was blank, just a mock letter so that it wasn't so terribly obvious she didn't have a betrothed, although everyone knew. She would open it later in case it was blank.

She drew in a deep, resolving breath and set her mind to earning the girls' respect. During their years in school they had called her horrible things, "circus freak," "man in a corset," "monster," among other cruel references to her abundant size. It wasn't her fault she took after her poppa's stature.

No, she wouldn't dwell on the past. Now was the time to forgive and forget. She had a long way to go to make up for her behavior toward them, and she would start by helping with their trunks.

Helen Baird and Jane Anne Taylor, were best friends and a bit snobbish. They watched Minnie lug their trunks to the veranda, but appreciation was not in their expressions. They would be the hardest to win over. Helen's family owned a bakery and provided the two loaves of bread in their baskets. Minnie would be sure to tell Helen how good it tasted.

Jane Anne's parents owned a tailor shop for men and women. Perhaps Minnie could talk to Jane Anne about making some new dresses with her purse from the benefactor.

Martha Grace Dickery cared for her parents until they died. Dixie Levine had grown up an orphan, and Minnie was an orphan now, too. Perhaps that would be their starting point for a renewed friendship.

Alice Canning leaned toward arrogant, like Helen, but she could make music out of any object. Minnie could make any object out of iron. Could that be their common ground? She'd do her best to try.

Last there was Lou Lou Lee. Minnie had said harsh things to her Poppa just the other day about Lou Lou's impoverished position. Minnie sighed. Now she had even less than that.

Minnie toted as many trunks as she could. Pastor and his son, Joshua, carried the remainder to the veranda where two wagons waited for them with matching dapple mares.

Minnie knew these horses, she and Poppa had made them new shoes just last month. She opened her basket and fished out two small apples. They whinnied their appreciation as she held out an open palm to feed both of them. She rubbed their necks and nuzzled their noses. "Thank you, my friends."

She tugged Jane Anne's trunks down to the wagons. The memory of Poppa shoeing these two saddened her so deeply, she had to lean against the trunks to keep from buckling to the ground. Jane Anne rushed up to her. "Careful!"

Minnie wavered slightly.

Jane Anne gasped. "You all right?"

Minnie just nodded and stiffened her legs. She had to be all right. What choice did she have?

Pastor Robertson helped the ladies into the bed of the first wagon and Minnie helped Joshua load the trunks in the second. Lou Lou's chicken crates were already on that wagon. Minnie climb in with her meager belongings and sat on her suitcase toward the back.

Pastor Robertson and his son drove the wagons to the train station where everything happened in reverse. The two men stayed with the brides until they and their belongings were loaded on the train, and Lou Lou's chickens were in the livestock car. Minnie stared out the window, anticipating Jet Butterfield or his cohorts arriving and dragging her off to his pool hall. Her foot vibrated against the floor and she chewed her lip. *Get this train going!* she muttered to herself. At last forward motion pressed her back against her seat. She sighed and closed her eyes. The further down the tracks they went, the safer she felt.

Ten days on the tracks and she'd be far from Butterfield and his brothel… and the only home she'd ever known. Minnie bowed her head in prayer. Then she looked up at the ceiling and whispered to her Poppa. "I sure hope you're right, Poppa. Thank you and Momma for watching over me from Heaven."

She lowered teary eyes. Helen stared at her with disgust, then smiled quickly and diverted her eyes to Jane Anne, the way one does when they get caught gawking. Helen leaned over and said something to Jane Anne and the two giggled.

They had no idea how much Minnie had been through to get here, but then again, neither did she know what brought them to this point. Her Poppa had told her not to judge. Now she knew why. Minnie sighed. "And the adventure begins."

Minnie stared out the windows as Portland, Maine moved farther away. She had always imagined traveling somewhere by train would be exhilarating.

Today, she was scared, desperate, and despondent. How had it all come to this? Just two days ago, she was content to be at her poppa's side, working the iron.

Her harsh words tormented her mind. "Poppa? Why would any self respectin' girl agree to make herself available to a perfect stranger in the lawless west? In Oklahoma, at that? Ain't it full of Indians that'd scalp ya as soon as look at ya, donchaknow?"

His answer that she had taken so lightly, now crushed her heart. "Aw, Honey, don't judge so harshly, Ayah." He had glanced up at her with kind eyes. "You never know what a person's circumstances might be."

Memories of her poppa's deep baritone voice threatened to draw tears she swore she'd keep under control from now on. Her eyes roved over the six women sitting in pairs in their Pullman Private Sleeper. The benefactor had provided very nice accommodations for the brides leaving Portland. This car was fancier than most. It set twelve comfortably and slept eight. Thank goodness or she would have had to make a bed on the short couch. Ten days of that would be exhausting, but still better than being forced to work at the brothel.

Why had this mysterious man taken such an interest in her home town?

She had said to her Poppa, "I went to school with all six of 'em. I don't see what their problem is to marry here in Po'tland?"

The Robertsons said this anonymous benefactor had a callin'. Could it be he knew her schoolmates would need to marry outside of Portland? Poppa had seemed to understand. "Princess, they each got their reasons for making a new start, donchaknow?"

Three days ago, she had no idea she'd be sitting here, in this fancy train car, with six women she hadn't spoken to since tenth grade. Helen sat across from Minnie with Jane Anne. They had been to the dining car together.

"Your momma's bread is so good, Helen." Minnie made good on her promise to compliment Helen. A very cold smile and a shrug was all Helen gave in return. Minnie took another bite of the bread and hard cheese she had sliced and turned to watch the Maine landscape slip farther and farther away.

Her conversation with Poppa played in her head. "I heard the church is providing baskets for each lady, donchaknow? Apples, hard cheese, dried fruit, hazelnuts. Helen's momma made them each two loaves of breads to tide them over so they won't starve to death on the train, but what will they eat once they get there? Oklahoma's too barren to grow crops, donchaknow?"

Minnie knew nothing about Oklahoma. Dixie, who spent all her spare time in the library, had researched the Oklahoma Territory and happily shared her wealth of knowledge to whoever would listen. Minnie listened closely. She needed to know what to expect and she needed to be kind to Dixie.

The rhythm of the tracks lulled Minnie as she reminisced about home. Like the train's rhythm, Poppa would set a cadence with his hammer and sing, in his deep baritone voice, while they worked the iron. Neither of them sang well, but it didn't matter when they were pacing the hammer strikes on a piece of iron.

The train's clickety clack, clickety clack, penetrated Minnie's mind as she drifted to sleep. She dreamed of working the forge with Poppa. Happy and content with things as they were. But her dream deteriorated into the gun blast that killed him. Butterfield's gold tooth and bad breath in her face. Desperately trying to gather her clothes. It was as if she were swimming

in molasses. She was running out of time and had to get everything done, but her limbs wouldn't move.
A loud bang startled her awake. She gasped and sat up straight. "Oh, I'm sorry." Martha Grace said sweetly. "I just come back from the dining car. You should check it out. They've got roast beef and gravy this evenin'."
Evening! Had she been asleep that long? "Um. Thanks, I'll go in a minute."
She needed to settle her nerves before she stood. Right now, she wasn't sure her legs would hold if she tried to walk.
"We haven't gone yet, if you want to go with us." Lou Lou and Dixie stood beside her. For once, Dixie wasn't holding that carpet bag. Minnie nodded and forced herself to stand. She stretched and yawned, then let them lead the way.
As she watched Lou Lou open doors and guide her and Dixie to the dining car, Minnie thought about those harsh words she'd said to her poppa. "And I heard Lou Lou Lee was so poor, dontchaknow, that Mrs. Hankshaw gave her four chickens in a crate for a dowery. That's just… sad, Ayah."

Poppa responded sharply. "Sometimes people do the best they can and that includes acceptin' some help so they can make a better life for themselves." And then he said something that pierced her heart. "Maybe, you've had it too easy to realize some people suffer and need a new start in life. Ayah?"

She couldn't believe her own father had no idea what a difficult life she had had being as big as she was. Now, she wished she had that life back. It was so much better than what she was facing in a few days.

The days passed slowly. Helen and Jane Anne's cold shoulders warmed slightly, but not much. Martha Grace, Lou Lou, and Dixie were speaking to Minnie and invited her to join them for meals. Alice spoke when spoken to. Even that was progress.

Dixie shared her books with the girls which helped pass the time. Jane Anne had a stack of books, too, but didn't offer to share them. Helen probably hadn't read a single book since school. She occupied herself by chatting or sleeping.

Minnie read Dixie's *Gulliver's Travels*, watched the landscape change, or thought about home.

Conversations in the Pullman often times drifted to the girls' betroths. Minnie smiled and listened to their hopes and dreams. Nonetheless, it saddened her. No man had ever asked for her hand.

Mentally, she shook her head. She didn't need no husband. None of the boys she knew in Portland were big enough to be her suitor. *They* were the *freaks*. They were tiny Gulliver's Lilliputians Island sized people. She chuckled to herself.

Perhaps men in Oklahoma grew taller, like her and her poppa. Why she had to move to some god-forsaken, dry, and desolate place such as Oklahoma to find a decent husband was beyond her.

But then she remembered Butterfield, and Graves, and Gray. She had been forced to do this.

On day six, Minnie had a chance to seal Dixie's friendship, and keep her from being kicked off the train.

Minnie noticed Dixie slipping food into her napkin and wondered if she had some poverty-minded disorder. It turned out, she was taking the food back to her berth to feed a dog she had hidden in her carpet bag. What everyone thought was a bag full of books, turned out to be a dachshund she'd brought with her.

When she accepted the opportunity to be a mail order bride, she didn't have the heart to abandon the dog she named Mr. Darcy, so she smuggled him in her carpet bag.

That fateful day on the train, Mr. Darcy escaped. Minnie could only imagine how cooped up he felt inside that carpet bag. The conductors were very upset to find Mr. Darcy running through the train and a despondent Dixie chasing after him.

Minnie's large size could be intimidating. So she drew herself up to her full height and stood her ground. The conductors cowed and decided one small dachshund would not be such a problem, as long as he were not allowed to run free. Minnie and little five-foot-nothing Dixie promised to keep Mr. Darcy contained.

Other friendships were forming. Lou Lou traversed the train cars every morning to check on her chickens in the livestock car. Gathering two to four eggs each day, she brought them back to the dining car and asked the cooks to fry them for her breakfast. When there were three or four eggs, she'd share with Dixie and Minnie. It was a treat to have fresh eggs.

At last the scenery outside her window had changed to flat prairie and red dirt. The girls did what they could to freshen up. They changed into their best dresses and helped each other put up their hair. They chittered with anticipation to meet their betroths. How tall would he be? How handsome? Was he kind as his letters seemed? Would his family welcome them? How soon would it be before they married? Commitments were made to stand with the other at their ceremony.

Minnie helped Lou Lou and Martha Grace with their hair. Dixie braided hers at the base of her head and wrapped it around her head like a band of ribbon. Minnie gathered her own in a simple round bun at the nape of her neck and pinned the hat Mrs. Robertson had given her from a previous rummage sale. She slipped on the pair of men's red gloves that just covered the pink marks on her wrists. The scars, like the memory of the horrible night that brought her to this, would always be with her.

She was as ready as she'd ever be to meet nobody.

Chapter Six

"Well," Doc Savage rubbed his hands together. "How would you like to get that cast off and put a less restrictive one on?"

Sam glanced at Emma Cherry, who had not left his side since the accident. She'd cooked three meals a day for Sam and Doc Savage, right there in the Doc's clinic. She bathed Sam, wiped his brow and held his hand through the pain and suffering.

She washed and pressed his shirts, bringing him a clean one every day. The Cherry's felt responsible for Sam's severe injuries, since he tried to save Emma from the runaway mule. Sampson had stopped in to see if they needed anything, but continued to distribute the town's firewood by himself. He even snuck some baling wire in so Sam could scratch under his cast.

Mary Etta brought his mail when he had it, but letters were few and far between.

Doc had helped clean Samuel in the more private areas after an elimination. But it was Emma who did everything else as well as any trained nurse Doc

Savage had ever worked with in his medical training. He was very impressed with her dutiful skills.

"Will I be able to sit up, Doc?" Samuel hated the weakness in his voice, but he had been flat in the bed for four weeks. His skin hurt even though Emma had rolled him over and rubbed a salve she concocted from honey, beeswax, oats, and castor oil on his back.

"I hope so." Doc smiled that practiced *everything-will-be-alright* smile which no longer convinced Samuel it would be. He had gotten to know the young Doc very well over the past month. In fact, he knew more about Doc Savage than he did anyone else in town, except for Emma and Sampson. After the long hours of nothing else to do but tell each other their life stories.

One day, for lack of anything else to talk about, Sam asked her, "How many children you and Sampson want, Emma?"

"Oh, Sam. There won't be no chil'en for Sampson and me." She shook her head sadly.

Samuel didn't know why that was, and now he wished he hadn't asked.

"It is wut it is, I s'pose." She shrugged.

Sam pressed his lips hard and agreed.

They knew about everything there was to know about each other. Except for one thing. Neither Emma nor Samuel knew Doc's first name.

He refused to give that secret up, despite every bribe they could think of. He held that piece of information very close to his chest, like a royal flush in a high stakes poker game.

Doc pulled out a saw and poured whiskey on it. Samuel swallowed with wide eyes watching Doc's every move. Emma held Sam's hand as the doc began carefully cutting into the plaster with a shallow sawing movement on one side and then the other. White dust floated in the air and powdered Doc's, Sam's and Emma's faces. Sam reached up and dragged his hand through the dust on Emma's face exposing her dark skin. "You look like a sugar powdered donut."

She laughed. "Aw, now I want some donuts." They all laughed and swiped the dust from their faces. The Doc then sterilized tin snips. Sam glared at him as he emptied the whiskey over the instrument. "Such a waste of good whiskey." Sam muttered. "Don't think of it as good whiskey." Doc set the bottle on the floor. "Think of it as a brigade of soldiers killing all the bacteria that would cause your leg to become infected."

Sam tipped his head back and nodded.

Doc cut the cast on the inside of Sam's leg. When he reached Sam's knee, heat filled his face. His eyes darted to Emma. "Emma, I appreciate all you done fer me, since my accident—"

Emma held up a dark hand. "It's all right Sam. I'll just slip out until Doc gets you taken care of."

She rose and kept her eyes diverted from Sam until she left the room. Doc completed cutting the plaster up Sam's leg and pried the top half from the bottom. Cotton stretched and clung to itself like a giant spider egg sack, but finally gave way.

Sam winced with anticipation of pain, but there was none. He lifted his head to looked at his body and quickly grabbed for the sheet.

"My God!" He couldn't believe how much his big, muscular legs had shriveled into skin and bones.

Doc patted his arm. "This is why recovery from this severe of an injury takes so long. It's not just a matter of healing the bone, there's the muscle recovery, too." He gently squeezed Sam's thigh, checking the break for weakness, and then Sam's shin.

The Doc pressed against the injury in Sam's pelvis. Sam winced and closed his eyes.

"Okay, so that still hurts." Doc chuckled.

"Yeah." Sam breathed the word.

"All right, so here's what I think we should do. I want to fashion a lesser cast for your legs for another two weeks. I'll not cast your pelvis, but you're going to have to be extremely careful. This will allow two things. One, you can sit upright, possibly even use a wheeled chair to get around."

Sam's expression told Doc he wasn't happy with this news. Sam was a man accustomed to being strong and independent.

"It's just for a few more weeks, Sam. Then we'll begin your physical therapy to get you up and walking again. I told you when we started this journey, you're going to have to be patient. It's so much better than a double amputation."

Sam's lip quivered. "When can I go home, Doc?"

Doc Savage rubbed his chin as if he had a beard. "You're a big man, Sam... Your apartment is upstairs... I just don't know how any of us could—"

Sam closed his eyes. "Okay, Doc."

"Besides, it wouldn't be proper for Mrs. Cherry to come to your home to care for you, which you and I know she's going to continue to do. She can keep coming here to the clinic. She's been a big help to me, with your personal care, and now you'll be able to sit up and move around. It'll all be part of your early therapy. I'll show you some exercises that will get your muscles started on building up strength and Mrs. Cherry will find you need her less and less. I think Mr. Cherry will appreciate that, don't you?"

Sam took a deep breath and nodded. "Doc, give it to me straight, what's going on at my shop?"

Doc Savage paled. "Sam, I'm not going to lie to ya. The folks here miss you… and your smithy work. But we're all rallying for you to recover and everyone is being as patient as possible. Believe me, you haven't lost your business. And when you get well enough to work again, you'll be busy for a long time." Doc tried to laugh, but he saw the anguish in his patient's eyes.

"I tell you what. I'll get you bathed up, get these new casts on your legs, and then we'll fashion you some long johns and britches that will fit over these new casts. Surely Cambridge has a pair a few sizes larger than you normally wear."

The Doc looked over Sam's larger than an average man's size and a glimmer of doubt passed behind his eyes. "Then, we'll go slow, because, I promise you, it's not going to be easy getting up for the first time. But if all that goes well, I personally will wheel you to the train station this afternoon."

Sam's brow came together in confusion.

Doc just smiled. "The Mail Order Brides arrive today."

Excitement filled the Pullman. Chatter was giddy and louder than what would be proper, but they couldn't help themselves. The train seemed to crawl as it closed in on their destination.

The land in Oklahoma Territory wasn't as desolate as they had imagined—as Minnie had imagined. While it was flatter than Maine, there were trees and lakes, creeks, and even rivers. Cattle dotted the landscape and some goats. They even spotted a herd of bison. The sky was bright blue and the air hot and humid, making hairdressing a challenge.

They all looked very pretty. Minnie was surprised how much Mrs. Robertson was able to do for her dirt-caked dresses. She had to admit, her clothes were pretty again, even if she were not. Of the three, she chose the dark grey light wool with black velvet straps, like suspenders, that tied at her waist with a velvet bow. The black hat and red gloves coordinated nicely and she did not look like a penniless beggar. Dixie held Mr. Darcy up to a window so he could see they were nearly there, but when the conductor made his rounds, she quickly tucked him back into her carpet bag.

At last a train station came into view and the train's whistle blew. The little town looked two blocks long with two and three story buildings on both sides of a wide, central street. There were homes flanking the main two rows and a covered wagon next to the depot that looked like it served food. How quaint. The girls jumped to their feet, giggling, and grabbing their bags and baskets, even though the conductors had sternly told them to remain seated until the train came to a complete stop. The brides lined up at the door waiting to get out.

Minnie stood at the back of the line behind Dixie. The screeching brakes and the momentum of the train stopping filled her heart with so much anxiety, she found it hard to breathe. Dixie felt it, too. She swooned and Minnie and Martha caught her by the shoulder before she went down. Lou Lou fanned Dixie's face with a black gloved hand. Jane Anne ran to the dining car. "Anybody got smelling salts?" she yelled. A kind woman answered and handed her the small glass bottle. Jane Anne grabbed it and a glass of water. Dixie sniffed the smelling salts and shivered, then she sipped the water. She still looked pale, but she could stand on her own now.

The train rolled to a stop. The girls bent to look out the windows. To their right was a water tower and a long coal wagon. The train would refuel and replace the water supply for the steam engine. To their left the town and several dozen or more people lined the platform. All were grinning and waving. Several young men looked uncomfortable in nicely pressed suits and string ties. They each held a piece of stationery. Minnie squinted to bring the signs into focus. They held the name of their bride-to-be. Minnie's heart sank. She had no suitor waiting for her. Instead she would be walking off the train and handing someone in charge the letter of introduction the Robertsons had given her, and praying they didn't put her on the returning train to send her back to Portland, Maine.

This was her new start. She couldn't go back home.

A large man in a wicker back chair with wheels caught her eye. Both of his legs were straight, like he was laying down, but sitting up, and a woven Indian blanket covered him to his boots. He looked pale, sickly even, and yet she couldn't take her eyes away from his. His shoulders were wide and muscular, and his face very handsome. Behind him stood a young man in a suit and a black woman in a simple day dress. They waved at the brides along with all the other people who seemed to be very excited about the brides' arrival.

He didn't wave, he didn't smile, and yet he intrigued her.

The people shouting, the girls giggling, it all faded as Minnie stared at this one man. What happened to him? Why did her heart stir at the sight of him? His huge build made her think of her poppa and she wondered if he could possibly be the town's smithy. A slight smile bowed her lips. This new start might not be so bad after all.

Chapter Seven

The conductor finally came to the door. His disapproval evident in the stern expression that held his mouth taut and raised an eyebrow on his forehead. Since the train had fully stopped, however, he did not say anything to the anxiously waiting women.

Helen stood first in line. She turned and squeezed her small gloved fists with Jane Anne's, before stepping out. Several minutes later she crossed to the depot with her betrothed and met a woman in black widow's weeds. Could that be Widow Drummond?

Minnie moved closer to the door. Her heart pounded in her ears. She watched the man in the wheeled chair. He seemed as disinterested as anyone could be. Why had he come to see the brides?

Jane Anne Taylor stepped out next. Minnie faintly heard her speak French to her betrothed. She strained to see who he was. The man had a delicate build. Could he be of French descent? Why else would she speak to him in the Canadian language? Every child in Maine knew at least some conversational French. Canada was just over the state line, after all.

Minnie's attention returned to the man in the wheeled chair. He had a rugged but handsome face. His beard needed trimming but his shoulder length hair stirred a desire in her to gather it in her hands and tied it back with a ribbon. Why would she care if a man had his hair loose about his shoulders? She tore her eyes off him and watched Alice step out. Lou Lou and Martha left the train together. Minnie looked back to the man who held her interest, but Lou Lou squealed, drawing Minnie's attention back to her friend. In all the excitement, her betrothed had grabbed Lou Lou and lifted her off the steps. Several women yelled at him for his inappropriate behavior, but Minnie laughed. Lou Lou would be happy with this one.

Minnie and Dixie exchanged a look of fear. Minnie smiled. "It'll be all right. Go on."

Dixie sighed, lifted her chin, and tightened her grip on Mr. Darcy's carpet bag. She turned and exited the train. Minnie stood alone. Should she step out with Dixie, like Martha did with Lou Lou? She watched Dixie descend the steps and speak with her intended. He reached for the carpet bag and Dixie scurried over to the depot with the other girls. The boy trailed after her. "Yeah, they're gonna have a time together," Minnie chuckled to herself.

The silence in the car pressed in on her like a dense fog. She looked around their lovely Pullman. The benefactor had made this transition as easy on them as he possibly could. But now was the moment of truth and she had to leave all these comforts and face her new start. She gathered herself to her full height, tucked her basket on her arm, her purse at her wrist, and her meager suitcase in her hand. She would walk out with everything she owned, all she had to offer. "Please be right, Poppa," she whispered as she stepped out the Pullman door. The toe of her large boot caught the threshold. She stumbled out onto the cut platform. The short distance she had to recover caused the basket to crush between her hip and the railing. She caught the frame to keep from bashing her head into the next train car. Food scattered everywhere. Her suitcase swung with the momentum.

"Oh God! This can't be happening." She paused for a moment with her eyes closed, then turned toward the steps. Her face filled with crimson embarrassment as she straightened to her full height.

The onlookers gasped in dismay and stared at her in silence. She was a freak!

No, she wasn't. It was the surprise of a seventh woman. They had no idea she was coming. She turned to face them with as much dignity as she could muster and drew in a ragged breath. This was it. She lifted her chin and stepped forward. The people stared at her as she took the steward's hand. Her large red glove covered his white gloved hand. She eased her foot down, being careful to step on each riser fully. The last thing she needed was to fall here, too.

Her boot touched the ground. She'd made it without another embarrassing catastrophe. She looked out across the sea of faces and straightened to her full five foot eleven inches. Half the men in Gunther City were as tall as her. Relief escaped her lungs. At least they weren't Lilliputians Island sized people.

Chatter rose among the citizens. The woman in black waved another woman over. They exchanged words and then the widow marched over to where Minnie stood. She scanned the people for the man in the wheeled chair. He turned to speak to the black woman. She bent to speak to him. His eyes locked on Minnie's and for a moment, there was nothing between, around, and behind her and him.

A tall man in a sheriff's uniform approached her. His shadow blocked the bright evening sun, waking her from her trance with the bearded man. She remembered her letter of introduction and quickly rummaged for it from her handbag.

"I have a letter from Paster Robertson," she said, hating her strong New England accent that stuck out like a bandaged thumb. She did her best not to sound like she was about to cry. She felt as if she stood in the exhibit booth under a sign that read, "the World's Largest Woman." Except she wasn't protected by a glass wall. Fear flooded her senses and she fought the urge to run back onto the train.

A Sheriff stepped up to her as the widow stepped beside him. "Thank you, Miss. I'm Sheriff GW Gunther and this here is Widow Drummond."

She squinted against the afternoon sun when he turned to gesture toward the widow. He looked her straight in the eye. "We weren't expecting a seventh" —he swallowed as his eyes washed over her stature — "b-bride."

She tried to hold her head high. "It's all in the letter, Sheriff." She waited for the inevitable rejection. What would she do then?

The Sheriff opened the Robertsons' letter and read it quickly, then he handed it to Mrs. Drummond. She read it and looked up at Minnie with mercy behind her tear soaked eyes.

"You poor dear. Of course you're welcome. We'll need a little bit to fix you up a room, but my boarding house is always ready for a bride-to-be."

Minnie started. She wasn't a bride-to-be. No one waited for her at this platform. Should she say something?

"All I'm asking is for you to allow me and Mrs. Gunther to spruce up your room all girly-like."

Tears trailed down Minnie's cheek. "Thank you, Ma'am. I, uh, you don't gotta go ta no trouble for me." She hated how small her voice sounded.

Widow Drummond reached out and took Minnie's large hand in hers and patted it. "Oh, yes we do, my dear, every bride deserves a pretty room and you'll have it at the Drummond's Bride House."

Minnie sighed. Her momma and poppa raised her to never lie. She hated that she didn't tell them the truth. But for now, if it made things so she could stay here and not be sent back, she'd go along with their assumption.

The man she had seen from the train windows, who sat in the odd chair with wheels, watched her closely. Sympathy radiated from his kind eyes. At least, she hoped it was kind sympathy and not hideous pity. She tore her eyes away from him and let Mrs. Drummond guide her to the shade with her friends.

The Sheriff jumped up on a bench and held his hand high in the air. "Folks, it looks like we have a surprise. We've got ourselves seven brides come to our humble little town. So, you men help me gather their luggage and get it over to the Drummond House. Let's let the women get settled in, rested up, and gussied up, then we'll see you all out at the Rocking F Ranch, where we'll have our first dance since the land run."

The crowd tossed hats in the air and cheers filled the train station. The brides all smiled and hugged each other. Even Widow Drummond looked pleased. Minnie allowed herself to smile, but still felt like she was the circus clown that came for dinner.

Chapter Eight

It had taken Sam much longer to get up, get dressed, and get into a wheeled chair than he had ever imagined. Having been flat on his back for these five weeks, his head swooned like a newborn foal when Emma and Doc helped him sit up.

Miss Emma's squirrel and dumplings stew ended up all over the floor. He hated the embarrassment, but he hated the absolute weakness more. Was getting outside just to see a bunch of homely, desperate brides come off a train worth all this? Doc and Emma seemed to think it was.

Then they tried to get him dressed. Shirts weren't a problem. Emma had been bringing him clean shirts every day since his accident. It was a matter of rolling from one side to the other and her slipping his arms into the sleeves. He could do the rest. But when they tried to get dungarees on him, it was almost comical.

He couldn't reach the end of his legs to slip into his pants. They had to pull the pants over his feet, for him, but found they wouldn't go all the way up because of the size of his casts. Finally, they opted to cut off his dungarees and put a Navajo blanket across his legs, which stuck straight out like two long sticks. Last, Doc put Sam's socks and boots on him. With a one, two, three, Doc pulled Sam into a standing position. Sam closed his eyes against the dizzy sensation that turned his stomach over. Doc said, "Keep your eyes open. Focus on one object." Sam opened his eyes and stared at an oval photograph of Doc's building when it was first built. Everyone had one of their own newly erected building. A feller named Eastman had been here last April when the buildings first went up. Sam supposed he'd made a nice bag of money printing out the photos. Sold frames, too, and moved on.

The nausea subsided and his sense of balance settled. Doc explained their next move. "Okay, Emma, on three, we'll turn him and seat him in the wheeled chair. Ready, one, two, three."

They pivoted him like a post, but it felt like they had spun him like a child's top. He wavered out of control. If it weren't for Emma and the Doc holding him up, he'd have collapsed. Then Doc said, "Now sit."

Sam fell back, hoping the chair was behind him. He panted and closed his eyes, thinking for sure he'd topple forward and fall to the floor, but Emma stood behind him and held his shoulders against the cane back. They waited until the dizziness subsided before moving to the next task: Wheeling him down to the train depot to watch the town spectacle.

A sense of anticipation filled Samuel when he heard the whistle of the approaching train. He didn't know why, he wasn't expecting a bride. Lord knew he didn't want one. Yet something about this train excited him.

When the first bride emerged from the steam and iron horse, it really surprised him. She was a beautiful blonde, not homely or desperate looking at all. Eddie Hutton, the banker, stepped up and escorted her to the shade in front of the ticket office. Widow Drummond waited for them to come to her. Samuel glanced away from the happy couple. What was this sensation blazing through his heart? Was he jealous? He truly had no interest in a wife. Why would he be envious of something he didn't want?

The second bride exited and the French architect, Mr. Foucart took her to the shade. Samuel smiled when she apparently surprised him with some French phrases. He wondered if she'd learned them specifically to impress Frank, or if she actually knew the language.

The next two brides were betrothed to the Forrest's eldest sons. Albert entertained everyone, except his mother and Widow Drummond, when he ran up and snatched his intended off the steps. Sam had to chuckle at that.

Deputy Andrew Ootaknih received bride number five, and the youngest Forrest's son received a cute little gal who clung to a carpet bag like her life depended on it. Samuel stared at that coveted bag. It had a wiggle inside of it. That was curious. The crowd giggled when she marched to the shade without taking Oliver's proffered arm, or letting him carry her bag. She seemed to be a volatile little stick of dynamite. Sam chuckled at this one, too. Oliver would have his hands full.

Samuel enjoyed the jocularity that passed through the townsmen who had come to see the new brides, but exhaustion seeped into his limbs and he hoped it would be over soon. He turned his head to tell Emma he was ready to go back, but something happened at the train. He turned back to see what everyone reacted to.

A seventh bride appeared. She tripped out of the train car onto the platform, smashing into her basket and spilling food onto the ground. The crowd gasped to see her and chuckled at her clumsiness.

Samuel didn't see clumsy, he saw grace and dignity as she recovered and stood tall and proud. A crimson hue flushed her face. It made her even more beautiful. Samuel sat up straighter in his chair. His heart slammed against his ribs. The rhythm of his blood surging through his veins filled his ears with a roaring sound.

Was this a side effect of being outside for the first time in so many weeks? Or was it this woman. She was tall and sturdy, but so beautiful. The square of her jaw line drew his gaze. He wanted to stand and walk up to her, to caress that jaw with his finger and thumb, and to take her into his arms. Her height sent a sizzle of excitement through him that he rather enjoyed.

Somehow he just knew she'd fit against his body perfectly. Not like these other women who looked like they'd break if held too tight.

But this woman! The seventh, unexpected bride, she was sent here just for him.

Samuel shook his head. He didn't want a wife. He hadn't participated in the mail order for a bride for a reason. What were all these crazy thoughts going through his head? He'd had too much of Doc's pain medicine. That had to be it. He was delirious, or… or something.

Samuel rolled his chair forward, but Emma's firm hand pulled him back. "Careful, Samuel. Doc said we should wait yere. Don't chu go do nuttin' to make yoself fall outta dat chair, I'd ne'er get chu back in it by myself."

"You don't understand. I—" He almost told Emma he needed to go to that last bride.

The Town Council had said six brides were to arrive. Didn't they? He should have paid better attention. Who was this one here to meet? No one approached her, except Sheriff GW. She handed him an envelope. It had to be a letter of introduction. Widow Drummond read the letter, too.

"Please don't send her back. I think she's here for me." Samuel said under his breath.

"Hmm?" Emma leaned down to hear what he had said.

"Nothing." Samuel hated the harshness in his voice. Emma didn't deserve it, but he couldn't admit to her or anyone else for that matter, that he just saw his future disembark from that train.

The sheriff and Widow Drummond didn't seem too upset. In fact, they walked her over to the shade with the other brides. Samuel breathed a sigh of relief. She was staying.

Maine must be Heaven, because Sam knew without a doubt this angel was sent here for him, but he couldn't approach her until he was healed. Doc had told him to be patient, but he couldn't, not any more. He set his jaw to regain his strength! He would stand! He would walk! He'd exercise with his hammers and build himself back up to where he was before the accident.

He had to, so he could ask her to be his.

Chapter Nine

Doc and Emma exchanged a look when the sheriff called for help.

"I'm all right." Sam reassured him. Doc nodded and left Sam's side to follow the other townsmen to the platform. Emma stayed with Sam.

There were seven trunks and a crate of chickens. Claude had loaned one of the Gunther Stable's wagons and a sturdy mule named Blanche to tote the women's belongings to the Bride House, and to take the ladies to the Rocking F Ranch this evening for the First Dance. Widow Drummond had planned to walk the brides to her home so they could get an idea of the lay of the town.

Wilma, and the widow oversaw every movement made to load trunks, gather the women and their intendeds, and lead them down Broad Street.

The other women continued to watch the activities with idle fascination. Mail order brides arriving was the most exciting thing to happen in Gunther City since April's land rush.

The other brides kept their gazes on the trunks until everything was loaded, but this one seemed uninterested. Sam wanted to carry her belongings for her and escort her into town. He moved his chair forward when she lifted the suitcase.

Emma gasped. "Whut chu doin' Sam?"

He sighed and let her pull him back. Was that suitcase all this last bride had with her? A need consumed his heart to fill a trunk with beautiful clothes, give her anything her heart desired, build a house and furnish it with the finest. He wanted her to lack for nothing. He wanted her… in his life.

The chickens clucked and frantically flapped about in their crate, drawing his attention back to the wagon. Wilma shook her head. "Claude, them chickens ain't gonna lay for a week after all this."

He nodded and shrugged. There wasn't much else he could do.

The intended suitors carried their brides-to-be's bags, except the one with the carpet bag, of course, and escorted them down to the Bride House. Widow Drummond led the procession, pointing out the businesses along the way. Wilma followed as rear guard, or co-chaperone, as it were. Claude drove the wagon at a pace in which he stayed behind her. The volunteer helpers walked behind the wagon. It was as close to a parade as Gunther City had ever had. Sam and Emma stayed at the depot watching the impromptu parade until they reached the widow's home. The women around him slowly dispersed, returning to their businesses or homes. Dahlia Cambridge hurried across the street to her mercantile, muttering about needing to find another color for this unexpected bride.

Sam glanced, longingly, toward the Bride House. The men who volunteered to help with the wagon carried the trunks in and came back for another. Sam held the wheels of his chair so that Emma couldn't move him from his spot. He watched until all activity ceased and Claude pulled the wagon on down the street to his stables. Sam's eyes stayed on the back of the wagon until Claude turned into the barn, then Sam's eyes cut across the street to his shop. His heart sank.

People had brought work to be done and piled it outside the smithy. It spilled off the boardwalk and into the dirt street. Sadly he shook his head. At least they weren't hauling it across the prairie to another Land-Run town. How he yearned to get that work done. If only he could stand.

He glanced down at his casted legs, loathing their weakness. He glanced back at the Drummond House. She was in there. Settling in, setting up her room, filling the wardrobe with what little she had in that suitcase. A piece of his heart went with her, longed to be with her. He had never felt so empty in his life. Doc exited the Bride House and walked across the street to his office. Sam needed to talk to the doc, right away. He wanted to get his hammers and start working these muscles. He had to regain his strength and he had to start now.

Sam turned to Emma. "I'm ready."

The brides were pleased to see the mercantile on their left and a tailor's shop next door to their new home. The ladies paused to inhale the scent of fresh baked bread that wafted toward them from further down the street. Helen commented on the aroma making her feel like she was home.

But Minnie spied the blacksmith shop at the end of the last building across from the stables. The smithy was far behind on his work according to the various items stacked at his doors, spilling into the street and in the prairie grass past the shop. Judging from what she could see, he was months behind. Curiosity filled her thoughts. She would ask about the smithy once she had a chance.

Widow Drummond smiled, seeing the girls pleasure in smelling the bread, and pointed across Division Street where Wilma Gunther ran the bakery. Wilma spoke up and promised the girls a fresh baked treat once they were settled in their rooms. Dahlia Cambridge promised to catch up in a bit and hurried to her mercantile.

Mrs. Drummond unlocked the front door and led the girls into the parlor. She waited for them all to enter. The suitors trailed after them, still holding their belongings, and gathered beside their bride-to-be. The widow cleared her throat and lifted her wooden spoon, shaking it at the men.

"This is as far as you go, gentlemen." She glanced out the window at the wagon with the trunks. "Except for today."

GW and the men began hauling the trunks in. Widow Drummond turned to the women. "Now, ladies, there are three floors with four rooms per floor. Thanks to Mrs. Cambridge, who's currently fussing over getting your room ready" —she tipped her head and gaze toward Minnie— "you ladies take your time and look at the rooms. Start on the second floor, though. Downstairs is where I live."

She smiled and took in a deep breath. "Now, they're all the same, mind you, except for the color scheme. We designated them by the curtain and bed cover colors. Your choices are: baby blue, dark blue, purple, pink, spring green, and dark green."

Again, she addressed Minnie. "I'm not sure which color Mrs. Cambridge will choose for you, dear, but I'm sure it'll be lovely."

Minnie pursed her lips. "What you have now, will be fine, I'm sure."

Widow Drummond wrinkled her brow and pointed her wooden spoon at Minnie. "No, Missy. Every bride in my home is going to have a pretty room, you included. You just caught us unawares, but we'll have things gussied up in no time."

Minnie's face flushed with heat and she lowered her eyes to the ground. She appreciated the attention, but hated it at the same time. She lived her life as an obstacle of attention. She had hoped Gunther City would be different. She had noted the men in the crowd were tall, like her. Some stood taller. That was one thing she had truly hoped for and thanked God for hearing her prayers on that one. Hopefully He heard some of her other prayers for this new start. She set the heavy suitcase down at her feet. There was no suitor to carry her things. She waited until Mrs. Drummond or Wilma Gunther released her to go find a room.

"Now," Widow Drummond continued. "At the end of the hall on each floor, you will find a bath and privy room. It's the finest you'll find in the west." She grinned from ear to ear.

Minnie chuckled to herself. Obviously, she was extremely proud of these bath rooms.

"There is a dumbwaiter on a rope to bring buckets of water to the rooms and a stove to heat the water right there next to your tub. You're gonna really appreciate the immediacy of the hot water and not having to haul it up the stairs by hand."

Mrs. Drummond paused to let the ladies absorb and appreciate this modern convenience. "Not even the Hotel up by the train station has such a nice setup. Then again, they have staff to haul water up for a private bath in the guest's room," she added.

Widow Drummond shook her spoon at the suitors. "Now you boys are gonna wait here while the gals go look at the rooms and decide which color suits them best."

She turned to the ladies. "You claim your room by setting your carpet bag or some piece of your belongings, in the hall by the door, then come back down here and let your feller know where to take your trunk."

Minnie's heart sank. She couldn't haul trunks for the girls. Except Jane Anne since she had two trunks. The suitors should do it for them. It was all part of the courting process. A process she was not part of. She decided to simply go find a room that wasn't decorated in gingham and claim it as her own.

Dixie looked panic stricken and Minnie knew why. She couldn't set her carpet bag down to claim a room and return to the parlor. There was no telling what Mr. Darcy would do without Dixie holding the bag firmly closed. Minnie stepped toward Dixie. "Let's go together and find a room next to each other, donchaknow?"

Relief washed over Dixie's taut expression. "Ayah. I'd like that."

Dixie's betrothed gave her a double take. He didn't look angry, but definitely annoyed. The two ladies scurried toward the stairs to look for a gingham decorated room next to a room that was not decorated for a bride.

"Let's go to the third level." Minnie suggested. Then lowered her voice to a whisper, "If Mr. Darcy does get out, we can corner him before he makes it down the stairs."

Dixie giggled. "Good idea."

Minnie heard the other Forrest brothers snicker and make comments about Miss Levine having his pecking order figured out. She frowned and hoped her helping wasn't causing trouble for Dixie and her betrothed.

Dixie chose the dark green gingham room which was next to a room with chocolate brown and brocade coverlet and curtains. It was lovely actually. Minnie rather wished they would leave it this way, but Mrs. Drummond made it very clear she would make the room more frilly, regardless of how much Minnie protested.

Minnie carried her suitcase, and Dixie's carpet bag into the chocolate room and closed her door. Mr. Darcy sprang from the bag the second she set it on the floor. He ran around the room sniffing and hiked his legs. "Eh! Mister Darcy. You must wait. I promise you will get to go soon!"

Mr. Darcy lowered his leg and continued his surveillance of his new surroundings. "Don't get too used to it, old man, this is my room not your's. Besides Ol' lady Drummond is changing the whole thing around tonight."

Tonight? They were all going to a First Dance tonight. What will Dixie do with Mr. Darcy then? Maybe Minnie should stay back at the Bride House and let Dixie go to the dance with her betrothed. Minnie had no reason to go anyway.

Minnie held Mr. Darcy close to her chest, but when he heard a man's angry tone, he squirmed and fought against her grasp. As Dixie's voice grew louder, he wriggled free and ran toward her door, barking for all he was worth. Minnie whispered very sternly, "Mister Darcy! No! Come here!"

Mr. Darcy ignored her and scratched at the door, barking and growling even louder.

"What's that?" Mr. Forrest's voice came closer to Minnie's door. She cringed. So much for hiding the dachshund.

Minnie listened as Dixie tried to coax Mr. Forrest back to the parlor and his continued insistence that she was hiding something from him.

Minnie couldn't take Dixie's anguish any longer. She opened her door with Mr. Darcy in her arms. "I'm afraid there is a dog in here, and it's my dog. I-I had no one, so I brought my little dog all the way from Maine, kept him closed up in a carpet bag. I did."

Oliver's eyes darted from Dixie to Minnie. Dixie stood with her tiny gloved fingers covering her mouth. Her face had drained of color and her hand trembled. His eyes roved over Minnie's tall stature. She stood firm. The dachshund squirmed and whined.

"You weren't carrying a carpet bag." Oliver said slowly.

Minnie knew that he knew. She sighed and stepped into the hall. "Listen. We meant no one any harm." She handed Mr. Darcy to Dixie. He leapt into her arms and licked her face. She hugged him tight and cooed calming words to him.

"Mr. Darcy is very special to Dixie. Please try to understand."

"Oh I understand, all right." Oliver stepped back from Minnie and turned on Dixie. His hands on his hips and a firm expression on his face.

"So, Miss Levine, you smuggled a dog out of Maine, on the train, and into the Bride House."

"Yes, but—" Dixie held Mr. Darcy to one side. Minnie was prepared to pounce on him and scream for help should he do anything remotely close to hurting Dixie.

"You!" Oliver's stern expression broke into a huge smile. "You are the most amazing woman I have ever met! I am so lucky you chose my letter. I knew there was something special the minute my eyes met yours. You are a dog person, like me!" He pulled her into his embrace and held her and Mr. Darcy tight.

Minnie stepped back to her doorway. She liked this Oliver Forrest already. If only she could find a perfectly matched missing rib like him. Dixie was one lucky gal.

Minnie stayed in her room while the other girls returned to the parlor. She had no one to tell goodbye and wanted to empty her suitcase right away. She only had three dresses, two petticoats, a pair of boots and some toiletries which Mrs. Robertson had given her. Thinking about the bundle Butterfield refused to let her take, saddened her heart so much she trembled as she put her meager belongings away. She tucked her poppa's things on top of the chifforobe for safe keeping and stepped back. This was it. Her new start. A tear broke loose. She sat on the bed and cried.

Chapter Ten

Dixie and Lou Lou's chatter returned to the third floor. They were eager to unpack and take a real bath. Tonight was the First Dance and they were excited to get ready. Not Minnie, she dreaded the whole idea. Now that Mr. Forrest knew about and approved of Dixie's dachshund, Minnie had no excuse to stay at the Bride House.

Minnie only had three dresses to choose from. She'd worn one on the train, so she'd wear another to the dance. The boots she had been wearing were more comfortable than others. She'd save them for church. Since she was already settled in her room, she took her turn in the bathroom. While the nice soaker tub full of hot water would melt away her aches and sore limbs, she had to wash quickly. The two other girls on her floor needed the wash room, too.

It was a good thing this boarding house had been turned into a women-only home because she no longer had a dressing gown. She wrapped herself in the chocolate brown bed cover and ran downstairs to ask Mrs. Drummond for some boot polish.

While Mrs. Drummond was shocked to see Minnie in her state of undress, she opened the supply closet off of the kitchen to proudly show Minnie everything available for her use. There was an efficient supply of everything a poorly equipped tenant could need, including leather polish and a small tin of saddle soap. Considering these people just set down stakes four months ago after the land run, Minnie was very impressed.

"May I ask you something, Mrs. Drummond?" Minnie hesitated before she turned to go back to her room.

"Of course, dear, and folks around here call me Widow Drummond. I don't mind it. My husband passed from this earth ten years ago. When I said, 'I do,' I gave him my heart. So when he died" —she turned and pulled a hanky to wipe her eye. "He took it with him. He truly was the only man for me and I'll never love another."

Compassion washed over Minnie. Her father's death was just twelve days ago. "I understand Widow Drummond. I wish there was such a moniker to let people know I lost my Poppa just before we came here."

Minnie bowed her head and pursed her lips, trying not to cry. Tears gathered and spilled over her cheeks nonetheless. She wiped them with her bed cover wrap.

"Oh, look at us." Widow Drummond chuckled. "You have a wonderful future to look forward to, and I'm troubling you with my heartache. I apologize."

Minnie tried to smile. "No need." She turned to go to her room, with her boot polishing supplies.

Widow Drummond reached out to touch Minnie's arm. "Your question, dear?"

Minnie tilted her head. Memory of her Poppa had washed all other thoughts away. Then she recalled her curiosity about the Blacksmith's shop. "I was curious. I-I know it's none of my business, I'm sure, but I noticed a Blacksmith shop at the end of Broad Street, but he appeared to be, I don't mean to judge, behind on his work."

She let the statement hang in the air as a question.

"Ah. You have a keen eye, Miss *Smith*."

Minnie glanced at the floor. "Well, I—"

"Our Smithy did a foolish but brave thing a month or so ago. He saved Emma Cherry's life, most likely."

Minnie's eyes widened with intrigue. "How so?"

"Well, Sampson and Emma Cherry are black folk, you see. Very nice people, if I do say so myself." Widow Drummond drew in a long breath. She had so much more to say. "They settled in a sod dug-out on their property from the land run. You know, there were no prejudice against who ran for their one-hun'ed and sixty acres." She nodded until Minnie nodded, too.

"Mr. Cherry is a hard working man, he chops down dead timber, cuts it down to yeah big." Mrs. Drummond held her thin, aged hands out to show how long the logs were. "And splits it all down to nice manageable sizes for stoves and hearths. Every morning they come to town with a wagon full of wood for the townsfolk. We either pay for the wood, or barter with our wares. He might get a ham from a pig farmer, a lotta bread from Wilma Gunther's bakery—"

"Oh, Helen would be delighted to know Mrs. Gunther is the one who owns the bakery. Her family made most of the bread back home, at least for those of us who lived in the Waterfront District."

"Yes, well," Widow Drummond nodded, not bothered with Minnie's interrupting her tale.

"Listen, dear. There are a lotta Gunthers in this town. You'll need to refer to them by their Christian name in order to make yourself clear." The widow chuckled. "Anyway, you get my point. The Cherry's sell firewood and the town gets nicely prepared wood without having to go out and chop it themselves."

Minnie watched Widow Drummond's far off gaze for a moment. She prompted the widow to continue. "And so Emma Cherry almost died?"

"Oh, yes. One day while Sampson Cherry was taking a load of wood into the hardware and Mrs. Cherry was holding the reins to their mule. Something spooked the beast and she took off running with poor Emma hanging on for dear life. Mr. Knight stepped out into the street and tried to stop the terrified animal, only he was trampled in the doing, the poor dear. He slowed the beast down and Emma was able to get her under control, but our poor blacksmith was left in the dirt, broken in several places.

"Thank the Good Lord above we have a young doctor straight out of medical school." Widow Drummond paused. "You know, nobody knows his first name. Folks here just call him Doc or Doc

Savage." Widow Drummond chuckled. "It's the darnedest thing…"

She realized her mind had drifted again.

"Oh, and so Doc knew the latest techniques for healing Mr. Knight. He wrapped him in plaster and linen from the waist down. It's been quite an ordeal for Mr. Knight, you can just imagine, but Emma Cherry hasn't left his side. She's helped Doc take care of our 12q smithy; bathing him, cookin' for him, and even warshing for him. She brings him a clean shirt every day, and now that Doc has been able to reduce his plaster wrapping down to just his legs, he's able to sit up… and get out. You might a seen him when y'all came in today." Widow Drummond smiled. Something mischievous passed over her expression.

"It was the first time he's been outta that back room of Doc's since the accident."

"Oh." Minnie recalled the curious man in the odd chair. "He's the man in the chair with wheels? A black woman stood near him. Was that Emma Cherry?"

"Yes, dear. You do have a keen eye." Widow Drummond's mouth twitched with a slight smile. "Anything else, dear?"

Minnie looked at her inquisitively. "Hmm?"

"Did you have anything else you wanted to ask… about the townsfolk?"

Heat flushed Minnie's cheeks. "No ma'am. I—my Poppa was a blacksmith. I s'pose you've figured by my last name, and so smithy shops are rather near to my heart. That's all. I didn't mean to gossip."

"Oh, Miss Smith, you'll never hear me repeating gossip in this house." She lowered her voice and leaned toward Minnie. "We step outside for that." She chuckled heartily.

Minnie giggled with Widow Drummond. She was a very likable person, despite first impressions and her wooden spoon. "I'm sorry for Mr. Knight. Samuel Knight, is it? I'm so sorry he was injured so badly. It'll take him months to get caught up once he's able to get back to work."

"Yes…" she paused to consider Minnie's interest. "I suppose so." Widow Drummond watched Minnie very carefully though veiled eyes.

"Well, thank you for the boot polish, I'll bring it back as soon as I'm done."

"No hurry, dear. I know where you live." An ornery smile lifted her thin lips. "You got a dance to get ready for, I can get the polish from you tomorrow."

"Thank you, Mrs., I mean, Widow Drummond. I appreciate everything you're doing for me, considerin' you didn't know I was coming and all."

"Don't you think anything of it. Everyone is welcome in the Drummond House." Widow Drummond chuckled. "Except men-folk of course."

Minnie smiled and thanked her again, then hurried back to her room. She needed to braid her hair and polish her boots. Mrs. Robertson had pressed her dresses before she left Portland, but it'd need touching up after being in the hand-me-down suitcase. She had a relatively small amount of time to be ready for the wagon to take the brides out to the Rocking F Ranch. Wherever that was.

Wonder if there's any chance Mr. Knight would be attending. She shook her head. He'd just left a sick bed to watch the brides arrive. Surely he wasn't up to attend no dance out in the country. Disappointment filled her heart as she sat down to scrub her boots clean.

Six anxious suitors sat in the Drummond Bride House parlor. They didn't dare make eye contact with Widow Drummond for fear they would get a whack from her wooden spoon. The Widow had her infamous weapon of discipline in her right hand and her arms crossed over her ample bosom. The hem of her skirt jittered ever so often, indicating she was patting her foot. Her unchanging glare through slitted eyelashes dared them to get out of line.

Mrs. Dahlia Cambridge smiled behind her cup of tea, enjoying the submissive postures of these six who were usually very confident and headstrong. Every male in Gunther City secretly feared the widow's wooden spoon and avoided her and it whenever possible. Mrs. Wilma Gunther lifted smiling eyes to Mrs. Cambridge often. They both enjoyed the future grooms' discomfort.

The brides were instructed to remain upstairs until every one of them were ready to go to the First Dance. It would be the last time they would be expected to travel with their intended as a group. Widow Drummond had made this clear while she explained how the dumbwaiter worked in the bath rooms.

A commotion drifted down the stairs. Widow Drummond's eyes fluttered from a ceaseless watch on the men toward the sound of bickering. She rolled her gaze to Wilma who immediately rose to her feet. "I'll see what's the matter."

She floated up the stairs.

Seven women stood in the hall on the second floor. Wilma was taken aback for the briefest of moments at their beauty. Their attention was centered on poor little Dixie Levine who was crying. Minnie Smith stood between the girls and Dixie, protecting her from whatever the other five were trying to take from Miss Levine. Wilma focused on what Dixie held.

"Oh, dear!" she gasped. These brides continued to surprise her with unexpected appearances. Miss Levine clung vehemently to a black and tan, long, skinny dog with large floppy ears, and a long slender snout. He had the shortest legs Wilma had ever seen on a canine. She almost laughed at the sight of him.

"What's this?" Mrs. Gunther hollered to be heard over the women's bickering.

Most of the girls turned to Mrs. Gunther and continued their complaints about Dixie's dog.

Minnie stood her ground to protect Dixie and the dog.

"She's gotta leave that beast here, donchaknow, in her room." Helen said.

"No, she don't." Minnie hollered back at her.

"Ayah, she thinks she's gotta take that thing everywhere she goes." Jane Anne planted her fists onto her hips.

"A dachshund doesn't belong at a dance, donchaknow? Make her leave it here." Alice nearly whined.

Mrs. Gunther suppressed a smile. "Is that what he is? A doxson?"

She pushed her way through the full skirts to reach Dixie. Minnie hesitated and then gave way. Wilma rubbed her palm over the trembling dog's head. "I've never seen such a long little doggy."

Dixie lifted tear soaked eyes. "My intended knows about Mister Darcy. He's fine with me havin' him with me. Please, Mrs. Gunther, you don't know what he's been through—what we've been through… to get here… together, donchaknow? I can't leave him here alone. Besides, Widow Drummond has seen him and said she won't have him here unsupervised."

Minnie nodded vigorously in an effort to convince Mrs. Gunther.

"Widow Drummond knows about your dog?" Mrs. Gunther glanced toward the parlor. "No, I s'pose the widow would be… concerned to have a dog left alone in her newly decorated room." Wilma smiled. "I tell you what—You say Oliver Forrest knows about… Mr. Darcy is it?"

She paused. Her eyes brightened. "You named him Mr. Darcy? From *Pride and Prejudice*?"

"Yes, ma'am. It's one of my favorite books."

"Do you have the book among your things, by any chance?" Mrs. Gunther's eyes widened with interest.

"Ayah, ma'am. I brought a couple a dozen books. I hope that's all right."

"Oh, my, yes. I tell you what, if you'll trust me to borrow your book, I'll, um…" She glanced around. "I'll sit with Mr. Darcy when you need to leave him home, so… so you and Mr. Forrest can have some alone time." She tilted her head with compassion in her eyes and scratched Mr. Darcy's long ear.

He panted and wiggled in Dixie's arms. "Mrs. Gunther, you can have all of my books, just let me keep Mister Darcy with me. Please!" Dixie choked on her tears, then cleared her throat.

"Miss Levine, if Oliver knows about your little dachshund, I'm positive it will be all right to take him with you tonight. And no, I only want to borrow your book. I know it's a treasure. I promise to return it. As long as you trust me to take good care of it for a bit." Wilma's eyes lifted to Minnie. Her shoulders relaxed. Wilma sighed with relief. She'd calmed the girls down and got an opportunity to read a book she loved. These new brides were improving things in this new town already.

"Of course." Dixie sniffed back her tears. "I'd trust you to the moon."

Mrs. Gunther handed Dixie a pretty handkerchief and wrinkled her brow. "You Maine gals do have unusual colloquialisms. I think I'm going to enjoy getting to know each of you better."

Her eyes perused the anxious faces. "I just mean you say things different from most folks around here." She smiled. "Now, this problem is solved, don't you think, ladies?"

Heads bobbed in agreement. The more aggressive girls, Helen and Jane Anne, frowned, but agreed. Mrs. Gunther turned to lead them all down the stairs. What a grand entrance they would make. She sighed. At the landing to enter the parlor she paused.

"Oh, Ladies." She turned to face the women. "With all the excitement over Mr. Darcy, I forgot to tell you."

The women stopped abruptly. Concern tightened their faces. Had one of their suitors not showed up?

"You all look just lovely." Mrs. Gunther's smile broadened.

Relief washed over them. They responded as one, "Thank you, Mrs. Gunther."

Chapter Eleven

Minnie followed the throng of girls into the parlor as suitors leapt to their feet. She stood alone and looked down at her dress. She didn't look lovely. This wasn't her prettiest dress, but it was the best she had. Besides, she didn't have an intended waiting in the parlor for her. What did it matter if she looked lovely or not?

Then Samuel Knight and his wheeled chair returned to her thoughts. Could she possibly hope he would be at the Rocking F Ranch? Only time would tell. Even if he were there, he couldn't possibly offer her a dance. Perhaps she could figure out a way to speak to him about his smithy shop. Would that be appropriate? She could only imagine how distressed he must be, knowing how far behind he was on his work. No, that would not be a topic to discuss with him. Perhaps she could think of some other subject to discuss with him— the weather, the presidential elections last year, No, her poppa had told her never discuss politics with a stranger. She could ask him about Gunther City. No, that'd be too presumptuous.

She sighed. She could find a seat near wherever he might have parked his wheeled chair. Surely something would come up where she could start a conversation with him. That is: if he was at the dance.

Claude Gunther drove a nicely groomed pair of black spotted appaloosas hitched up to the same wagon that delivered the brides' luggage, only the wagon had been decorated with ribbons and bows, and a string of lanterns were lit giving a festive look. It was a lovely way to travel the four miles to the Rocking F Ranch. Sheriff GW Gunther hopped down from the buckboard leaving Claude to stay the horses.

The girls and their escorts lined up in a promenade style to exit the Drummond Bride House. Minnie lingered at the end of the procession. The couples proceeded to walk out to the wagon, gasping and commenting on how lovely the wagon was decorated. The sheriff stepped into the home and yanked his Stetson from his head, revealing a very receding hairline.

"I'm sorry I'm late, Miss Smith." He extended an elbow to Minnie.

She stared at him a moment, confused by his gesture, then smiled and took his arm. "Thank you, Sheriff."

"My pleasure. We can't have an unescorted lady running amuck in our town." He chuckled.

Minnie giggled. "Indeed, that would be ghastly."

They laughed and walked out the door. GW aided Minnie as she gingerly stepped on a small step ladder, which had been placed at the back of the wagon to help the ladies in without lifting their skirts. GW placed the ladder inside and joined her on the long board attached to the sides for a more comfortable ride out of town.

The brides chatted with their intendeds and each other along the way. Dixie held Mr. Darcy tightly, while Oliver Forrest casually draped his arm behind her. The other Forrest men teased their younger brother for finding a dog-loving wife. Dixie blushed and Oliver frowned, but Mr. Darcy enjoyed the attention given him nonetheless.

Minnie appreciated the kindness of the sheriff to accompany her. He was a handsome man and he stood as tall as she. That was such an enjoyable experience in itself. Back home, the only man as tall as she, was her own Poppa.

She watched the sheriff interact with the other men and women in the wagon and wondered if there was any chance he could take an interest in her. Could she be a lawman's wife? She was strong and sturdy. How could she contribute to a sheriff's home other than cook and clean, and give him children? That thought made her look away from him. Heat flushed her cheeks and she covered them with her large hands.

"Are you all right, Miss Smith."

Her eyes rose to meet his and she yanked her hands down to her lap. "Yes, I'm fine."

"If you're cold, we have wraps for you ladies." He indicated a trunk against the buckboard.

"No, it's warmer here than back home. I assure you, I'm quite fine."

Helen's glare caught Minnie's attention. She seemed to disapprove of Minnie calling attention to herself. Minnie lowered her eyes and listened to the rhythm of the two horses, wondering what specific iron Mr. Knight had used to shoe them.

She noticed a slight break in their rhythm and observed their gait. The one on the left had a slight rise in his hind end. She would call Mr. Knight's attention to it as soon as she could speak to him. She stared ahead of the wagon at the buildings, noting a hardware store, a saloon, and the smithy. It was the last shop on Broad Street before the prairie. Loud noises spilled from the opened door and windows of the saloon. A lively tune on a piano, people singing, laughter, and hollering all made for so much clamor.

Minnie wondered how Mr. Knight slept at night. Of course, she knew after a long day of smithing, he was probably so tired he could sleep lying next to a railroad track leading into Grand Central Train Station. She giggled to herself, remembering her own fatigue and asking her poppa if they could eat a cold supper.

He had agreed. Breakfast could be their hot meal and supper would be something that didn't require cooking. Some evenings, even that was too much to do in their weary state. Often she had gone to bed without eating at all, but woke before dawn famished and would cook a meatloaf and boiled potatoes.

Then she'd put it away in the icebox for supper that night.

Just then, the wagon rumbled past the blacksmith's shop. Minnie studied the items waiting for the smithy to repair. Things were stacked one on top of another. It saddened her to see a gate, an infant's iron bed, a large iron chandelier, some candle stands, several wagon wheels, a broken yoke and chain. Other items were buried too deep under the piles to tell what they were. She knew how badly these things were needed by the people who had left them here. All of which she could repair, if she could just get into the shop.

But that was a ridiculous thought. No one here would let a woman work the forge. Only her poppa allowed her to work the iron. It was unladylike, as Helen insisted on reminding everybody. Minnie stared out across the prairie. What if she could get in there and get some of Mr. Knight's work done? She shook her head. What a crazy thought. First of all it would be breaking and entering. She glanced at the sheriff sitting beside her. Second…

She couldn't think of another reason not to do it, except no one would allow it. To do such a thing would drive off any and every prospective suitor within a hundred country miles. She would seal her fate as a spinster if she let anyone know she knew the trade.

Minnie sighed heavily.

"Are you sure you're all right, Miss Smith?" The sheriff leaned out to look at her face.

She smiled. "I was just thinking how I miss the sea. But when you look out across this prairie I can see a similarity to the waves. The wind's the same, except it doesn't carry the taste of salt with it."

GW chuckled. "No, we don't got salt in the wind, but we got plenty of red dirt."

"Yes, I suppose you do." She laughed, hoping her comparison to the ocean appeased his curiosity about her weighted sigh. Her true thoughts had to remain her own.

Chapter Twelve

The Rocking F Ranch's large timber gate came into view. It looked like felled tree trunks that had been buried in the ground, three varied sizes from a smaller one that stood about fifteen feet above ground, to the largest one standing twenty feet tall and topped by one smaller tree trunk. The center of which was hewed to make a bare-wood oval and the brand, an F over a rocker bar, was burned in its middle.

The girls twisted in their seats to see the ranch house and the large barn where they had been told the dance would be held, but the buildings were down a dirt path, lined by trees and a creek. It made for a lovely ride, but difficult to see the buildings.

Light spilled from the large barn once it came into view. A timber framed walk led from the house to the barn. The eldest son, Henry, explained the lay of the ranch and that since the Forrest's three sons were legal adults the family had claimed six hundred and forty acres.

Several out-buildings set back from the big barn. One building was a smokehouse, another was the spring house. It straddled a creek and held milk, eggs and meat. Across the creek stood the ranch hand's bunkhouse.

Minnie admired the amount of construction that had been accomplished since the land run in April. Here it was only August and between the town and this ranch, it was no wonder the lumber store across from the train station was stacked with so much lumber. It was needed in abundance.

Martha Grace, Alice, and Dixie were very interested in the ranch house. This would someday be their home, too. At least until the sons built their wives separate homes.

Buggies, wagons, and carriages were parked all around the large barn. It looked like everyone from town, with the exception of the ones in the saloon, Minnie thought, were already here. The brides and their escorts were the last to arrive. Pete and Gladys Forrest stood near the barn's double doors, greeting people as they walked in. The ranch hands took the horses into the corral, and put the carriages, buggies, and wagons in the smaller barn.

GW jumped from the wagon and set the step ladder for the brides to be able to get down with ease. Minnie hesitated before lowering her foot to the little ladder. It didn't look precarious going up the small ladder, but coming down looked like a tumble just waiting for her. She held up an index finger to the sheriff, turned her back to him, and held out her hand to Oliver Forrest, who stood next to Dixie and Mr. Darcy. Oliver automatically received Minnie's hand and she eased herself down backward to the ladder. The toes of her boots going into each step of the ladder. She felt secure in her descent.

GW stood at the ready should she fall, but avoided touching her skirts and being accused of improper behavior. He chuckled when she touched the ground. "There's more than one way to skin a cat."

Confusion washed over Minnie's face. "Why on earth would anyone want to skin a cat, Sheriff?"

He shrugged and the two of them laughed.

Dixie looked at her betrothed, shrugged her shoulders, tucked Mr. Darcy snugly under one arm, and held Oliver's hand as she too descended backward to the ladder. GW paused to be sure she made it to the ground safely. And so it went with the brides exiting the wagon backward, having their hands held by their intended and another's intended watching for their safe landing.

The Sheriff placed Minnie's hand at his bent elbow and walked her into the barn. "Miss Smith, I have a feeling things are going to be a lot different with you around."

Minnie considered his statement. Thinking about the smith's forge sitting idle, the possibility of herself working the iron in Mr. Knight's stead, and helping him to get caught up as he recovered. "I hope you're right, Sheriff."

She smiled and turned to be introduced to Pete and Gladys Forrest. Mr. Forrest seemed agitated. He greeted Minnie with the briefest of handshakes and then ignored her completely. Curiosity lingered with Minnie, but she allowed Sheriff Gunther to lead her further into the barn.

As the seven brides and their escorts entered the barn, a fiddler lifted his bow and played an exaggerated two notes that sounded like "Ta Dah." The dance floor had been designated with end-to-end hay bales framing a cleared area on the barn floor. A man stood next to the fiddler with his arm resting on a bass cello.

The attendees applauded and then the fiddler set his bow to strings to play a waltz. The other man accompanied him in a bass clef rhythm. Minnie looked to her sister-brides, but they had immediately been swept out onto the floor with their intendeds in a three step and spin dance she could never imagine herself doing without stepping on her partner's feet, or tripping over her own.

Nevertheless, Sheriff Gunther bowed his head. "Miss Smith, I know I'm not your intended, but I am your escort, and as such I am honored to begin the First Dance with you." He put out his hand. "May I?" With all eyes now on her, because the other six brides were dancing, including Dixie with Mr. Darcy tucked under one arm, Minnie nodded in agreement. GW took her hand in his, placed his other hand at her waist, and whispered, "One, two, three; one, two, three."

She followed him out on the floor, softly counting to the beat of the music. He was tall like her and easy to follow in his graceful rhythm. Without realizing it, she was waltzing with ease and loving every minute of it.

When the waltz ended, the fiddler kicked up a lively tune, and the couples switched to the appropriate

dance for that song. Minnie's eyes widened and the sheriff smiled. "How about we check out the lemonade table and then get ourselves a beef dinner. I heard ole Pete cooked half a cow on a spit just for this event. Probably why he has such a sour face tonight. He's not the most generous settler among us. "I'm surprised Gladys talked him into having the dance out here in the first place. He's not much of a social person, either. Especially with all the time and man power it took to get this whole thing ready. I heard he's been fit to be tied ever since the town council asked him to do it." The Sheriff laughed heartily. "But the Misses got her way to have the First Dance here. Just like most of you females do." GW escorted her to the food and drink table. Barrels with stools had been set outside of the hay bales for sitting. Behind a long table stood two identical women who dished up food. The table was covered with a large platter of sliced beef, dozens of vegetable choices, cakes, pies, and trays of golden brown cat-head rolls glazed in butter. GW lifted his hand to gesture toward them. "These are my twin sisters, Dorothy and Debra."
Minnie inhaled the yeasty aroma.

GW smiled. "They make these rolls. It's a town favorite and no one has been able to duplicate their recipe." He chuckled. The twins giggled and waved off his compliment.

"Pleased ta meet ya." Minnie nodded.

Their eyes rounded as they took in her large size. Dorothy smiled and insisted she have a "healthy" portion of beef and vegetables. Debra fussed at her sister about always overfeeding everybody. It was quite comical. Minnie liked these two immediately, but what she really wanted was a double portion of those rolls.

She thought of Helen's momma who made excellent bread, but this recipe beat the Baird family's bread, hands down. Glancing over her shoulder, she wondered what Helen would do about all this. Would she be gracious, or would she be the same ole spoiled, chip-on-her-shoulder girl that Minnie had grown up with?

The lemonade was fresh squeezed and sweetened with honey and mint. Debra proudly leaned into Minnie to whisper it was another Gunther family secret recipe and winked. Minnie accepted the cup and smiled. Why didn't these two open a restaurant? Everything they made was based on a family recipe that tasted superior to anything Minnie had ever eaten back in Maine.

A large bowl of watermelon punch was available, too, and several huge pitchers of sweet tea were set out on the drinks table. The barn grew hotter with all the dancing and people. Minnie fanned herself and sucked down more lemonade.

She perused the people to see if Mr. Knight was present. No wheeled chair or smithy with broken legs sat among them. She did see the black woman who had accompanied him at the train station. Emma? Was that her name? Berry? No, Cherry. Emma and Sampson Cherry, Minnie brought the information to the front of her mind. They stood to one side clapping their hands with the music. Would it be proper to approach her and ask how Mr. Knight was doing? She'd learned of his accident through idle gossip although Widow Drummond claimed it wasn't. Minnie snickered. No wait, she said she never *repeated* gossip in her house. They had to step outside for that.

Minnie laughed to herself.

"What's funny?" Emma Cherry said softly. An enormous grin exposed her brown mottled teeth, with one or two missing.

Minnie started. When had Mrs. Cherry walked over to her? "Oh, I was thinking about something Widow Drummond said today."

"Huh, and it made you laugh? That's a good sign."

"What is?"

"Widow Drummond strikes fear into most folks' heart with her wooden spoon." Mrs. Cherry leaned her head back and laughed from her belly. "But once a body gets ta know da woman, she's such a dear. Would do anythin' fer a body. Even us black folk." Mrs. Cherry's eyes sparkled.

"Yes, I find that to be true." Minnie smiled remembering the widow making her abundantly stocked supply closet available to Minnie earlier that day. The widow had taken one look at Lou Lou's chicken crate and ordered Albert Forrest, Lou Lou's intended, to go out back and section off the poultry yard with a surplus roll of chicken wire and to slap a lean-to on the side of her chicken coop, so Lou Lou's chickens could roost and have a laying box to themselves.

Every bride's needs were met upon arrival. Some, but for the asking, and others without. Mrs. Drummond had an eye for detail and unspoken needs.

"You gonna fit in yere right nice." Mrs. Cherry turned to the fiddler and clapped with the music. Minnie let her eyes follow the couples who were dancing. She tapped her foot to the music. As the song ended, Alice Canning pulled away from her suitor, walked over to the barn wall and lifted a hand saw from a nail. She climbed onto the riser where the fiddler and bass player stood. Her betrothed, Henry Forrest, watched from the dance area. He looked concerned, maybe even agitated, as he glanced around. Oliver sidled up next to his oldest brother and shoved an elbow into his ribs. Minnie smiled. This was going to be good.

Alice walked up to the fiddler and put out her hand. The man turned to the people and shrugged his shoulders. Everyone laughed. Henry's face reddened. He gestured for Alice to come to him. She ignored her betrothed, and gestured again for the fiddler to hand her his instrument. Reluctantly, he eased the fiddle toward her. She shook her head, then touched the fiddler's bow. She gestured for the fiddler to hand the bow to her. When she snapped her fingers, he handed her his bow, letting his fiddle hang limp at his side.

She sat on a three-legged stool, which had been put on the riser for the fiddler to rest, placed the saw tip down, bent it slightly, and drew the bow across the straight edge. The crowd had been chattering, wondering what she was up to, but when she drew the bow across the flat side of the saw, she played the most beautiful version of Amazing Grace Minnie had ever heard, everyone silenced. Even Henry's shoulders relaxed.

Alice bent the saw to change the note and cause a vibrato in the long notes by shaking the handle slightly. Back home it had been said that Alice could make music out of anything. Minnie had to agree, it was true.

Everyone stood, entranced at the sound she was making with an old wood saw and a fiddler's bow. When Alice finished, she stood, and held the saw and bow out from her body as if it were hot to the touch. The people applauded and cheered. She had won their hearts, and the oldest Forrest son appeared to be even more smitten by his bride-to-be.

The other brides applauded their sister-bride. Her whole family was known for their musical talent. This was no surprise to them. Their family's business was making string instruments that were coveted by

European artists. It was said Alice had music in her blood. Tonight she proved it with a simple saw and bow.

Alice held up the bow, presenting it to its owner. The crowd busted out laughing because nearly every hair on the bow was frayed and curled like a busted cat tail weed. The fiddler frowned as he accepted the ruined bow, but then he smiled and lifted another from his fiddle case. The people cheered. He began another waltz and the couples resumed dancing.

Minnie turned to Mrs. Cherry. "I don't mean to be rude, but could I ask you a question?"

Emma's eyes were moist from witnessing Alice's performance, but with Minnie's inquiry, her eyes widened. "I believe that would be all right," she agreed, but caution washed over her tranquil expression.

"I was wondering… Mr. Knight is the town's blacksmith, Ayah?" Her Maine accent so different from the woman's southern drawl.

Suspicion filled Mrs. Cherry's eyes. "Yes, he is."

Minnie touched the woman's arm. "Oh, I didn't mean… I just was wondering when he would be able to get back… I couldn't help but notice he had a lot of iron work waiting for him to—"

Mrs. Cherry's large lips trembled, holding back emotions.

"Oh, Mrs. Cherry. I'm so sorry. It's none of my business, I'm sure. It's just my Poppa was a blacksmith, donchaknow, and smithing is dear to me, I couldn't help but notice the work waiting for Mister Knight. Please don't cry."

Mrs. Cherry wiped her eyes and sniffed. "No, no. It's all right. I just feel responsible fer his gettin' hurt is all. He saved my life, you know?"

Minnie lowered her chin to her chest. A flush of embarrassment filled her face. "Yes. I knew that."

A full moon cast an eerie glow over the land as the bride's and their betroths returned to town in the same festive wagon. The lanterns were lit and Sheriff Gunther sat at the end with Minnie. For some reason everyone had sat in the exact same spot going home as they did going to the Forrest Ranch. Several of the women slumped over onto their intended's shoulder and slept as the wagon rocked and bumped along the stretch of road that led back to Broad Street.

Minnie found herself fighting the lull of the wagon, but remained awake all the same. Sheriff Gunther served not only as her escort, but as chaperone to the other couples. When they pulled into town, Minnie turned to look at the iron work waiting to be repaired. The Turner Saloon was still lit up and lively. The piano playing was loud enough to wake the dead… or cover any noise that might be made next door.

Three men spilled out of the double swinging doors and stumbled up Broad Street. The smithy shop was the last building at the edge of town, but, Minnie noticed, people leaving the saloon would always go up the street, or across, if they were headed to the stables. Her eyes met Sheriff Gunther's. He had been watching her working thoughts through her mind. He smiled. "The saloon owner's a woman. Katherine Turner. She's a decent person and a smart business owner. You may find that you like her, despite her occupation."

Heat of embarrassment filled Minnie's face. She wasn't judging anybody. Least of all a woman who filled what would be thought of as a man's position in life.

No, she wasn't judging anybody. Not anymore anyway.

Chapter Thirteen

Minnie fell into her small bed but didn't cover up. Even with the windows open for cross ventilation, it was so sultry. Maine had its heat and its humidity, but it was nothing compared to this Oklahoma sweat-box weather. The crickets sang their night song. The full moon lit up the room with a soft light. She closed her eyes and willed sleep to come, but she couldn't go to sleep. The smithy shop was heavy on her mind. Could she make her way down to it and check it out? With the moon as bright as it was, someone would see her. But if she went out behind the Drummond Bride House, and around the stables, perhaps, no one would notice her.

She looked down at her bright white sleeping gown. In the moonlight it nearly glowed. She'd need something dark. Her poppa's clothes! She had chastised herself for bringing them. Could it be that Poppa had led her to take them for this very reason? "Thank you, Poppa," she whispered and changed into his clothes. His pants were too big, but she tied the tail of his shirt around her waist to help hold them up. With her boots and his hat, she could pass as a man traversing the streets. If no one looked very close.

She'd have to be so, so quiet. If Widow Drummond thought there was a man in her boarding house, she might shoot him with her shotgun and ask questions after. Minnie pursed her lips and slipped out of her room. The stairs creaked as she eased down them carefully to the first floor, out through the kitchen, and into the back street between the boarding house and the Mayor's home.

Minnie hurried, staying close to the back of the buildings and rounded the stables' corral. The horses whinnied as she slipped past them. She cooed calming words like her poppa had taught her when they shod a skittish horse and zipped across the street.

If Mr. Knight was like her poppa, he'd have made a twist of iron for a lock on his back doors, because he was the only one in town strong enough to open it. She slipped around to the back of the smithy shop and stood before the alley doors. She'd made it. One look at the door handles and she snickered. The lock was the same as Poppa's, but she was strong, too. Soon she was inside, and thanked God for light of the full moon. The forge was more than a month cold. She opened a large box next to it. The charcoal box was empty. First she'd have to locate his woodpile and make some charcoal. She glanced out a window at the moon. It was well into the night. She had enough time to get some charcoal started and tomorrow she'd see if she could fire up the forge to start on some of this work.

Looking around, she saw Mr. Knight organized his tools, like she did for her poppa. They hung on the walls in a working order. She smiled. "So his hardwood would be…" she turned around. "Ah." He kept his hardwoods at the back door, just like Poppa. She gathered several pieces and put them in the charcoal kiln. Mr. Knight had his shop set up so similar to her poppa's, she had no trouble figuring out what to do. His flint lighter hung on the wall, where she expected it to be. She placed some softwood in the forge, and lit it. Once she had a nice burn going, she scooped it with a shovel and filled the kiln. It would continue to burn and cause the kiln to heat, charring the hardwood inside. The kiln warmed the shop.

She sat back against the anvil and wiped her brow. The evening had cooled but the shop was at a familiar temperature that would be miserable to an average person. Looking at the back doors, she wondered, did she dare leave them open to let the heat out and fresh morning air in? She considered the thought.

The saloon activity was dying down. Minnie figured it would be light in a few hours. Normally, she would never leave a kiln burning, but she needed to get back to the Bride House and get some rest. Exhaustion was consuming every fiber of her being and she longed to rest. Mr. Knight's kiln was self contained and Minnie assessed she could close the shop with the kiln burning and everything would be all right. As small as the kiln was, she figured, Mr. Knight probably had charcoal charring every day and burned it in his forge the next. With any luck, no one would question the heat.

She hoped.

Breakfast smells waft up the stairs, gently waking the brides. All but one. Minnie heard the padding of her sister-brides' feet as they made their way down.

Giggling and chatter faded to the first floor. Minnie had only been in her bed for an hour. She turned over and ignored the call for breakfast. Her need for sleep was greater than her need for food.

Soon the chatter and giggles returned as the girls dressed. A knock came to her door. She sighed heavily. "Yeah?"

"Minnie?" Dixie called to her.

She dragged herself from the bed and opened her door just a crack. Dixie and Mr. Darcy peeked through. "What, Dixie?"

"Widow Drummond wants everyone in the parlor in ten minutes." Worry laced her tone.

"Why?" Minnie yawned.

"We're going to discuss our chores and… I don't really know."

"All right." Minnie closed her door and flopped back into bed. Just five more minutes, and she'd get up.

Another knock woke her. "Minnie! Widow Drummond is waiting on you downstairs!" It was bossy Helen Baird.

Minnie sat up but didn't answer.

"Minnie!" Helen pounded on the door. "Get up, you lazy girl! Surely you're not that tired from the dance? You hardly—"

Minnie yanked the door open. "I'll be down in a minute!"

Helen looked her up and down. "You've not even begun to get dressed. Hurry! Widow Drummond is waiting on you."

"I'll be down in a minute, Helen." Minnie growled. She slammed her door and sat on her bed.

A light tap woke her again. When had she laid back down? "What!"

Dixie called her name. Minnie sighed heavily. She couldn't be mad at Dixie. She opened the door and Dixie handed her a mug of hot coffee. "This should help. You really need to come down. Mrs. Drummond said you may come in your dressing gown."

Minnie shook her head. "I don't got one."

"Oh." Dixie's eyes dropped to the floor. "Well, just wrap up in your bed covers and come down. No men are allowed in the house before ten."

"Okay. I'll be down." Minnie yawned. "Thank you for the coffee."

"Not a problem." Dixie's brow drew tight as Minnie eased her door closed. She sipped the coffee and pulled the red gingham quilt Mrs. Cambridge had made and placed on Minnie's bed while she was at the dance last night. The red gingham curtains did make the room brighter and she really appreciated the change.

Barefoot and wrapped in her new quilt, Minnie descended the stairs. Still yawning, but sipping the coffee Dixie had brought her, she joined the girls in the parlor. Hostile glares didn't affect her as she sat and lifted sleepy eyes to the widow. "Sorry."

Widow Drummond cleared her throat. "Well, now that I have you all here, we need to discuss chores and expectations."

Minnie drank her coffee and looked around to see if the pot was nearby. Mrs. Drummond had it sitting on the pot-belly stove near the dining room. Minnie rose and poured herself some more, than sat back down, while Mrs. Drummond discussed a cooking, cleaning, and wash rotation. Two girls were assigned each task, with Minnie being the odd number, she would be with Lou Lou and Dixie. Thank God she wasn't paired with Helen or Jane Anne.

Alice and Martha Grace took first turn for cooking. Helen and Jane Anne had laundry, which took two days, and Minnie, Lou Lou, and Dixie had clean up: Dishes, counters, and floors, including sweeping the downstairs. Mrs. Drummond glared at Minnie when she stated, "…and alcohol is not permitted in the boarding house ever!"

Minnie turned to Dixie with an innocent crinkled brow. She had not been drinking alcohol. But to defend herself would require she reveal she had been at the blacksmith's shop most of the night.

Mrs. Drummond led the girls on a tour of the kitchen. Cooks were expected to plan the meal for their assigned day. A slate board hung in the pantry. They were to write their menu selections and check to see if anything was needed from the mercantile. However, Widow Drummond proudly informed them, her pantry was well stocked. They were to be sure to check in there before suggesting any purchases.

The widow made breakfast this morning, but they would be responsible for breakfast, lunch and supper for all of the brides beginning today. Only supper was *required* to be a hot cooked meal, the other two were up to the cooks. The gentlemen suitors were allowed to join them for supper. So the cooks were required to ask if any gentlemen should be counted for supper.

Minnie yawned. Mrs. Drummond glared at her but went on. Minnie considered speaking to the landlady later to emphasize she had not slept well and was not hung over from the fire-water drink. Mrs. Drummond emphasized this was an excellent opportunity for the brides to demonstrate their cooking skills, and she strongly suggested the cooks invite their betrothed the night they were on cook duty.

Sunday would be a day of rest for the brides, Widow Drummond and Wilma Gunther would prepare a late lunch which would serve as supper, because of church services. Unless the brides were invited to another's home for supper, or on a picnic with their betrothed, they were expected to eat at the Bride House. Mrs. Drummond smiled. She appeared to be excited for all the activity that was expected to take place in her home because of the courting practices. Minnie blinked heavily, trying to stay awake. She refilled her coffee twice more. Her team had *clean up,* so when the widow finished her lecture, Minnie walked into the kitchen to see what needed to be done. She wanted to get it finished so she could go back to bed. Sometime she needed to figure out a way to check on the charcoal she had started last night.

Samuel Knight woke before the sun. His sleep had been filled with dreams about the seventh bride. He sat up on his own. The spinning would stop soon, he hoped, and the nausea had to subside. He hadn't eaten anything since Emma brought him to the Doc's back room after the brides disembarked.

She had given him butter sandwiches and beans with salt pork for supper, but he wasn't hungry. She insisted he eat. How could he make her understand, ever since he saw that woman emerge from the train, his appetite had disappeared? Thankfully Emma was in a hurry because of the First Dance and didn't stay to badger him into eating.

He reached for his two hammers. He had to get back to his forge, otherwise, what did he have to offer. He'd never cared about being a provider other than for himself, but now, since this angel from Maine had come to town, he wanted to be a better man. Until he could stand at his forge and generate an income, he could not even consider asking permission to court her. No woman deserved a lame husband from the get go. He wouldn't broach the subject with her or Preacher William Gunther, until then.

He shook his head slowly. His brain felt like jelly that sloshed inside his skull. This was no good. He pulled a hammer up to his shoulder and lowered it slowly, feeling its weight in his arm. Then he lifted the other. With his eyes closed, to stay the nausea, he continued to work with his hammers, until a knock came to his door. Emma had breakfast.

"You're up?" She entered with a tray covered by a drying towel.

"Mrs. Cherry, I need a favor."

"Why Samuel, we be long past chu callin' me dat, but whut can I do fo ya?"

"I need to get into my shop."

Emma gasped. "Doc said you still need to take it easy."

"I know, I know. But I need to get some things done, so when I'm better, I can get straight to work."

"Well, is it somethin' me or Sampson could do fo ya?"

Samuel considered her question. "I don't know, probably. Does your husband know how to make charcoal?"

Emma smiled. "He shore do."

"Great. After I eat, could you help me dress and see if Sampson could meet me in my shop?"

"No." Her smile melted into a frown. "But I can ask Sampson to go to yo shop and get sum har'wood charring fo ya."

Samuel sighed a long deep sigh of resignation.

"Fine. If he could do that, it would put my mind at ease. Thank you."

"Shore 'nuff, Sam. My Sampson be happy to do it fo ya." Emma placed the tray in his lap and removed the towel. Steam rose from beef hash, cornbread, and four fried eggs. She left the room and came back with a tin cup of coffee along with the coffee pot. She set it on the little wood-burner stove to keep it warm and folded her hands in front of her apron. "Is there anythin' else I can bring ya?"

Samuel's stomach answered for him. He chuckled. "No. I think this will be fine."

"All right. I'll go talk ta my Sampson and I'll be back to hep ya dress."

"Thank you, Emma, and thank Sampson for me, too."

"I will. Now you eat." She looked stern, but a smile gave away her true compassion.

Sampson Cherry finished his route, delivering firewood to the townspeople. Emma had asked him to char some hardwood for the Smithy. He had left some good pieces in his wagon and pulled it around to the back of Mr. Knight's shop. It was past midday, so he could spend the rest of the day watching the kiln. Emma wouldn't be ready to go home until she had fed Mr. Knight and helped him to bed. Maybe she'd bring him a tray if he were just down the street working on charcoal.

He examined the smithy's twisted iron through the door pulls. He'd have to put his back into it, but he most likely could twist it open. He tried, and then drew in a deep breath, and tried again. He clenched his jaw and strained until the iron slowly gave way. He opened the doors and smelled the kiln already burning. "Hmm."

He chuckled and shook his head. That smithy couldn't wait. He's already been down here and started his charcoal a charring. Sampson left the doors open, to release the heat and walked over to the kiln. Hardly any smoke rose, a small flame flared every so often, otherwise it all looked good. Just like his daddy had taught him back in Virginia, the charcoal was heating through quite nicely. He pulled over a wooden bench, leaned his back against the wall and stretched out his long legs. He'd keep an eye on it, while he waited for his wife to bring him supper. Maybe catch a wink or two while he was at it.

Chapter Fourteen

That evening, after the house had completely quieted down, Minnie laid in her bed until the moon crested her window. She donned her poppa's clothes and eased down the betraying stairs. Why hadn't she chosen a room on the second floor? Oh, right, she was trying to help Dixie, when she suggested the third. She chuckled as she eased the back screen door closed and scurried down the back street to the stables.

A different group of horses whinnied and she made a mental note to bring apples next time. Stroking their noses, as they lifted their heads over the split rail fence that held them in, she cooed calming words. "Shh, my friends. Don't tell anyone you saw me, ayah?"

The horses shook their heads and stamped their feet. She knew how they felt. She wasn't exactly where she belonged either. But if she could get Mr. Knight's work caught up for him, she'd have a purpose here in Gunther City. She looked forward to working with the iron again. At least she could be of some help to someone who sorely deserved it.

From what others were saying about Samuel Knight, he weren't much social, but after his accident, everyone hailed him a hero for the self-sacrifice to save Emma Cherry. Few women survived a runaway wagon without losing their life or getting severe injuries of their own. Mrs. Cherry wouldn't have survived the injuries Mr. Knight had sustained. Mrs. Cherry was lucky Mr. Knight had been where he was when her mule took off. He was like the polished armored clad knights of Dixie's books, questing to find damsels in distress. Minnie smiled. Perhaps he could be her knight in shining armor, too.

Hurrying across Broad Street, Minnie rounded the smithy shop and stood at the back doors. She noted the iron bar had been twisted the opposite direction in which she had left it. Had Mr. Knight come down here somehow to check on his shop?

Oh Lord, the kiln! He'd know she had been in his shop! Her breath quickened. She glanced up the back street. Should she run home? Forget this foolishness? No, he couldn't know it was her. No one knew. Whoever had been in here would only know that the kiln had been lit. She gritted her teeth, leaned into the iron, and untwisted it. Maybe they'd think some good Samaritan had charred up some charcoal for Mr. Knight. She looked around the forge. She hadn't left any signs to lead back to her. Her hand clasped her poppa's collar. Her heartbeat slowed to normal. She would stay, get the work done she had intended, and make more charcoal before she left.

The back doors had to stay closed for now. She'd just have to endure the heat. Maybe later in the night she might open them for ventilation. Hopefully the town would be sound asleep by then, and the Turner Saloon would be loud enough to cover up the noise she was bound to make. She also prayed the people in the saloon would only enter and exit through the front doors, like she had observed the other night. Pulling the large doors together, she checked on the charcoal in the kiln. It was perfect. She transferred it to the charcoal box, and lit another round of hardwood. The stack seemed larger than yesterday. Maybe Mr. Cherry'd replenished the supply.

Would he notice the wood was being used? If he did, would he tell anyone? "God," she prayed. "If I get caught, please let your mercy shower down into their hearts and know that I meant well."

She opened her eyes and turned to the forge. Filling it with just the right amount of charcoal and kindling, she lit the fire and pumped the bellows. While it burned, she opened the front door just enough to slip out. Her eyes scanned the stables, Broad Street, the boardwalk. All was quiet. She turned her gaze to the things needing repair and assessed which pieces she should work on first. From her experience in her poppa's shop, she knew the wagon wheels probably were needed the most. She dragged them into the shop and closed the door. Pumping the bellows some more she watched the coal turn red, then yellow, and finally white hot. She lifted the wheel onto a long sturdy table and removed the broken iron. Mr. Knight's apron and gloves hung near the forge, she needed them to keep from getting burned.

How she wished he had an extra pair that she could sew up to fit her hands, like she had done with Poppa's gloves. But this was what she had and this was what she'd work with. Setting a strip of iron in the fire, she placed it on the anvil, paused to listen to the rhythm of the piano next door, and began working in four-four time on bending the iron to the circumference of the wheel.

It made the work fun, matching the piano player's beat which changed seldom from a lively tune. She supposed saloon music was basically the same gay song, just different words.

Before too long, four wagon wheels were complete. She looked around and found a large desk in the opposite corner. Inside the middle drawer, she found a pad of Bill of Sale slips and a bottle of ink and a nice pen. Not knowing who the wheels belonged to, she simply wrote: "4 Wheels Repaired," and the cost she assumed was fair.

At least it would have been fair back home. If she overheard any complaints in the gossip at the supper table, she'd adjust the prices tomorrow.

She considered that thought. How would they pay Mr. Knight? Maybe she should put a slotted box, like the orphanages back home used at their stoop for people to make anonymous donations. People could just slip the money in the box and she could stack it on his desk when she came back the next night. Then she remembered Widow Drummond telling her that a lot of business was paid with bartering wares.

She chewed on her bottom lip. Well, if anyone wanted to barter the work for meat or chickens, they would have to square up with Samuel Knight when he got back to his forge. Surely people were honest about such things. Why else would they just leave the work to be done and not have some journal entry recorded.

A shock of fear ran through her heart like a flash of lightning. What if they took their payment to Mr. Knight's sick bed. Would he figure out she had broken into his shop? Blacksmiths were extremely protective of their hearth. He'd send the sheriff to investigate the break in.

She swallowed the lump of fear. She just couldn't worry about everything. For now, all she could do was get as much work done before daylight and get back to the Bride House before breakfast.

Minnie slipped out the front door for the next item to fix. The cool evening air refreshed her sweaty brow. She paused to enjoy the coolness. A boot heel sounded on the boardwalk. She stiffened. Her eyes shot open.

A beautiful woman stood in front of her, with fists on hips. Her dress was made of the finest material Minnie'd ever seen, and her hair was beautifully swirled and tucked on top of her head, with feathers, lace, and beads woven in.

"What's going on?" The woman whispered loudly.

"I-I'm just" —Minnie looked back at the shop— "I'm helping Mr. Knight. I know smithy work. My Poppa…I know what I'm doing. I just wanted to help." Minnie stammered.

"You're a girl?" The woman looked her over. "You dress like a man. You almost sound like a man, but you're not a man."

"Yes." Minnie stood to her full height. Her tallness usually intimidated people. "So are you."

The woman glared at her a moment, then she broke out in a laugh, but quickly covered her mouth and looked around. "I'm Katherine Turner. I own this saloon. And you are…?"

Minnie's eyebrow shot up. Katherine Turner. The woman the sheriff told Minnie about while they rode to the First Dance. Would she be an ally or would she tattletale on her? "I'm Minnie Geneanne Smith. I come in on the train from Portland, Maine, but I ain't got a betrothed." Tears choked her words. "My Poppa was killed and I had to get outta town. Our pastor put me on the train with the mail order brides. I got three dresses to my name and I lost my favorite pair of boots."

Minnie gasped for air. She'd spilled her guts without a breath between words, now her lungs were starved. "Please don't tell no one, Miss Turner."

Katherine Turner tilted her head slightly, a scoop of beads hung down from her hair. "You're a mighty unusual sort of gal, aren't you? I think I like that about you. And I'm pleased to see another woman who ain't skeared a doing what's considered men's work."

She nodded her head. "Yes, ma'am. I like you already, Miss Minnie Geneanne Smith. You keep on doing what you're doing. I won't tell a living soul. Shoot, I won't even tell a dead one."

She threw her head back and laughed, but quickly covered her mouth and looked around. "I keep forgetting it's so late. I'll tell Frank to crank up the piano, so we cover your hammerin'. Don't you worry none. If need be, I'll even tell folks that sound they're hearing is a new instrument we got to help Frank keep the beat and they can just kiss my be-hind." Katherine turned and laughed all the way back into the saloon.

"Kiss my be-hind." She repeated, pleased with her own words, as she stepped through the double swinging doors.

Minnie closed her eyes and let her head fall back. That had been close. She perused the items waiting for repair and chose a gate. She could see where it had broken and the hinges were rusted through. She pulled it inside and pumped the forge back to white hot.

Minnie slipped in the back door and hurried to her room. She had just enough time to wash and get dressed. Her team had cooking duties today, so there was no point in trying to get any sleep before breakfast. She'd eat, make some excuse that she was still tired, and slip back upstairs to get some rest until lunch time. The familiar exhaustion from working the iron all night was both comforting and punishing. She quickly folded her poppa's clothes, placing them at the top of her wardrobe, and slipped into her camisole, bloomers, and corset. Because Minnie had lived alone with her father and had no mother or sister to help with dressing, Mrs. Tucker had kindly restructured Minnie's corsets so that she could bind them in the front and not the back, like most were made.

She was just as grateful for this feature now, because she could dress herself and not bother any of her sister-brides. She tossed her dress over her head and wiggled until it fell down over her undergarments. Padding feet hurried from room to room as the girls sought help with their foundations. Minnie chuckled. It was no surprise when a light knock came to Minnie's door. Dixie in her unmentionables and Mr. Darcy in her arms, rushed in when she opened it. Dixie set Mr. Darcy on Minnie's bed and grabbed ahold of the poster at the foot rail. "Not too tight, please. I prefer to breathe." She giggled.

Minnie pulled the strings, working down Dixie's back, and tying it above her bottom. Dixie's waist was so tiny, she didn't need the foundation for a fashionable figure, but any respectable woman wouldn't dare *not* wear her corset, even out here in the wild western plains of Oklahoma.

"There you go." Minnie yawned. "See you in the kitchen."

Dixie turned to look Minnie over. "You better wake up, sleepy head."

She gathered Mr. Darcy and padded to her room. Minnie buttoned her dress, slipped on her boots, and wrapped her braid around the crown of her head, tucking it under with a single hair pin. She yawned and glanced longingly at her bed. Dixie hadn't noticed it had not been slept in yet. Hopefully she thought Minnie had already made it. She hurried downstairs and was the first to enter the kitchen. She went straight to the pantry and gathered potatoes. The slate was wiped blank after the evening clean up. She didn't know what her chore partners had in mind, but surely breakfast would include fried potatoes. She lifted the chalk and wrote, "Breakfast." Then under that, she wrote, "Fried Potatoes."

Mrs. Drummond had shown all the brides where her utensils were kept during their tour. Minnie laid the potatoes on the butcher block table, pulled out the peeler, and shaved the dark brown skins.

Lou Lou entered the kitchen, yawning. "Good Mornin'."

"Mornin'." Minnie suppressed a yawn. "You want to fetch water and start the coffee?"

Lou Lou yawned again and picked up the water pail. "Sure." She staggered out back to the pump.

Dixie rushed in. For the first time, she wasn't holding Mr. Darcy. "What are we making?" Her eyes were wide with excitement.

Minnie shrugged and turned to Lou Lou stumbling in the back door with the pail of water. Minnie hurried to her and set the bucket on the pie cabinet, and turned back to Dixie but was speaking to both women. "Menus are up to us. Either of you know how to make hotcakes?"

Lou Lou and Dixie nodded. Lou Lou prepared the coffee pot and placed it on the stove, filled the wood box and lit a fire. "You're obviously going to fry those, I'll go gather eggs. How about hot cakes, biscuits and gravy, fried eggs, fried potatoes, and…"

Minnie nodded. "There's sausage in the cellar."

Dixie nodded. "…And sausage. I love sausage gravy." She wrote the selections for breakfast. "Okay, and what for lunch?"

Minnie thought. "Are there any leftovers?"

"I'm not sure." Dixie disappeared into the pantry. "Martha made several loaves of bread, and there's a ham hanging in the cellar. How about ham sandwiches, sliced pickles, sliced turnips, and peaches… and cream if there is any?"

Minnie continued to shave the potatoes. "Sounds good to me. How about supper?"

Lou Lou came through the back door with her apron held out in front of her. "I've got eggs. Did I hear you ask about supper?"

Dixie and Minnie nodded.

"Are we allowed to butcher those chickens?" Lou Lou lifted the eggs from her apron and placed them in a large brown bowl.

Minnie considered her question. "I suppose so, we had chicken stew yesterday. The Forrests' sent some beef home with somebody the other night, I saw a good chunk of it wrapped in cheesecloth in the root cellar."

"Well," Lou Lou emerged from the pantry. "I was thinking chicken and dumplings for supper, but since we had chicken yesterday, how about that beef… and dumplings? cornbread, and… I noticed a whole lot of canned vegetables in the pantry, how about greens, and glazed carrots? And maybe we should make another batch of bread for tomorrow's team."

Minnie took the big knife from the drawer, slid it across a wet stone in both directions, and diced the potatoes. "Are you kidding? Helen and Jane Anne are cooking tomorrow. Let her make the next batch of bread. We'll stick to the quick breads."

Lou Lou frowned. "Gosh, yes. What was I thinking?" The girls laughed.

Dixie completed the menu on the slate and pulled out two skillets. Lou Lou had lit the stove for the coffee so all she had to do was add some lard and let them warm up. She turned and measured out flour, salt, baking soda, sugar, and lard. Blending it with the pastry blender, she hurried down into the root cellar and brought up a jug of milk. Soon she had the dough ready, but so was the melted lard. "Minnie, you want to fry, and I'll get these biscuits cut out and in the oven. Then I'll make the hotcakes."

"Sounds good to me." Minnie yawned.

The women set about their tasks and soon had breakfast ready to serve.

Chapter Fifteen

Claude Gunther stood at the doors of his stable, scratching his head. He had no idea who had repaired the wagon wheels, the gate, or the iron baby bed. But people had come to him throughout the day trying to pay him for the work. Said they had a bill of sale attached to their items and wasn't sure it was all right to put the money in the box next to the smithy's door.

It was a mystery to Claude. He told them if that was the instructions on the bill of sale, then that was what he'd do if he were them. One family had four chickens to give the smithy for his work. They'd need water, maybe some feed.

Claude suggested they bring them to his stables. He had the crate from one of the bride's and he'd watch over the chickens 'til Mr. Knight was back in his shop to claim them. The whole thing seemed stranger and stranger as the day went on. He hadn't noticed Samuel over there working, and thought for sure he was still at the Doc's. He'd just been at the train station in a wheeled chair and his legs were still in casts, surely he wasn't well enough to be over in his shop working.

Sampson came by with his supply of firewood and Claude rushed out to greet him. "It's the darnedest thing, Mr. Cherry. How you s'pose them iron works is gettin' done?"

"Beats the heck outta me. Mr. Knight asked Emma to have me go by dere yesterday and char up sum har'wood so when Mr. Knight be ready ta come back, his hearth would be ready ta go. But when I gots in dere, Mr. Knight had already started da wood charring." Mr. Cherry pulled his hat from his head and wiped his brow with a handkerchief. "Now that I think 'bout it, it might notta been Mr. Knight. But who could it a been?"

"Lord only knows, Mr. Cherry. Lord only knows." Claude shook his head and paid Cherry for his supply of firewood.

Mr. Cherry climbed into his buckboard and drove his mule on down the back street. Eventually he came around to the smith shop. The wood pile had been used. He unloaded some more hardwood and walked up close to the back doors. Heat spilled through the crack between them. He examined the twist of iron that locked the smithy's doors. It was backward from how he had left it. Someone had definitely been inside. If it weren't Mr. Knight, then who was it? When he finished his route, he decided he'd go talk to Mr. Knight.

After breakfast, Minnie's team was free to do what they pleased. Lou Lou and Albert Forrest had a morning appointment with Preacher William Gunther. She would be back in time to help with lunch. Dixie, Mr. Darcy, and Oliver were going out to the Rocking F Ranch. Therefore, Dixie wouldn't be back until time to help with supper. Albert and Oliver were expected for that meal. Minnie crawled up the stairs, peeled out of her dress, untied her corset and let it fall to the floor. She collapsed into bed, wearing nothing but her camisole and pantaloons. She was asleep before her pillow warmed.

A clamor at her door woke her in what seemed like five seconds later. She could hear Helen's hateful voice and Widow Drummond trying to calm the girls. Minnie sat up, trying to get her bearings, and pulled the quilt over her shoulders, she opened her door.

"Well, there you are." Martha Grace said with authentic concern.

"It's about time!" Jane Anne's voice grated Minnie's nerves.

"My God, are you sleepin' again?" Helen spoke with venom in her tone.

"Now, ladies, we are all working on getting used to a schedule." Widow Drummond tried to settle the women.

Minnie just stared at the anxious faces.

Widow Drummond cleared her throat. "Yes, well, it seems the hour has passed for our noon meal and your teammates have not returned from their outings. I'm afraid you are on your own to prepare lunch and" —she glanced over her shoulder— "it appears everyone is quite famished."

Minnie closed her eyes and yawned. Lifting heavy eyelids, she turned away from the door, then turned back. "I'll be right down."

She closed her door and slipped into her dress without the corset. She'd be returning to bed anyway. Helen stomped away but her voice penetrated

Minnie's door. "She'll never find a husband if she's going to be this lazy!"

"Shut up, Helen." Minnie muttered as she buttoned her dress and slipped her boots back on.

She brought the ham up from the root cellar and set it on the butcher block table. She had just set the coffee to boil on top of the stove, when Lou Lou came rushing into the kitchen. "I'm sorry I'm late, Minnie. What can I do?"

"I've just started carving the ham, slice up the bread, and get those pickles out from the pantry." She yawned. "I'll butter the bread and make the sandwiches. Open three jars of peaches and see if we have cream." She glanced at the slate on the pantry door. "Oh, and bring out them canned turnips. We'll just warm them on the stove."

Lou Lou did as Minnie asked, all the while examining Minnie's demeanor. "You all right?"

Minnie looked up slowly. "You're meeting with Preacher Gunther sure took a long time."

Lou Lou blushed. "Well, not so much. After our meetin' with the preacher was over, we walked around the church grounds and… talked."

"Uh huh." Minnie glared at her. "So, is he a good… talker?"

Lou Lou's face brightened to crimson. "I'll say."
Minnie couldn't help but chuckle. "Well, then I forgive you. But let's get these starving brats served their lunch before they gnaw Widow Drummond's leg off."

Lou Lou giggled and disappeared out the back door and into the root cellar in search for cream.

Sampson yanked off his hat as he entered Doc Savage's office. "Afternoon, Doc."

"Afternoon, Sampson. You needing Emma?"

"No, sir. I's here to speak to Mr. Knight. May I go on back?" Sampson waited until the Doc nodded.

Emma had just cleared Samuel's lunch tray and nearly dropped it when Sampson opened the door.

"Oh, Sampson. What ya—? Ya needing yo dinner?"

"No, wife. I's needin' ta talk ta Mr. Knight."

"All right, but don't be long. He usually takes a nap after his meal."

Sampson smiled at his wife and walked up to Mr. Knight's bed. "Yo lookin' better."

"Thank you, Sampson. I'm feeling better. I'm going to get up after a bit and see if I can talk the Doc into letting me go down to my shop. Could you go with and help me get that lock open?"

Sampson rubbed the back of his head. "That's kinda why I come to see ya, Mr. Knight."

Samuel perked up. "Why, what's wrong?"

"Not sure anythin's wrong. I wen' down to yo shop like Emma asked me ta, ya know, ta make chu some charred wood. But—"

Samuel sat up straighter and tilted his head. "But what?"

"Well, there was already some wood charring in yo kiln. I assumed it were you so I didn't thin' nuttin' mo' 'bout it, 'til today. Claude Gunther's been gettin' people trying to pay him for arn work and he don't know nuttin' 'bout it getting' done, neither."

Sampson turned his hat like a barrel head in his hands. "It's the darnedest thing, Mr. Knight."

Samuel stared at his friend. "I'll say." He glanced at the door. "Listen, I've gotta get out of here and check on my shop. Can you please help me?"

"Wul, whut I gotta do?"

Sam scooted to the edge of his bed and swung his plaster wrapped legs over to the floor. "Pull that chair over here, and help me get over into it." He pointed at the wheeled chair and scooted closer to the edge. "I think I can do the rest."

Sampson hesitated. Would Emma kill him for doing this? He complied and helped Samuel over into the chair.

"Thanks." Samuel sounded exhausted already.

"Now" —Samuel pushed the wheels and propelled himself forward— "to figure out how to break outta this poky."

He winked at Sampson.

Sampson smiled. "I think I gotta way." He positioned himself behind Samuel's chair and pushed him out the room and around to the back door.

"We'll go the back way."

"Works for me. Thank you, Sampson."

"Just do me one favor." Sampson whispered.

"Anything."

"Don't tell Emma I done this."

The two men snickered as they slithered down the back street to the blacksmith shop. Sampson untwisted the iron bar with great effort and pulled the back doors open. Charcoal smoldered in the kiln. Embers were grey but warm in the forge. His smaller hammer lay next to the anvil and the iron pieces had been rearranged, picked through, maybe. Moving to the front door, he gestured for Sampson to open them. He complied.

Samuel found completed iron work that had not been picked up by the customer. It had a bill of sale attached to it and was stacked neatly to the left of his front doors. The price on the bill of sale was a little higher than he would have charged. He wheeled himself up close and leaned over to examine the work.

It was good. Clean. Well done, actually. He sat back. Very well done. He had to admit, he was impressed. Bewildered eyes lifted to meet Sampson. "Who could be doing this?"

Sampson shrugged. "Dunno."

Samuel inspected another iron lamp stand. "Whoever it is, he's really good at it, but why all the secrecy?"

"Mr. Knight, I has no idea." Sampson searched the premises for a clue who had been in there. "Want me to stay the night, an' see who's coming in?"

Samuel considered his offer. "No, you got your wife to go home with and you got your firewood work to take care of." He sighed. "I'll figure something out." Samuel gave the place one more look over. " Whoever he is, he's not causing any harm, really.

Just makin' a mystery, and the work that he's doing is good—really good, so I can't complain, you know? I just feel weird about him doing it without telling me." Sam considered the work.

"Maybe that's why he's charging more than I would. Maybe… he's padding his share for doing it." Sam ran a trembling hand through his hair and down his face. His beard had gotten long and out of control. Kind of like this mystery blacksmith doing his work, it was out of his control. He should ask Emma to wheel him over to the barber.

Samuel shook his head. Why was he worrying about his beard? His shop had been broken into and all he could think about was sprucing up for a woman who doesn't even know he exists. Why would she? He's lame and a burden on everyone right now. How could he possibly make himself known to her? Again, he shook his head. Someone had broken into his shop!

…And fixed things that needed to be fixed for his customers.

…And put a bill of sale for the people to pay for the work.

Samuel got an idea. "Sampson! Let's close up and go talk to Miss Turner. Maybe she's seen something."

"Good idea." Sampson hurried to stand behind Samuel's wheeled chair and push him out into the back street. Samuel helped by pushing his wheels and made his way to the back of the saloon. He knocked as hard as he could to be heard. Eventually the door opened and the bartender, Joe, glared at them. His dark shiny skin gleamed in the sunlight. "Whach'all needin'?"

Samuel scooted up closer to Joe. "Is Miss Turner available?"

The man's smile dropped into a frown. "Whach'all needin' her for?"

"I just need to ask her a question. Please. My shop's next door and... it got broken into. I'm wonderin' if she saw anything unusual last night."

The man cocked his head back as if he didn't believe Sam. "I know who you are, Smithy."

"Please." Sam begged. "I'm living in the Doc's back room right now and can't watch the place myself. I need to know if Miss Turner saw anyone going in or outta my shop."

The bartender didn't say a word, but backed into the saloon. A few minutes later, Miss Turner emerged in a slinky immodest gown. "How can I help, Samuel?"

Sam explained his dilemma. Katherine just smiled. "I can't say I saw any *men* going in or out of your shop, Sam. Sorry, but if you gots somebody who cares enough about the work you cannot do right now while you are" —her eyes swept over his plaster wrapped legs— "I say you got a pretty good deal going on over there and maybe you should just let the chips fall where they may. Maybe fate's working in your favor for once." Her smile widened. Samuel's expression of distress softened her smile. "Look, honey, if I see any *men* going in over there, I'll send word down to the doc's and let you know. Deal?"

"That's all I'm asking, Miss Turner." Sam nodded. Katherine closed the door.

Samuel looked up at Sampson. "I have an idea. Help me back to my shop."

Sampson pushed him back into the shop. Samuel rolled over to his desk and took out a piece of stationary. He scribbled a message on it and placed it in his lap. "Could you help me with the front doors again?"

As Sampson pulled the front doors open, Samuel rolled over to his tools, and lifted a small hammer and a nail. He joined Sampson on the boardwalk, and handed him the paper, hammer, and nail. "Here, put this up there. This will tell me just how talented our mystery blacksmith is. Maybe, after this, I'll hire him on as a partner." Samuel looked over the pile of work. "Lord knows I can use the help."

Sampson tacked the letter to the front door and followed Samuel back into his shop. He closed the front door and secured the iron bar.

Samuel sighed. "I'm tired, my friend. Could you push me back to the Doc's?"

Sampson closed the back doors and twisted the iron bar.

Chapter Sixteen

By supper, Minnie had rested, albeit perforated sleep to fulfill her chore requirements. Dixie and Lou Lou were back. The three of them entered the kitchen at about four o'clock to get started on the supper. Minnie made a double batch of biscuits because the breakfast biscuits were devoured with many grand praises. So twice as many would be needed tonight since several of the girl's betrotheds were joining them.

Dixie was giddy with stories about Mr. Darcy and Oliver's prize border collies. It seemed Mr. Darcy took to ranch dog duties the minute Dixie's foot touched ground on the ranch. At first, she was terrified her dachshund would get trampled, but his instincts came out the moment he saw the herd and he out maneuvered Oliver's best herder.

The Border Collie's registered name was Della's Best, but he called her Delli. In fact, during their outing at the ranch, he screamed her name so many times, Dixie could barely breathe to tell the story.

Oliver's pride was sorely wounded when Mr. Darcy spied a dozen cows and their calves. He had leapt from Dixie's arms, herded ten of the bovine into a tight circle and directed them into a split rail corral. While Delli had gathered two and a calf.

Oliver admitted later, that he had needed to get the calves in the corral for worming, branding, and castration, but was planning to put it off until the next day when Dixie wasn't visiting. She begged him to take care of them while they were contained. She held Mr. Darcy and stood on the bottom rung of the fence to watch Oliver and his brothers complete the tasks. If she had been wearing the appropriate attire, she'd have helped.

Mr. Darcy wriggled and barked when they let the cattle back out into the pasture to graze. It seemed Mr. Darcy felt the cattle needed to be kept close at hand and not allowed to wander too far from his sight.

"I was terribly concerned Mr. Darcy's performance would be too much of an upset and Oliver would call off the betrothal." She sobered in telling her tale. "But we laughed on our way back to town. He finally admitted he was impressed with the Mister Darcy's skills."

The three laughed and expressed sympathy throughout Dixie's story, while they prepared the evening meal. Soon, the supper table was set, coffee, tea, water, and milk was offered to those who waited in the parlor with their future spouses. Dishes lined the big, long table, and the supper bell was rung. Widow Drummond said grace and the table came alive with dishes being passed, chatter and laughter, stories, and food consumption.

Tomorrow it would be Helen and Jane Anne's turn to cook and Minnie, Lou Lou, and Dixie would get two days to do their laundry. Alice and Martha Grace had *clean up*, so when the meal was devoured, Minnie excused herself to return to her room. Before she stood, however, she cleared her throat. "Widow Drummond?"

The widow's eyes sparkled with jubilation. She enjoyed having the brides and the suitors in her home. It had been transient boarders for too long. "Yes, dear?"

"I was just curious. What does Mr. Cherry ask for his firewood?"

"Oh, you needn't worry about that dear. I cover those expenses for the house."

"No, I was just curious… my future husband and I will be purchasing it from him, also. I just wondered."

Widow Drummond nodded. Appreciation washed over her expression. "Good thinking, Miss Smith." She explained to all the girls what Mr. Cherry delivered and how much he charged for the bundle sizes.

Minnie nodded. "Thank you. May I be excused?" Helen's voice trailed Minnie's approval. "She'll never find a suiters the way she keeps to herself."

"Shut up, Helen." Minnie muttered as she opened the door to her room. She would read until everyone was in bed, then she'd make her way down to the smith shop and get some more work done. She prayed the quality of her workmanship would outweigh the fact that she broke into Mr. Knight's shop.

Once she changed into her poppa's clothes, she'd slip down into the root cellar for some apples. There were horses in that corral that would be holding her to her word. She chuckled and tried to let the fear of being caught subside.

How much trouble could she get into, really? She worried her cuticle, chewing until it bled, while reading another of Dixie's books, "Tom Sawyer."

As she reached the stables, the horses whinnied as if they were expecting her. She cooed to them and handed each an apple in the flat of her palm. As she ran across the street toward the back of the smith shop, she spied a piece of paper tacked to the front door. Once she fired up the forge, she'd see what the note said, and then pull the undone work inside. After untwisting the iron which was twisted the opposite from how she'd left it, she hurried to the kiln and placed the charcoal in the bin and started the forge. She refilled the kiln and started another round of wood charring. Widow Drummond had told her how much Mr. Cherry charged for the wood. She unlocked the front door, brought the money box in, and counted its content. Pleased there was more than enough to pay Mr. Cherry, Minnie found a stack of stationary and tore a strip to wrap around the money. She tied it to a piece of split wood with twine and laid it on top where the twine showed, but the money did not.

Everything was ready to begin.

First, the note on the door. She opened the door enough to take the note and read it by the forge fire. A smile slowly curled on her lips. Someone was challenging her and she loved a good challenge. The note asked for left handed tongs, fourteen inches in length to handle logs in a hearth.

"Come on!" she whispered. "Make it a hard challenge, would ya." She looked at the iron available, and chose three-quarter inch round steel for the tong bits. Then she lifted a half inch round rod for the handles. These she'd cut down to the fourteen inches requested. A one-quarter rod for a rivet and some borax for a nice weld flux and a sturdy wire brush. There, she was set to begin.

She rotated the metal away from her body counter-clockwise so the grip would be comfortable for this left-handed customer. When the tongs were finished, the reins were in the proper orientation to keep them from rolling out of the customers hand when he used them to move the wood.

She held up the finished tongs and admired her work. Her poppa would be pleased. She wrote out a bill of sale and placed them to the left of the front door for the customer to pick up tomorrow. Next she assessed the items she'd brought in and determined which was most important. She continued her work. A rooster crowed across the street at the Gunther's Stables. She hurried to snuff out the forge, put the tools away, and locked the front door before scurrying out the back. This time, she smiled when a thought came to her. She twisted the iron rod the way whoever had been getting in during the day had done. Perhaps he was the left-handed customer requesting special-made tongs for his comfort. Her tell-tale sign of entrance at the back door was disguised for now.

Dawn peeked over the horizon and she needed to hurry. Today was laundry for her team and she wouldn't be allowed to sleep past noon. But at least she could skip breakfast and gain some sleep. If only Helen would leave her alone. Maybe she'd write a note and pin it to her door. "Please let me sleep."

In her room, she sighed and stripped down to her chemise and drawers, folded her poppa's clothes, and collapsed into bed. Breakfast be damned... was her last thought.

Sampson's conscience tormented his soul. He needed to let the sheriff at least know there had been a break-in to the blacksmith shop, even though Mr. Knight had told him there was no reason to report it because there hadn't been any harm done. Knight's trip down to his shop had worn him out and he was sleeping soundly when Sampson left his room. Sampson crossed Broad Street and tapped on Sheriff Gunther's door.

Deputy Andrew Ootaknih greeted Sampson. "Mr. Cherry? What brings you back down here? You delivered our firewood this morning."

"Yes, sir, I know I did." Mr. Cherry turned his hat in his hand like rotating a wheel. "I need ta speak ta ya or the sheriff, although I wuz told not ta."

Curiosity wrinkled the deputy's brow. "Well, then you better come on in and have a cup of coffee. Just put a pot on a few minutes ago."

Cherry glanced back at the Doc's office across the street, then entered the Sheriff's.

"I'm much obliged." Sampson accepted a tin cup of coffee and sat. He told Deputy Andrew about the break-in and how work had been done. "Mr. Knight says the arn work been done real good, too. So he's not turibly upset by it. But—"

Andrew smiled. "But you're worried about the break-in."

Sampson looked up with surprise. How'd the deputy know what he was trying to say? "Yes, sir."

"Well, I'll talk to the sheriff, but I suspect he's gonna agree with the smithy, and as long as he doesn't file a complaint there's not a lot we can do."

Sampson's eyes widened.

"But—" Deputy Andrew held up a hand. "We'll keep an eye on the place for Mr. Knight."

Sampson sighed with relief. "Good."

A gentle tap woke Minnie. The sharp angle of sunlight told her it was noon, or nearly noon. She sighed. "Coming."

Lunch would be served soon and wash needed to be started. She didn't have much. She only owned three dresses and two sets of under things. Most women had to start at sun up to get their belongings washed and hung to dry. Minnie knew her wash would only take a few hours and she could iron and hang them all back in her wardrobe by this evening. She opened her door just enough to see who wanted her.

Widow Drummond with worry in her eyes peeked in.
"Are you ill, dear?"

"No, Widow Drummond. I stayed up late… um… reading. I'll be right down."

"All right, dear. Your sister brides were getting worried."

I'll bet, especially Helen. Minnie grumbled under her breath and closed her door.

Lunch was vegetable soup and cold bread. Minnie had hoped for meat, but didn't complain. Widow Drummond had given Minnie her late husband's overcoat, so that she could wash her three dresses and underthings. She considered the possibility of washing her poppa's clothes as well. If Lou Lou and Dixie finished and left her to herself, she could sneak them in with her dresses and hang them in the middle between her dresses and the bed linens to hide them from prying eyes.

She agreed with Dixie to hurry the wash along and added her whites to their tub. They had already combined their darks and had them hanging on the line. Minnie returned to her room and bundled her bed sheets and dresses over her Poppa's clothes. Back in the yard, she stirred her dark clothes into the cold wash. Dixie and Lou Lou hung the various whites.

Minnie rung out her darks and left them in the bushel basket while she helped the girls hang the rest of the whites. She promised to bring their whites in with her, in hopes that they would leave her to hang her dark clothes.

Although they hesitated, she convinced them they had done enough for her already. Finally, they went back in the house. Minnie quickly hung her wash, spreading the skirts of her dresses along the two outer lines in order to strategically hide her Poppa's pants and shirt on the two inner lines.

Minnie finished her task as quickly as possible and went upstairs since she wore nothing but a man's overcoat. She thanked the good Lord no traffic came down the back street while she had been outside with her laundry.

The sun was so hot even in late August, although the air was humid, Minnie hurried down to check her clothes in about an hour. Dixie and Lou Lou were distracted and never saw her return with her bushel basket full of her meager belongings and their whites. She folded her Poppa's clothes and placed them in their hiding spot at the top of her wardrobe.

The dresses, she laid out to smooth as best she could. She folded their unmentionables and returned them to their rooms.

Before she could seek out Widow Drummond for an iron, Dixie brought Minnie two irons. She closed her eyes and thanked the stars she had folded her poppa's clothes first. Now she could get at least one dress pressed and be proper by supper. Little did anyone know, she also pressed her poppa's clothes and returned them to their hiding place. There was still time, so she quickly pressed her second dress and hung it neatly in the wardrobe. Suitors were coming for the evening meal and although she didn't have an intended, she needed to look her best—Well, second best. Her best was saved for church and the sister brides' weddings.

A knock came to her door just as she finished pressing the dress she had designated for church. She had slipped the other over her head but hadn't fastened it all the way when she answered her door. It was Dixie. Her eyes were wild and she spoke very quickly.

"Hurry, we're wanted downstairs. There's been some trouble!"

Minnie's heart slammed against her chest. Someone figured out she'd broken into the smithy shop. Somehow she'd left a trail and they figured out it was her. She closed her eyes and steeled herself to walk down the stairs as innocently as possible.

When she descended the stairs enough to see into the parlor, her breath caught. It was Samuel Knight, in his wheeled chair, and Emma Cherry at his side.

This was it! She had been found out.

She placed a trembling hand on the rail to steady her steps and continued into the parlor. His eyes widened when he caught sight of her, convincing her all the more, he knew it had been her in his shop.

"I—I can explain…" She thought to say, but Widow Drummond stepped out and gestured for the girls to be seated.

Chapter Seventeen

Mr. Knight smiled as the women settled into their settees and fire-side chairs. Mrs. Cherry sat next to his wheeled chair with a pleasant expression. Surely they weren't here to accuse Minnie. They'd have more stern faces. Besides, why would they want all the brides in the parlor if they were here to point a finger at Minnie? Her heart began to settle down a bit.

Except for one thing—

Mr. Knight had been to the barber and his face was even more handsome than the day she had first seen him.

Wait! What was she thinking? Here she was about to be nailed for breaking into the man's shop and all she could do was admire his recent beard-trimming. His hair had been smoothed back and tied with a leather strip at the nap of his neck. The length of it hung down below his collar. How she'd love to undo that leather and run her fingers through those curly locks—

"I'm Samuel Knight, the local blacksmith" —he paused— "and this is my friend Mrs. Sampson Cherry."

Mrs. Cherry smiled warmly, although she appeared to be uncomfortable with his introduction.

Minnie's heart swooned. The sound of his deep baritone voice did things to her insides she'd never felt before. She wanted to take his hand and help him stand from that chair. She would wrap herself in his arms, and lay her head on his chest so she could listen to his voice as he spoke.

Minnie blinked, realizing she wasn't listening, and forced herself to focus on Mr. Knight's words.

"… So if you ladies see anything suspicious at the end of the street… where my shop is. It's the last shop at the end of town… across from the stables… let the sheriff or Doc Savage know as soon as possible. So far there hasn't been any harm done." He chuckled. "In fact, the guy doing this is helping me out more than causing harm. But that's not the point, is it?"

Minnie's eyes met Mr. Knight's and an angelic harp started playing in her head, or was it simply the blood rushing past her ears? Did she hear him right? The work being done was helping? She pursed her lips and mustered up the courage to ask, "So… what you're saying, Mr. Knight, is whoever is getting into your shop… and completing the iron work, is… doing a good job?"

Mr. Knight's eyes penetrated her soul. He had beautiful eyes. She could stare into those dark pools for the rest of her life. Lord help her, here she went off the deep end of the pier again. What was she thinking?

"I have to be honest with you, Miss…?"

She lifted her chin. "I'm Minnie Geneanne Smith, and you are Samuel Knight, the blacksmith." Goodness gracious, now he'd think she was making fun of him. Here was her first chance to converse with this man of her dreams, and all she could do was repeat what he'd already said.

He chuckled. "Yes, that's me."

Minnie ducked her head, but kept her eyes focused on him. "I heard about your accident. How much longer 'til you can get back to your forge?" She asked.

His face dropped into a morose half smile. Had he understood her question with her heavy New England accent? Until she stepped out on the Oklahoma red dirt, she had not been so acutely aware of how she and her sister brides enunciated their r's differently. The Oklahomans had a more southern drawl. It would take time for both to learn to understand each other. She focused on his sad face, was he deciphering or just overwhelmed with emotion?

"I don't know. Doc says I got several weeks to get these plaster braces off, then several more" —He looked directly at her for a moment, then swallowed hard— "I'll be back at my forge in no time."

His face flushed. Had she made him mad? It was a very personal question, she knew that. Oh Lord, help her, she couldn't say anything right around this man.

"That's why I'd like to figure out who's been working in my forge. I think I want to offer him a job, at least temporarily. I'll be back on my feet real soon, but I've got a lot a work and could use an assistant."

Minnie swallowed. Should she tell him it was her? Would he believe her? Would anybody believe she could handle such a strenuous man's work? The other brides knew. Would they tell on her?

Helen cleared her throat. "Well, I for one, will certainly keep my eyes open for any suspicious activity. Whoever is vandalizing your place of business belongs in jail, Mr. Knight. Forgive our sister-bride, Minnie. She's love struck with blacksmithing and can't realize that you have been violated!" Helen crossed her hand over her chest as if she were offended and huffed.

Minnie's eyes rounded. Oh God, it would be Helen to let the cat out of the bag.

"Love struck with blacksmithing?" Mr. Knight smiled slightly. "What do you mean?"

Shut up, Helen! Shut up! Shut up!

Helen tsked her tongue. "Her poppa was a blacksmith. She's been working at his forge since she was a girl. Quit school to work for him. It's so… unladylike." Helen shivered and rolled her eyes away from Minnie, then wrinkled her nose as if she smelled something rancid.

Widow Drummond stepped over to Helen. Her lips thinned and her hand flinched for her spoon, but she gently touched Helen's shoulder. "Miss Baird, we don't need to be unkind."

Helen's mouth dropped open. She tossed a glance toward Jane Anne. "Well, I never!"

Helen marched to the stairs with Jane Anne close behind her. Widow Drummond turned to Minnie who fought tears for the callous mention of her poppa.

"I'm sorry, dear. Miss Baird apparently is having a... difficult day."

"Widow Drummond, Helen has always treated me that way. That's the real reason I quit school, not because of my poppa's smith shop." Minnie glanced at Mr. Knight. Heat filled her cheeks. "I'm sorry, Mr. Knight. We were out of line."

"No, I didn't mean to disrupt your... routine. I just wanted to ask" —he paused with such discomfort, Minnie worried he was in pain— "for your help... and keep an eye out for who might be getting into my shop." He glanced at Emma. She rose and said goodbye to Widow Drummond and the girls. Then she helped Mr. Knight wheel himself out of the Bride House.

Sam's heart stopped for a beat or two when that seventh bride entered the parlor. He nearly forgot what he'd come here to say. He wanted to stand, and tell her she was the most beautiful woman he had ever seen, and could he please court her. He knew he had a stupid grin on his face, but he just couldn't help himself. She caused him to do stupid things no matter how hard he tried to control himself. Perhaps if he introduced himself. And so he began.

"I'm Samuel Knight, the local blacksmith" —Sam resisted slapping himself on the head. Everyone knew he was the blacksmith. Why had he said that? — "and this is my friend, Mrs. Sampson Cherry." Emma smiled warmly, but he didn't miss the strange look she gave him.

He'd never used such formality with Emma since he met her nearly five months ago. This seventh bride made his brain turn to mush. He explained why they were there and asked them to help him by reporting if they saw anyone at his shop.

Lord, he had never said so many words at one time in his life. Why was he rambling? He tore his eyes away from the beautiful, sturdy woman who already had won his heart and tried to focus on the sour faced blonde he had seen with Eddie Hutton. Boy, was Eddie going to have his hands full. Good thing he had a mind for running a bank. He was going to need that knowledge and those funds to keep that one happy.

"So if you ladies see anything suspicious at the end of the street… where my shop is." God, he could not shut up! He just rambled and rattled on and on about where his shop was located, like they didn't already know. Why couldn't he just point down Broad Street and leave it at that? It wasn't as if there weren't a huge sign out front.

He told them to report any suspicious activity to the sheriff or the doc. Then he just rambled on about how the intruder had done him a solid favor be finishing his work and how he had been impressed by the work. Sampson rolled his eyes at himself. Would he ever stop flapping his jaw.

He even heard himself chuckle like a lovesick school boy. He closed his eyes, trying to center his thinking. Then an angel from heaven spoke. Her words were like a divine harp to his ears. She asked if the work that had been done was any good. It shamed him to admit it, but whoever had broken into his shop had done an excellent job. Maybe better than he would have done. He had to answer her truthfully, but he also used this opportunity to find out what her name was. "I have to be honest with you, Miss…?"

When she said her full name, he felt as if it were etched upon the inner layer of his heart. "Minnie Geneanne Smith."

And she knew his name! How did she know his name? Oh, of course she did. He'd just introduced himself and told them he was the blacksmith. He resisted slapping his palm to his forehead.

Besides, Widow Drummond had most certainly been a channel of information that missed very little details or opportunity to tell what she knew, and filled everyone in on who all the people were and their background in Gunther City. Every resident in this boarding house probably knew who he was before he entered the parlor.

Sam chuckled again. "Yes, that's me."

He cringed. Mercy! Would he ever speak with an ounce of intelligence around this Miss Smith? Even Emma kept turning questioning looks at him. She knew he wasn't himself. Did she know why? Women have a sixth sense about these things, or a huge heart full of wishful thinking. They desire everyone to be matched with another.

"And, I heard about your accident…"

His face dropped. *No, no! Don't pity me! I'm not a weak man. I'm strong. I'm brave. I'll make a good husband. Just as soon as I get my strength back, I swear!* He stammered on, "I don't know. Doc says I got several weeks to get these plaster braces off, then several more…"

What was he saying? He couldn't let her know how lame he actually was. Suddenly, he refused to accept these limitations the Doc had put on him. He needed to heal and he needed to do so immediately. Otherwise this beautiful angel was going to catch another man's eye. He couldn't miss his chance to ask her to let him court her.

He swallowed hard. "I'll be back at my forge in no time."

Then he heard himself ramble on and on about how he wanted to find the person who had been secretly working at his forge and that he might hire the guy. If Sam were to be matched with a woman, this woman was his perfect match. Not only because she surprised the entire town when she showed up without an intended waiting for her, but because of her size and strength. She was unique. She was exotic. She stole his heart the minute he saw her and scrambled his brain and his tongue.

He didn't care what Doc Savage had said about his recovery timetable. He would be back on his feet and at his forge in two weeks, Lord willin'. He'd show her he was a solid man who could love and honor, provide and protect, 'til *death do we part*.

Then the sour-faced blond spoke. Her voice was like nails scraped on a slate.

In fairness, though, he had to stop calling her sour-faced blond. She had a name and deserved to be known by it. Eddie Hutton's betrothed, wasn't good enough either. He had to think. Heidi? No, that wasn't it. Helga? No… Hell— something. Sam nearly chuckled. She was a bride from hell all right. Slender and lean, sharp tongued like a hellcat. That's it… Hell-lean cat. He smiled. Helen!

Focus, Sam! He chastised himself, forcing himself to listen to Helen's information.

"…love struck with blacksmithing and can't realize that you have been violated!"

Blacksmithing! Minnie Geneanne Smith is love struck with blacksmithing? What was this woman saying? Minnie knew blacksmithing? Could this seventh bride get any more perfect? She was sturdy enough to swing his hammer. Could she lift an anvil? He considered that. Probably, if she was smart about it and used basic mathematics and leverage to do so.

He shook his head, mentally. A woman couldn't be a blacksmith. Not that she couldn't physically do the work, just that it was man's work. She couldn't possibly—

The hellcat tsked her tongue. It sounded like a stick snapped in two.

"Her poppa was a blacksmith and she's been working at his forge…" Sam's mind stopped listening to the hellcat. Minnie Smith actually worked at a blacksmith's forge, back in Maine?

The hellcat wouldn't shut up. "It's so… unladylike."

That was all Sam could take. He wanted to tell the hellcat to shut up. She would never again speak so harshly about his woman. Then he wanted to leap out of this con-founded wheeled chair and take Minnie Geneanne Smith into his arms and beg her to marry him. Right now! This minute!

But he couldn't stand. Not yet anyway. But soon. Widow Drummond reached for her spoon, and Sam nearly laughed out loud. Hellcat was in for it now. Instead, the widow patiently put Helen in her place. Of course she demonstrated her true brat-like personality and ran up the stairs. A hellcat-follower ran with her. They always travel in pairs, he mused.

With them gone from the room, he could turn his attention to the woman he would soon marry. Minnie blushed and somehow it made her even more beautiful. This just wasn't possible, but there it was. She glowed like an angel. All he wanted to do was bask in her radiance.

Her voice was like a perfectly tuned gold bell, forged and formed in the passionate fires of a seraphim from heaven. "I'm sorry, Mr. Knight. We were out of line."

"No, I didn't mean to disrupt your… routines. I just wanted to ask" —you to marry me. No, he couldn't say that— "for your help… and keep an eye out for who might be getting into my shop."

He glanced at Emma, hoping she would rescue him from his bumbling tongue and get him out of there before he made it worse. He'd made a fool of himself in front of the one person on earth he wanted to impress the most.

He'd be back, and when he came back, he'd be standing on two strong legs, worthy to ask permission to court her.

Emma and Sam entered the boardwalk with intent to go to the next person, but Sam turned in his chair to look at Emma.

"Could you do me a favor?"

"Of course, Sam."

"Could you and Sampson finish telling folks about my shop, and could you take me back to Doc's?"

"Shore. Ya needin' rest?" Concern filled her dark eyes.

"No. Emma. I need to talk to the Doc. I've gotta get outta this chair, and quick. That girl's gonna find a husband and I gotta make sure it's me."

Emma's dimples deepened when she smiled. "Why, Sam. Is that why chu were stammerin' in there? I wondered what was wrong witchu." She tossed her head back and laughed.

Heat flushed Sam's face, but he didn't care. "Just get me back to the doc, please. You can have your laugh with Sampson."

Emma's laughter died down into a chuckle. "Sam, chu and Miss Smith are a match made in heaven. I knew it the minute I saw her step off that train. I just didn't know you knew it, too. Of course I'll get you back to the doc. Let's see if we can find Sampson first though. I ain't got no business goin' in people's places without chu or my husband."

"Oh, Emma, this is the Wild West, we don't hold to such protocols."

Her glare hardened.

Samuel bowed his head. "Yes, let's find Sampson first. It's the least I can do for you, dear Emma."

As it were, Sampson was filling a firewood box just around back. Emma rushed to him and explained the situation, including Sam's heartfelt confession.

Samuel rolled his eyes. He didn't want everyone in town knowing his heart's desire, until Minnie knew. Sampson wouldn't tell, he was sure of that. It was Emma he worried about.

Chapter Eighteen

Emma and Sampson Cherry completed their task. Everyone along Broad Street had been asked to notify Mr. Cherry or Doc Savage if they saw any activity in the smithy's shop, Samuel was settled down for the night, and all of the firewood had been delivered. They climbed into their buckboard wagon and Emma snuggled up against Sampson's large arm.
"Wha' chu wantin', wife?" Sampson eyed her suspiciously.
"Nuttin' husband." She smiled up at him.
"Uh huh." He slapped the reins on the mule's back. "'M'on home, Bessy."
Emma squeezed his arm. He glanced down at her again. "Woman, whachu wantin'?"
"Just wonderin'…"
Sampson sighed. "Wonderin' what?"
"Do you know what day it is, Mr. Cherry?" Emma fluttered coy eyes at him.
He thought a moment. The sway of the wagon tossed him against her. Then she smiled. "Five years ago today, we jumped da broom."

"That's right." He smiled sweetly. "Whachu got in mind?"

Emma sat up straighter. "I was thinkin' it might be nice to eat in town."

"Hmm." Sampson twisted on the board and looked over his shoulder. "Chuckwagon's closed down for dah night. S'pose the hotel restaurant is still open?"

"Only one way ta find out." Emma smiled a huge grin.

Sampson gazed at the joy in her face. There weren't nothing he wouldn't do for his Emma. "Let's see." He pulled the reins to make Bessy turn around.

When they reached the opposite end of town, across from the train station, Sampson helped Emma down from the wagon. Taking her arm, he led her into the hotel. The restaurant was empty, but Jeremy Blackwater, the maître d' for the Gunther City Hotel, stood half asleep at a polished wood podium. Sampson approached him. "Could a body get a bite ta eat?"

Jeremy smiled. "Kitchen is still open, Mr. Cherry."

"It's our anniversary." Emma announced proudly.

"Well, then, in that case, let me show you our best table." Jeremy led the way and seated them in a two top near the window. The sun was setting and the sky displayed pink and purple strips of fading light. "Will this do?"

Jeremy placed menus before them and bowed. "Your waiter will be right with you. May I get you something to drink? Champagne, maybe?"

Emma widened her eyes at Sampson. "Oh, Sampson, should we?"

"We'd love a glass of champagne." Sampson said without hesitation.

Emma squirmed in her chair. She'd never had wine, let alone champagne. This was going to be a delightful celebration.

Jeremy came back in a moment and set a silver bowl beside their table. A green bottle peeked out of a white linen cloth. Jeremy expertly twisted a wire and eased the cork out. It popped and Emma squealed. Jeremy poured a small amount for Sampson to sample.

Sampson looked it with the question on his face. Jeremy leaned over and whispered in his ear. "You smell it, taste it, and tell me if it is all right. Then I'll pour Mrs. Cherry a glass and fill yours the rest of the way."

"Oh." Sampson leaned his head back slightly. He did as Jeremy instructed and gave his approval. Jeremy filled their glasses and returned the bottle to the chilling bowl.

"Now, have you had time to look at your menus?"

Sampson chuckled. "I thought you said our waiter would be here in a moment."

Jeremy shrugged and smiled. "Ah, alas, he is I."

They laughed and told him what they chose.

Sampson wanted fried chicken, mashed potatoes and carrots, hot bread, and a bowl of pudding for dessert. Emma wanted the roast beef and gravy, mashed potatoes and vegetable du jour. She laughed when she spoke the French word. "And creme brûlée." Again she giggled. Ordering with French words was as much fun as eating in the restaurant.

"Excellent selections." Jeremy stated and left them to their private celebration.

Plates were wiped clean with the hot bread, the champagne bottle was empty, and Emma and Sampson were delightfully satisfied with their meal. Emma sighed and Sampson gazed at her with pure love in his eyes. He couldn't wait to get home so they could celebrate some more as husband and wife. Night had settled over their sleepy little town. It was a good thing Bessy knew her way home and Sampson wouldn't need to do much guiding. He planned on holding his Emma all the way to their sod dugout. The couple climbed into their wagon and he flipped the reins on the mule's back. She started forward at a slow but steady pace.

As they reached the last two buildings before leaving town, Sampson looked toward the Smithy shop. Although the saloon's music blared into the street, a steady rhythmic pounding resounded. Was it coming from Mr. Knight's shop, or was it the new drum Miss Turner had been bragging about?

Sampson considered stopping his mule to check, but a horse in the corral to his right whinnied hysterically and a loud crack rent the air. Emma gasped, and Sampson stood up in the wagon.

The horse broke the top rung of the corral's split rail fence. Sampson jumped down and ran to the broken rail, lifting it into place to hold the horses back. He had to fix this or all the horses would get out. Mr. Gunther was surely asleep. He couldn't go get the man without risking the horses escaping.

"Emma!" Sampson shouted. "Go wake Claude!" Emma slid out of the wagon and hurried up the stairs to Mr. Gunther's apartment above the stables. In minutes, Claude ran down in his dungarees and long johns. His boots were on his feet, but not tied. Emma ran behind him. Sampson let Claude and Emma hold the broken rail while he went to his wagon and lifted an ax. He rounded the building and found a right sized tree.

The champagne filled his head with a dizzying sensation as he swung the ax over his shoulder. He slung the ax down toward the base of the tree, but the action made his head swim even more. The ax came down but didn't connect with the tree. Rather, it wielded past it and split his foot open.

Sampson screamed and fell to the ground. Emma rushed to him. "Oh God! Sampson! What do I do?" Sampson panted. "It's too far to get Doc, go to the Smithy's and whoever's in there, have them come with a hot iron."

"Nobody's in the Smithy!" she cried.

"Yeah, der is. Go! Gotta cauterize it, Emma, or I's gonna bleed to death."

Emma stared at him.

"EMMA, GO!" He bellowed.

Minnie waited until well after supper, same as the night before, changed into her poppa's clean clothes, and left the Bride House by way of the back door. A quick trip into the root cellar for some more apples and down the back street. The horses whinnied as she rounded their corral. She giggled and gave them an apple each. She still had some in her other pocket that she'd save until she was making her way back to the house at dawn.

Slipping into the back of the smithy's shop, she noticed Mr. Cherry's payment had been received and more hardwood was stacked in its place. So far, her system was working. Once inside, she walked to the front door and opened it just enough to get the money box and some items needing repair.

Switching out the charred wood with fresh, she set the kiln to make more and fired the forge. While the pit heated, she counted out Mr. Knight's money and stacked it neatly in the drawer.

The repair work included two gates and four iron stands. She would need several three-quarter inch round steel rods and the same number of half inch rounds. She placed them in the embers of the forge and pumped the billows. The fire glowed orange and yellow. Sparks blew up into the air and she drew in the aroma of the charcoal.

She loved the smell of a fire. Memories flooded her mind of her working beside Poppa, teaching her his skillful methods. She had learned to make a rose by cutting the end of a rod several ways and bending it back for petals. She considered making a few for the gate she was about to repair. Just to make it special for the woman whose yard it would protect. A smile pressed on her lips as she tried to stay the tears.

Suddenly, a loud pounding came to the blacksmith's door. Minnie jumped, nearly tripping backward. She recognized the woman's voice screaming for help. It was Emma Cherry. She wasn't supposed to be in here. Should she disregard the woman's pleas to protect her secret?

But then Emma said the words that Minnie could not ignore. "My Sampson's been hurt. Please! Help us!"

Minnie pulled the door open. Emma's eyes were wide with fear, and yet she was taken aback by the appearance of Minnie at the door. "We need your help! Sampson's hurt bad. He needs you to bring a hot iron… to-to cauterize the ax wound."

Ax wound! Minnie had seen her father cauterize many a wound. Gunshot wounds, knife wounds, even ax wounds. She knew how it was done, but she'd never done it herself. Her poppa had explained how it could save a man's life by stopping the blood from completely draining out of his body.

Minnie looked past Emma. Horses were leaping over the corral railings, but she didn't see Sampson. "Where is he, Emma?"

"Ahind the stables. Please hurry!" Emma cried.

Minnie had those irons heating, they would work. She grabbed Mr. Knight's oversized glove and lifted one of the three-quarter rounds and followed Emma.

Claude knelt beside Sampson. He had a hold of Sampson's leg. Blood covered them both. Claude did a double take when he saw her with the hot iron. "Hurry!"

Minnie didn't think, she just ran up to Sampson and sank the orange hot end of the rod into the gash in his foot. Sampson screamed. Minnie cringed but held the rod steady.

Emma ran to Sampson and held his head in her lap, crying over his unconscious body. She closed her eyes and leaned into Sampson's face. "Please don't die. I love you with all my heart, Sampson Cherry. Don't you go and die on me now!"

The smell. The sound. It was nauseating. Steam rose from Sampson's foot. Minnie felt like swooning herself, but gritted her teeth and held the iron to the wound. The blood boiled and dried instantly, darkening to a black stain.

Claude suddenly leapt up. "I'll get Doc!" He ran into his stables. Hooves beat the ground as he rode off. Soon, Claude and Doc Savage leapt from the horse and hit the ground running to Sampson. "Miss Smith! Pull the iron back."

She hesitated. Would he start bleeding again if she took the iron away? Lifting it from Sampson's foot, she stared at the black iron. She had no idea what to do with it now. Looking around, she plunged the hot iron into the soft soil and turned back to Sampson. Would he lose his foot? Had she made it worse?

Doc Savage yelled something at Claude and he ran away. Minnie stared at him as he rounded the corral. Then she heard the horses whinny from the prairie grass. They started when Claude careened around the corral with Mr. Cherry's wagon and trotted further from the stables. Doc and he loaded Sampson in the back and helped Emma in. She scooped Sampson's head into her lap and held him as they took off toward the Doc's office.

A cloud of dust billowed behind the wagon as Doc Savage slapped the reins and careened around the stables to Broad Street and continued up the street to his office.

A horse whinnied. Minnie remembered the apples in her pocket. She ran out to the grass where the horses were now grazing, like nothing had happened, and whistled. They lifted their heads and looked her way. She held out an apple in the flat of her palm. One horse whinnied.

"Come on," she cooed.

Minnie nearly jumped out of her hide when Claude spoke behind her. "That's working, coax them into the stable. I'll lock them up for the night."

She made kissing noises with her lips and brought out another apple. The horses strolled up to her and followed the apple into the stable. Mr. Gunther closed the bottom half of the stable doors behind the last horse and fell up against it. With a trembling hand, he wiped his brow. "Dear God, I hope Mr. Cherry will be all right."

"Me, too." Minnie bent over at the waist, staying the nausea, and trying to breathe normally.

"Aren't you that seventh bride?" Mr. Gunther looked her up and down. "Why you dressed like a man?"

Chapter Nineteen

"Because, she's been working in my shop at night." Samuel Knight's voice boomed from the dark street. Minnie gasped. Her eyes darted around the stable. Should she hide in a dark corner?

No, she was caught. It was too late. "I-I can explain!"

"No need." Samuel wheeled his chair up to the dutch door and peeked over. "Minnie Geneanne Smith. So, it's *you* who has been working at my forge?"

Minnie's eyes dropped to the ground. What could she say, except the truth? "Yes."

"Can you come out here? I've worn myself out wheeling down this boardwalk as fast as I possibly could."

Her eyes lifted to meet Claude's. His eyes rounded with concern and opened the stable door for her to exit.

She pulled Mr. Knight's glove from her hand as she left the stable.

"Good luck." Claude whispered as she passed him.

She handed Mr. Knight the glove and walked away from him to retrieve the iron rod. "I just wanted to help."

She hated the whine in her voice.

"I know. Come with me." He wheeled himself across the street to the still-open doors of his shop. "Sit down."

She pulled on the door to close it.

"No, don't close the doors." He wheeled himself further into the shop. "You're not with an escort, and I'm not fit to be your chaperone."

Minnie stared at him with confusion. "Why not?"

"I'm a single man, Miss Smith. And... I'm in love with you."

Minnie dropped the iron rod. It thudded to the ground. "What?"

Samuel crammed fingers into his long black hair. It was no longer tied behind his head, but loose across his shoulders. "I-I wanted this to go different... I wanted to be standing when I said it..." He hit the chair with his fist. "Damn this chair!"

Minnie flinched. Did he intend to hit her?

Samuel looked up startled. "I'm not mad at you! It's just... I wanted to be standing when I tell you—"

He looked down as if he were searching for something. "Miss Minnie Geneanne Smith, would you allow me to court you? I fell in love with you the minute you stepped off that train. Well, you stumbled off, actually," he chuckled. "but I immediately knew you were the one for me."

Minnie stood statue still. Her mouth opened and closed a few times. "I-you mean, you're not angry? I broke into your shop and fired up your forge?"

Sam stared at her. "Did you hear what I said?" He clenched his jaw. "No, I'm surprised you're a woman. What I mean is, I'm surprised my burglar turned out to be you… I mean…"

Minnie stared at his handsome face. His hair, loose just as she had imagined, made her want to grasp his head and press her lips into his. She closed the gap between them. "I think I know what you mean."

She bent at the waist, with her hands on his arm rests, and leaned into him to place a kiss on his lips. He mumbled a word, but she didn't know what he had said. He kissed her back, and his hands took her shoulders to pull her in closer. She nearly tumbled into his lap, which stopped the wonderful kiss. She laughed and regained her balance. He laughed, too.

"Yes." She whispered. Still bent at the waist and darting her eyes from his right and then his left eye. "Huh?"

"I heard what you said and you may court me, Mr. Samuel Knight, the blacksmith."

His eyes widened. A smile slowly rose on his still moist lips. He leaned into her and caressed her lips with his, then pushed her away.

She staggered back, confused.

"Then you need to do one of two things."

"What?"

"Get us a chaperone, or get out of my shop. We are betrothed, Miss Smith and cannot be trusted to be alone without a guardian of your virtue."

Claude cleared his throat.

They looked up. He stood at the smithy's doors.

"I've been here the whole time, Knight. Her virtue is witnessed, and by the way, congratulations!"

Claude escorted Minnie back to the Bride House with Samuel rolling in his wheeled chair next to her.

She had to go in the back door, because she had left it unlocked.

"I'll come by in the morning, Miss Smith." Samuel kissed the back of her hand. "And announce our betrothal to Widow Drummond." He smiled. "Thank you."

"For what?"

Claude stepped away, absorbed in something to do with the water pump in the yard.

"For being you. For being perfect. For accepting my request to court you."

She nodded. Words wouldn't come to her. She just couldn't express how happy she was at this moment.

"And…" He glanced over at Claude. "We'll figure out a way for you to help in the forge until I can stand on my own. But I want you to know, I'll be working as hard as I can to get to that point. You won't have to work alone. I'll be there every day, at your side. It should be a help to me to get my strength back if I'm in there doing what I can to help."

She nodded. "Sure."

"And we'll figure this chaperone thing out, too." He glanced at Claude again.

Claude heard the cue and approached them. "We'll work something out. No problem for me to keep an eye across the street. Long as you keep both sets of doors open in your shop, Knight, I don't see the ole biddies objecting… too much."

They laughed. Minnie stared at him a moment longer. She couldn't believe this was happening. He squeezed her hand and let it go. She held it close to her heart and turned to enter the house.

He wanted her to work *with* him in the forge. He'd be by her side healing and regaining his strength. Best of all, he wanted to court her. She no longer had to sneak around at night or be up until dawn. She eased up the stairs and disrobed. Sleep still didn't come, she was too excited.

She couldn't wait to tell the girls her news.

It was Minnie's team's turn to cook. She rose just as the sun spread its pastels across the sky. Mornings were so beautiful here in the wide-open plains of Oklahoma. She dressed and braided her hair, pinned it around her head, and slid on her boots. It was she who tapped on Dixie's door. Mr. Darcy growled until he recognized Minnie, then he ran in circles and jumped at her skirts.

"Come on, lazy head. We gotta make breakfast." Minnie giggled.

Dixie yawned. "I'll be right down." She eyed Minnie suspiciously. "What's with you, so wide awake and full of... something?"

Minnie just smiled. "I have an announcement!"

"What?" Dixie called after her, but she was halfway down the stairs.

Minnie loaded wood in the stove and lit the kindling. She stepped out the back door and filled a bucket with water at the pump. Hauling it in, she set it on the pie cupboard and filled the coffee pot. Measuring out the coffee beans, she turned the crank to grind it nice and smooth. *How does Sam take his coffee? Strong or weak?*

Lou Lou staggered in, yawning. "What are you doing up so early?"

Minnie glanced up from pouring the grounds into the coffee filter. "It's a beautiful day. Why waste a moment of it?"

Lou Lou considered her a moment, then shrugged and disappeared into the pantry. She came back with an armload of potatoes and set to peel and cut them for frying. Dixie came in, looked at both women with furrowed brow, shook her head, and pushed the back door to go collect eggs.

Minnie just smiled and scurried down to the root cellar for bacon. When she returned, she pulled out the large bowl and began mixing biscuits, patting them out to roll and cut. Soon everything was frying, baking, or percolating.

Dixie circled Minnie, glaring at her intently. Then she snapped her fingers. "I've got it!"

Minnie started. "What?"

"You're in love!" Dixie squealed. "It's true. I know a love stricken face when I see one!"

Lou Lou looked up, startled and grinned.

"You, Minnie Smith, are in love!" Dixie said in her sing-song manner "Who is it? Please tell us!"

Lou Lou chimed in. "Oh, Minnie. Please tell us!"

Minnie grinned and cut her eyes to the left. "You'll find out along with everyone else."

"Oh, that's not fair!" The two women whined.

They continued to beg but Minnie wouldn't give in. They finished cooking and set the table. When all the brides were in their places and Widow Drummond had said grace, Minnie rose from her chair and cleared her throat. All eyes lifted toward her. "Mr. Knight will be coming by this morning and you all need to be properly dressed to receive him."

She sat back down. Dixie and Lou Lou widened their eyes at Minnie. They now knew but didn't say a word.

"Why?" Helen quipped. "Did he find the culprit who's been vandalizing his shop?"

Minnie smiled as she split her biscuit and buttered it. "You'll just have to wait and see."

Dixie giggled. Minnie glared at her. Lou Lou shook her hands as if they were on fire. "Oh, I can't stand it! Minnie's in love with Mr. Knight!"

Minnie gasped and turned a hard stare to her friend. "Lou! You promised."

"I did no such thing." Lou Lou laughed.

Widow Drummond smiled. "Well, Miss Smith, congratulations, and does Mr. Knight return your affections?"

Minnie dropped her eyes to her plate. "Yes, ma'am."

"Oh, how wonderful!" Mrs. Drummond buttered her biscuit and took a bite.

"Huh?" Helen spat. "Betroths aren't allowed in the Bride House until after ten o'clock."

Minnie's smile dropped to a flat, expressionless line. "For your information, we were going to announce our betrothal to you all, before somebody couldn't wait to spill the beans" — she glared at Lou Lou— "And he wanted to formally let Widow Drummond know so that everything was proper with the bride's committee."

Minnie nodded toward the widow.

Martha cut up her fried eggs and dipped a biscuit in the yolk. "Oh, Minnie, tell us all about how this happened?"

Minnie chewed her bacon and swallowed, washing it down with a sip of coffee, she wiped her mouth and returned the linen napkin to her lap. "Well…"

All eyes were on her and the breakfast sat half eaten on their plates.

"It was the result of an accident, actually." Minnie smiled and let her eyes meet each girl's curious gazes. Only Helen acted disinterested and continued eating.

"Mr. Cherry injured his foot with an ax last night 'round back of Gunther's Stables, and Mrs. Cherry ran over to the blacksmith shop to get help."

Helen lifted her eyes and turned a hard eye as she listened.

"I had a half inch round in the forge, and—"

"WHAT!" Helen stood so fast, her chair fell back and hit the floor. "YOU are the thief?"

"I'm no thief, Helen!" Minnie pursed her lips. "But I am the one who's been working in Mr. Knight's shop."

Widow Drummond's mouth dropped open. "Is this true, Miss Smith?"

Minnie turned to the widow. "Yes, ma'am. But I can explain—"

"Widow Drummond," Helen planted her fists on her hips. "We should send for the sheriff immediately! We have a thief among us!"

Minnie glared at Helen. "I'm not a thief. Mr. Knight knows I've been working in his shop."

"Oh, Miss Smith." Widow Drummond wrung her linen napkin. "Is this why you've been so tired during the day? Have you been sneaking out at night and… and…"

Mrs. Drummond lifted the napkin to her mouth as if to cover the words she couldn't say. Tears formed in her eyes.

"See!" Helen yelled. "You've upset Widow Drummond." She rushed to the widow's side and patted her hand.

The widow waved the napkin at Helen. "No, no, I'm all right."

Helen turned back to Minnie. "She belongs in jail for breaking and entering. She had no business sneaking down there in the middle of the night." Helen's eyes widened. "I wonder if her reputation has been compromised, not to mention…" Helen gasped. "What exactly happened last night? Now you're all 'in love' and prancing around here, having a man over to the Bride House before ten o'clock. You're gonna have to get married right away aren't you! You shameless wanton brazen hussy—"

"Shut up!" Minnie leapt to her feet. Her lip trembled. Her eyes darted from one girl to the other. They all stared at her with stunned accusatory glares. Even Dixie and Lou Lou looked shocked.

Minnie tossed down her napkin. "Mr. Cherry lived, in case you're wondering!"

She ran to her room, slamming the door and diving onto her bed. Tears poured from her soul. Her wonderful, beautiful morning was ruined.

Chapter Twenty

"That will be enough, Miss Baird!" Widow Drummond stood, lifting her wooden spoon. "Now, let's all calm down! We don't know the whole story." She glared at Helen. "Sit! Down!"

Everyone settled back in their chairs.

"Now." Widow Drummond composed herself. "We need to give Miss Smith a chance to explain what happened and then I will talk to Mr. Knight. He's a trustworthy gentleman, I'm sure he has conducted himself in an upstanding and proper manner."

Widow Drummond waited until all the girls were seated before she returned her spoon to her apron and sat down herself.

As if summoned, the front door bell shook. All the women turned at once to see the bell jiggle on its curlicue iron work.

Widow Drummond folded her linen napkin and laid it gently over her untouched food. "Ladies, let's retire to the parlor and discuss this calmly with Miss Smith and Mr. Knight."

She walked to the door and opened it. "Mr. Knight, do come in."

Samuel's smile melted from his face the minute Mrs. Drummond opened the door. The atmosphere in the Bride House was tenser than an eight-day clock wound far too tight. He nodded to the widow. "Morning, Widow Drummond. I'm sorry to call on you so early in the day, but I stopped by to make you aware of a change in the status of one of your boarders."

He looked around her to see if he could see Minnie. From his angle in his wheeled chair, several women were seated in the parlor. But Minnie was not among them. He wheeled his chair back a little and waited for the widow to open the door.

"Yes." Widow Drummond said in a sing-song manner left from her east coast living that Knight had come to know meant she was not happy.

"Is there something wrong, Widow Drummond?"

"Well…" She blinked and fluttered her hand at her throat. "Possibly, we're not sure. Do come in. We need you to help clarify some things."

Samuel wheeled himself into the house and glared at the many emotions exhibited on the ladies' faces. Eddie's hellcat looked the most venomous of them all. "What is all this? Where's Miss Smith?"

"She, well, she went to her room. I'm afraid we upset her." Widow Drummond lowered her eyes. "I'm sure you can straighten everything out, Mr. Knight."

He turned with rage, staring at the staircase. There was no way he could go to her.

"Why don't you tell me exactly what happened?" He spoke through gritted teeth.

"I'm sure it's all just a misunderstanding," The widow said. She glanced at Helen and back to Sam.

He turned angry eyes to the hellcat. "You! What did you do?"

Helen's eyes rounded. "I-I" She lifted her chin. "I know she's the one who has broken into your shop. She should be arrested." Helen glanced around to the others. "She claims she's in love and I, well, I think she used her feminine wiles to seduce you so that you wouldn't call the sheriff. And—"

"Stop!" Heat filled Sam's face. His jaw muscles hurt from clenching so hard. He wanted to leap out of his chair and strangle that busy body she-vixen. He turned to the widow.

"Will someone go get my intended and ask her to join me down here?" he growled.

Dixie darted up the stairs. Soon she had Minnie in tow. Her eyes were red and swollen from crying. She saw Sam and ran to his side. "Oh, Mr. Knight!"

He wrapped his arm around her hip and pulled her into him snug. "Hush, now. It's all right."

He turned back to the room full of women. "I will have you know your own Minnie Smith saved a man's life last night. She is not a criminal, nor did she use her feminine wiles to persuade me not to call the sheriff." He glared at Helen for a long moment. Helen shrank back into the settee.

"Miss Smith has saved my b—" he cleared his throat. "She has done me an enormous favor by getting into my forge and catching me up on the work needing done. And last night…"

He looked up at her.

"I came over here to stand with—"

He scowled at all the gawking faces and then at Widow Drummond. Determination hardened his face. He grit his teeth tight, then leaned over and, using his hands to help move his legs, he set his feet on the floor. He winced but continued. He closed his eyes, and pressed his back teeth together, pushing himself with all his might upward. His arms vibrated with the strain, as he pushed himself up to stand. He was unsteady, wobbly even. He swung an arm back toward Minnie for balance.

Minnie gasped and grabbed his arm to help steady him. She realized for the first time he was taller than her, and she smiled. His balance centered, and he looked each of the women in turn square in their eyes. His voice hardened. "I came here this morning, to stand beside Miss Smith and announce to you all that we are betrothed. Claude Gunther witnessed the entire event with Mr. Cherry and later when I confessed my feeling for her, if you need confirmation of her *moral standing*."

He loosened her firm grip on his arm and placed her hand at his elbow, as if they were casually standing together, so he could pat her hand. "I loved this woman the minute I saw her come off the train." He glanced at her. Their eyes locked for a moment. He had to tear himself away from her beautiful pools of bronze and gold. "I knew it was just a matter of time before I asked her to let me court her. Some of you may have a problem with her ability to do smithing work."

His eyes bore into Helen Baird and she shrunk back even further.

"Let me set your mind at ease. Miss Smith is not only a talented smithy, she's better than me in her ability to craft the iron and you should be darn" —he glanced at the widow— "excuse my language, happy she's here in Gunther City, because any fancy iron work you're going to be asking us to do for you will be done by her, and I guarantee you're going to love the work once it's done."

Samuel glanced at Minnie. He placed his hand tenderly on the side of her face and kissed her cheek. Several of the ladies gasped.

He ignored their indignation and kept his eyes glued to the windows of her soul. "I'm sorry you had to go through this alone."

She smiled a watery smile.

"Now…" The word escaped Samuel's lungs like an exhale. His strength gave out and he toppled back into his wheeled chair.

Minnie did her best to catch him and ease him back. Holding his body as he crumpled awkwardly into the chair sent a tingly sensation through her. She longed to be held in his arms. To mold into his body and share her love with him.

But not yet. He was too weak. Concern filled her heart. Would he ever stand again?

His breath came rapidly as he closed his eyes and endured the pain that it obviously cost him to literally stand up for his woman. Finally, he caught his breath and he looked up. "Widow Drummond, I will make arrangements for proper chaperoning, but I need Miss Smith to be in my shop by nine o'clock. There is a lot of work that needs to be done and, as you can see, I am not completely myself yet."

The widow nodded. A quivering tremor lifted a corner of her mouth. "Oh, of course, Mr. Knight. I would think that if you kept your two sets of doors open, front and back, and Claude Gunther continues to keep a watchful eye on you, that will be sufficient. Should you need anything from me, just send one of the Gunther children down to fetch me."

Samuel smiled. "Thank you, Widow Drummond. I appreciate that."

He reached up and took Minnie's hand. "Now, I realize you've been wearing your poppa's clothes, but surely we can fashion something more appropriate for you to work in?"

Minnie nodded. "Oh, yes, back home I had a calf's skin leather apron, it's lighter in weight and more flexible, and I refashioned some of Poppa's fire gloves to fit my hands. Also, I sewed me some sleeves out of Poppa's double weave aprons to cover my arms."

"Well, sounds like we need to do something similar to that for you here. What do you need from me?"

"Well," she thought out loud. "A tanned calf hide, some sinew for thread and a good tooling needle."

"Done. We'll stop by the tannery after I pick you up later this morning."

"Thank you, Mr. Knight."

He smiled. "Please, call me Samuel."

She blushed bright red. "I'd like that, Samuel."

A week became two in no time. August became September, although the weather stayed quite warm. Trees remained green. It was so strange to not see yellows, reds, and oranges wash over the treed areas like it did in Maine in September.

Samuel and Minnie kept their word. Minnie worked for Samuel in his blacksmith shop, while he worked very hard to regain his strength.

They opened the front and back doors each morning and kept them open while they worked the iron. It helped to keep it from being an oven, and let anyone who passed by witness their propriety. Claude Gunther kept his top half doors open on the stables at all times. Customers came and went for smithy work and served as additional witnesses to their appropriate behavior.

Although, not everyone approved of the seventh bride working like a man, all of their customers were satisfied with the work they received. Samuel's business was once again thriving.

The bartering customers filled their chicken pen, root cellar and smoked meat pantry. The cash customers were good for their pay. The bank had been so prosperous, Eddie Hutton was allowing bank notes backed by gold coins.

Samuel's bank account grew to a healthy balance. He had visited with Mr. Hutton and had set Minnie up with an account of her own. He had made sure half of the shop's earnings were deposited in her account and she had access to the funds in her name for whatever she needed.

Jane Anne, who now worked with Ruby Tanner, the town's seamstress, measured Minnie for a dressing gown, two day-dresses in a light-weight cotton material, and two in wool for winter. Plus two shirtwaists for work, which would be made using the double woven material Samuel's aprons and pants were made from to prevent them from being easily burned by the loose embers. Then she had picked out some silk blend material, that Mrs. Cambridge had bought for the mercantile before the brides arrived, in a golden yellow and a robin's egg blue for Sunday dresses.

Minnie had one very special dress in mind. The pattern would have to be from her memory and Mrs. Tanner had to ask Mrs. Cambridge to order just the right material for it. Minnie didn't dare tell Jane Anne about this dress. She knew it would not be a secret very long if Jane Anne or Helen knew anything about it.

Mrs. Tanner's husband, Wiley, owned the hide tanning shop where Samuel bought the soft calf leather for her apron, and he asked Newt Cambridge to order some heat resistant gloves to fit her hands from the catalog in the mercantile.

With the exception of the anonymous benefactor who gave each of the brides a dowry purse before they left Portland, Maine, Minnie'd never had access to her own spending money like this. Since she had lost every piece of clothing except three, when she ran for her life from Jet Butterfield, she was so happy to be able to get new dresses, and it wasn't even her birthday or Easter. A sad smile crossed her lips with the thought of her Poppa's generosity.

In the evenings, they snuffed out the forge, set work that had not been picked up by customers out front with bills of sale attached to them, like she had been doing when she worked through the night. They closed the back doors first and walked to the front of the shop to close and lock the front doors.

Just as they neared the double doors, Samuel pulled her aside into the shadows and wrapped her in his arms. His strength was definitely returning. She could feel it in his bulging arms and thickening chest. She sighed with pleasure.

"Samuel," she breathed.

"I love you, Minnie," he growled, and lowered his lips onto hers. Tenderly, his mouth caressed hers. She knew they shouldn't, but she couldn't hold herself back any longer. Like the sizzling fire of the forge, her passion consumed her wits. Her heart pounded rhythmically in her chest, like her hammer slamming against the white hot iron, shaping it, forever changing it, into something it had not been before.

Working beside him every day, her desire to be in his arms grew to an intolerable level. The heat of the shop was nothing compared to the heat building inside her. She found herself beating the iron so much harder than she would have because of the unrelenting passion blooming in places she had no idea had feelings. She longed to be his wife and to be in his bed every evening. She grew to hate sleeping alone in the Bride House. Why didn't he ask her to marry him?

A throat cleared.

Sam gently pushed her away and stepped out of the shadows. "Hello, Claude."

Minnie picked up an iron rod, trying to make it appear it was the reason she had been in the shadows, and stepped out behind Samuel. She hefted the rod and then leaned it against a stone wall.

"Sam." Claude wouldn't make eye contact. He simply nodded and turned to walk back to his stables.

Minnie helped Samuel close the front doors and stood on the boardwalk as he leaned into the iron bar to twist it as the lock for his shop. They now knew Sampson Cherry was the only other person in town strong enough to untwist Sam's system for locking up his shop, but weren't concerned. Mr. Cherry had proven he could be trusted.

His foot had healed, although he had a distinctive limp, it didn't prevent him and Emma from chopping, stacking, and delivering firewood again. The town was very happy to have their blacksmith and their firewood delivery functioning again.

The Cherry's had become dear to Minnie and Samuel, and they had discussed a special gift they would make for them come Christmas.

Minnie tried her best not to giggle as they waved good night to the stable owner. He glared at them sternly as he closed down his stables. Minnie thought she noticed a slight smile as she turned back to see him latch his doors. She squeezed Sam's hand as they walked. He nodded. He saw Claude's silent reprimand and was sure Widow Drummond would be holding out her wooden spoon by tomorrow morning.

Samuel escorted his bride-to-be to the Bride House, as was their routine, and joined the women for supper, along with the other brides' intendeds who were in town. Widow Drummond allowed Samuel to use the basement washroom to clean up before the meal. A privilege extended to no other male in town. While Minnie cleaned up from her hot sweaty day in the third floor's washroom. It was Lou Lou who generally called Minnie from the bath, when she fell asleep in the soaker tub, to come down for supper. Typically a betrothed couple would retire to the parlor after the evening meal to talk and get to know each other better. It was an opportunity to hold hands and even steal a kiss on those rare occasions when Widow Drummond left the room to freshen the tea or take care of a matter in the kitchen.

However, Minnie and Samuel would bid one another good night directly after the meal. Just like back home in Maine, it took all her strength to return downstairs for supper rather than to go to bed without food. She was too exhausted to do much of anything else.

Thank God, she had been dismissed from house chores. That had gone over like a lead balloon with Helen and Jane Anne, but Minnie didn't care. She was the happiest she had ever been in her life and the three friends whom she had grown to love like sisters, Dixie, Lou Lou and Martha, were happy for her. Martha pitched in without being asked to clean Minnie's room and wash her laundry.

She told her not to, but Martha being the nurturer she was, did it happily. Minnie'd come home to find her dresses washed, pressed, and hanging in the wardrobe. Her boots would be polished and her unmentionables would be neatly folded and put away. Even her bed linens were washed and put back on her bed. She pondered something especially nice to make for her when she and Andrew Ootaknih married.

Chapter Twenty-One

Samuel found himself staring at Minnie when she bent over the forge, priming the fire with the bellows. Although he had promised Widow Drummond, Claude Gunther, and the whole town, for that matter, that he would hold her reputation in the highest regard. He longed to caress her rounded derrière. The way her body moved as she slammed the hammer on the iron and anvil. He wanted to mold himself into her form and kiss her soft, full lips until they both were overwhelmed with the fervor of their love.

When the heat of the forge veiled her skin with moisture, he could smell the Carolina sea air of his youth, and pine bark, and something so unique to her. Discretely, he drew in drafts of her essence, like a good cigar, letting his desires for her fill his chest. He loved being near her and made any excuse he could to help her with heavy items, so that he could enjoy her nearness.

Thank God for the heavy blacksmith's apron to hide his obvious yearnings, daily. He promised himself he would ask for her hand in marriage, as soon as he had all of his strength back and could stand like the man he had been before the accident to fulfill the marriage vows to love, honor, and protect her until his dying breath. He just prayed his willpower was stronger than his hunger.

Customers were impressed with Minnie's work. Samuel received daily compliments on the quality of the work they were receiving from his shop, and occasionally mentioned how much better the details were since he had come back. He nearly busted his buttons with pride and quickly let them know his sweet Minnie deserved all the credit.

It set his heart on fire knowing she could please his customers with such quality work. He couldn't believe his luck, out of her misfortune, to have her show up here, in Gunther City, just when he needed her. She was the perfect helpmeet for him. He prayed he was half as perfect for her. This was his goal from here on out: to be as good to and for her as she was for him.

Katherine Turner stopped by from time to time to wish Minnie and Samuel well, and offer a free drink anytime the happy couple wished to celebrate or cool down after work. Minnie declined, of course, but appreciated her friendship when half of the brides in her house were much less friendly.

So it wasn't unusual one afternoon when Miss Turner strolled over to the blacksmith shop. But she just stood around as if she were looking for something. Minnie pulled off her gloves and approached their new friend. "Miss Turner?"

"I don't believe in spreading alarm, especially when… part of what I do… what I hear is ninety percent alcohol and less than five percent… truth." Her eyes roamed over the shop.

"Miss Turner, what are you trying to tell us?" Minnie touched her arm.

Katherine drew a deep sigh. "There were some men in my place last night. They'd just come in on the afternoon train. We seem to get travelers more and more now that our town is settling down… you know, after the land run? I don't mind, more business for me, of course." She drew in a ragged breath. "They come in, spend the night, and generally buy some horses, a wagon, some supplies, and move on. Everybody has heard of the West and how exciting it is, you understand?"

Minnie bent her neck to peer into Miss Turner's eyes. "Katherine? What's wrong?"

She sighed again and looked deep into Minnie's eyes. "It's just… they asked a lot of questions about the town's prosperity, how the bank was situated, what kind of security it had, you know. Things that a drifter just don't normally ask."

Samuel stepped over to the saloon hall owner. "Miss Turner, you thinking they're aiming to rob the bank?"

Katherine turned to look out the door, and then back to Minnie and Samuel. She pursed her ruby-red lips, then turned her head slowly. "I don't believe in spreading alarm."

"Well." Samuel put his arm around Minnie's shoulder. "It never hurts to voice a concern. Maybe we should go talk to Eddie."

Katherine nodded. "If you think it's enough to cause an alarm?"

Samuel smiled. "It wouldn't hurt to voice your concern."

She nodded again. Samuel walked out with her onto the boardwalk.

Suddenly, a gun went off and a woman screamed. Two men vaulted onto two chestnut mustangs tied to the post in front of the bank. Both horses bore the Forrest's Rocking F brand. Each man had a saddle bag slung over his shoulder. Another gun fired in the air. Eddie Hutton stood on the boardwalk holding the smoking shotgun. Henry and Albert Forrest rushed out behind Mr. Hutton, their guns aimed at the robbers. Eddie looked terrified. The two bank robbers rode past Minnie, Samuel, and Katherine who were gawking in shock.

As they rode past, their eyes met Minnie's. One grinned. The other frowned. She gasped. Her hand covered her mouth.

Alford Graves and Hayden Gray leaned over the neck of the horses they had just stolen and kicked the horses into a full gallop, then gave them their head. The horses ran like the devil himself were behind them.

Samuel touched Minnie's arm. She turned feral eyes on him and spoke from behind her hand. "I know them."

Mary Etta Gunther hurried across the street as fast as her arthritis stricken knees could carry her toward the bank. Panting, she hollered, "Mr. Hutton! Are you all right?"

Eddie turned from the dust cloud following the robbers to Mrs. Gunther. His eyes were wild and wouldn't settle on any one thing. The Forrest boys shouted, "We saw them. They didn't even cover their faces, Mrs. Gunther!"

"All right." Mrs. Gunther lifted an arthritic knobbed hand to her chest. "Go get the sheriff."

Henry leapt off the boardwalk and ran toward the sheriff's office. GW and Andrew had heard the commotion and had already leapt up into their saddles. They galloped past Henry and everyone still on the street in hot pursuit of the bank robbers.

Helen Baird ran across Broad Street. She disappeared through the bank door. Wailing could be heard as Helen obviously expressed her concern for poor Mr. Hutton. Samuel glanced at the bank doors. "Eddie truly will have his hands full once he marries that one."

Minnie looked at him in confusion. "You have no idea."

GW and his deputy returned exhausted and defeated. He and the deputy rode straight to the bank. Claude Gunther ran out and pulled their horses from the hitching post and led them into his stables. They were covered in froth and needed to be cooled down. The stolen mustangs outran them and disappeared along a creek bed. He and the deputy pulled Eddie and the Forrest's sons back into the bank to write down their account of what had happened.

Minnie and Samuel stood among the gathering throng of citizens listening at the bank door. Katherine Turner entered the bank also. "I know what they look like, Sheriff," she said in the heaviest southern drawl anyone had ever heard her speak.

"All right, Kitty. Give me a minute." He said with an odd expression. He turned to his deputy, "Go get Wilma, she's got a knack for sketchin' and can draw a pretty good likeness of the men from the witnesses' descriptions."

Andrew nodded and ran across the street to the bakery. Soon he and Wilma hurried through the bank doors.

Minnie pulled away from Samuel's protective embrace and shoved through the door. "I-I know who they are!"

Startled eyes turned on her. Sheriff Gunther, who had been bent over with one boot on the cross support of a chair, an elbow resting on his knee, listening to Henry Forrest's recollection, stood to his full height. "How could you— all right, Miss Smith, who were they?"

Minnie glanced back to the door. Sam hobbled in after her leaning heavily on a cane, and placed both hands on Minnie's shoulders. He stood behind her. He could feel the strength infused from his presence as she stiffened with courage. "I-uh, their names are Alford Graves and Hayden Gray."

Surprise washed over the sheriff's face. "And how do you know these two bank robbers?"

Sam squeezed her shoulders. She lifted her chin. "They work with Jet Butterfield in Portland, Maine."

Helen gasped. "Jet Butterfield owns a brothel in Portland." Her eyes darted to Eddie and the witnesses. "How on *earth* could you know *him*? Unless—I knew it! You *are* a soiled dove!"

Everyone in the bank gasped. Sam felt Minnie's shoulders round with discouragement.

Minnie staggered back from Helen's harsh words. Sam nearly stepped around her, but then Minnie continued.

"I know them because… they killed my Poppa… an- and stole everything from me." She swallowed. "They're the reason I had to come here without a betrothed. They-they threatened to kill me, too." Tears clotted her words. "I had to run for my life, Helen."

Sam turned Minnie toward him.

"That's what brought you here?" He held her against him and squeezed her close. She cried on his shoulder. His heart filled with anger. Helen Baird was indeed a hellcat. How could she be so mean? Eddie had better get control of his bride-to-be before Sam took control of her. He would not have his precious Minnie treated like this in public or private. Then his anger turned on the men who had violated the entire town. Why were these men here in Gunther City? Could it be coincidence they got off the train in the very same town his Minnie Geneanne had settled in? Were they after her, too? Or was it just dumb luck on their part? "Minnie? Why didn't you tell me?"

Now her tears turned to sobs and she leaned into his broad shoulders. "I couldn't."

Sheriff GW walked closer to Minnie. "It's all right, Miss Smith. Between Sam, here, and me, and the deputy, we're gonna do our best to protect ya" —he shot a displeased look at Helen— "and to find these men. They don't belong anywhere except in jail, and it's my job to make sure that's where they get put." He nodded once with such affirmed conviction. Minnie sighed with relief.

The sheriff meant what he said, but Minnie doubted Graves or Gray would ever be caught. If Butterfield had anything to do with this robbery, they would be well hidden somewhere beyond this sweet little town. Butterfield got away with murder! He had powerful connections in Portland, surely his power reached out here in the West. Why else would his goons have come out here with intent to rob the bank.

That thought made her knees weak. She fought to remain standing. If it weren't for Sam supporting her, she might have collapsed right then and there.

She nodded at the sheriff to let him know she understood, but words wouldn't move past her tears. Sam tugged at her shoulders. "Let's go back to the shop. The Sheriff knows where to find you if he has any more questions."

Minnie's sad eyes met Sam's. She glanced back at the sheriff, who looked over Wilma's shoulder. She worked on both likenesses because the witnesses couldn't settle their recollections on one robber at a time. She would soon have them completed.

GW looked at Minnie. "I'll bring these to you to identify which is Graves and which is Gray, if that's all right, Miss Smith."

Minnie's eyes darted to the drawings. She swallowed hard and nodded. She could already tell which was who, but she'd been through so much telling her worst nightmare, and then being accused by Helen of such impropriety. She just didn't want to tell the Sheriff right now. She'd go back with Sam and get her bearings.

The sheriff tipped his head back, giving approval for her to leave.

She turned back to Sam. "Ah-all right, let's go."

Chapter Twenty-Two

When things settled down and Mr. Hutton could finally collect himself to determine how much had been stolen, the entire town stood outside of the bank waiting to hear how bad the damages were. A very pale Eddie Hutton walked slowly onto the boardwalk.

Samuel and Minnie approached the crowd to listen. Eddie held his derby in trembling hands and wiped his mouth with a white handkerchief bearing an embroidered EFH. Helen stood beside him, with her best fair-queen smile plastered across her face, in show of solidarity for her betrothed, but she, too, looked to be in shock.

"How much did they take?" Newt finally asked. Eddie's eyes rose from his hat and met Newt's, then he panned the crowd and swallowed hard. "They... got... it all." He staggered back against the people who had crowded behind him. "Every solid coin in the vault. They got it all."

The crowd gasped as one. Mrs. Tanner swooned. Doc Savage waved some smelling salts under her nose and helped her to stand. Whimpering and sobbing broke out among the women. The men turned to the Sheriff and demanded he form a posse. He agreed and chose the younger men to get their horses and ride with him. Claude brought them fresh horses. GW'd go to where they had lost sight of their tracks and work down the creek until they could find any evidence of where they went.

Samuel turned to get a horse from Claude's stables, but GW stopped him. "Sam, I need somebody levelheaded to stay in town with the women. You and Newt's shops are at either end of town, I need y'all to watch from both ends to make sure those scoundrels don't double back."

"But G Dub!"

"Sam, please!"

Sam stared at the sheriff, then he looked at Newt. "The Sheriff's right." Newt shrugged. "Someone strong and levelheaded needs to keep an eye on the women in town and handle those two should they try to come back for — for whatever reason."

Sam swung around to find Minnie. The fear in her face resolved the whole issue for him. He nodded.

Mary Etta patted her apron pocket. "Oh! Miss Smith. I forgot all about this." She held up an official looking letter and handed it to Minnie.

She stared at the return address. "It's from home."

Sam wrapped an arm around her and turned her back to the blacksmith shop. "It looks important. Let's go back to the shop so I can keep an eye on this end of town, and you can read your letter."

She nodded, but worry filled her face.

Sam dragged a chair out onto the boardwalk so he could sit while keeping watch. He hated to admit it, but he hurt and was exhausted. Minnie went inside their shop and snuffed out the forge. They weren't going to do anymore work this late in the afternoon. In truth, she was stalling. She dreaded seeing what news was in this letter from home. The return address was a law firm along the waterfront. What could they possibly have to tell her? Had her poppa's body been found? Butterfield had claimed her poppa's debt gave him rights to their house and all within, was this some form of papers telling her he owned the property outright? All she had from home were her memories. But at least she had those.

With everything readied to close the shop, she pulled a chair out beside Samuel and held the unopened letter in her hands. He looked over at her with one eyebrow raised. "Don't ya wanna know?"

She sighed. "I'm not sure."

Sam nodded. "Well, it's yours to do with as you please. If it were me, I'd wanna know."

"Sam," she said thoughtfully. "What will we do with the bank being robbed?"

He stared down the street a long time. "I'm not sure. I s'pose we all gotta start over."

"But, without the money in the bank, no one'll be able to pay for nothing. The economy in our town is ruined. All we got is bartering. How we gonna get by with just that?"

Sam took a deep breath. "I don't know. Before the land run, there was them who had coin and them who only had goods to barter. I s'pose we'll go back to that and build our way up again."

Minnie stared at her envelope. If only she had that gold Mr. Butterfield had killed her Poppa over. She could fix the bank's problem and life could continue as it had been in Gunther City. "I think I'll take this home with me. I don't know if I'll open it or not." She stood.

"Here." He stood with some difficulty to steady himself. "I'll walk you home."

"No, you can watch me walk home from here. You need to stay at your post until those two come back or the posse does."

Sam kissed her cheek. She half-heartedly kissed his and turned to walk herself to the Bride House.

Minnie scurried down the boardwalk to Division, the small street between buildings. She dodged a buggy and three riders to cross Broad Street, leapt onto the opposite boardwalk, hurried past the Town Hall, and paused at Widow Drummond's door.

She turned to wave at Samuel, indicating she was all right before she entered the Bride House. Although she was anything but all right.

Minnie's heart was too heavy to smile or be pleased that he had not taken his eyes off her as she traversed the two blocks to get home. She locked the door as she closed it behind her, and dragged herself upstairs, ignoring Widow Drummond's call to supper.

Gunther City was supposed to be a safe haven for her. Instead, her presence had tainted everyone's lives. She was the bad apple that spoiled the whole barrel. Her tears began to fall the minute her body landed on her bed. She cried into her pillow until it was soaking wet. Why couldn't Butterfield and his goons just leave her be?

Her heart ached with sorrow. She'd never been wealthy, but her poppa had always been able to feed them with his iron work skills and provide a roof over their heads. It hadn't been a bad life.

Until Butterfield and his men came, and turned her life upside down.

Coming here to Gunther City had been terrifying and lonely, but all that had changed since she met Samuel Knight. He was the love of her dreams. They had worked together harmoniously in the smithy and he and his business were back on their feet.

Then Butterfield crashed into her life again. They were ruined financially. The whole town was. Not only did Graves and Gray ruin her life, they ruined everyone she knew and cared about.

A tap at her door drew her from her pit of despair. Dixie called her name. If it were anybody else, she'd have shouted for them to leave her alone. But Dixie.

"Minnie? Please let me in."

Minnie forced herself up and opened the door. Dixie slipped into her room with Mr. Darcy and the two of them sat on Minnie's bed. Mr. Darcy jumped into Minnie's lap and licked her tear soaked face. Minnie couldn't help but chuckle.

"Down, Mr. Darcy," Minnie fussed at the dachshund, but in truth, she had grown to love the sausage dog and appreciated Dixie's unrelenting friendship.

"It's all my fault." Minnie confessed.

"How could it possibly be your fault?" Dixie gathered Mr. Darcy into her lap.

"Jet Butterfield sent Graves and Grey here to destroy my happiness, just like they did in Portland."

"Why would Butterfield care about whether or not you were happy?" Dixie looked deep into Minnie's eyes. "Seriously, what difference does your life make to a wealthy man like him?"

Minnie thought about her question. He had been after her poppa's gold, not her. The only reason they killed Poppa was because he wouldn't give them the treasure. She wasn't sure he even had a treasure to give them. They probably shot him over nothing. The whole idea of that caused a sob to catch her breath. She grabbed her throat and fought to breathe. "Oh, Dixie. I… don't… know."

She tossed herself onto her pillow and bawled.

Dixie rubbed her arm and cooed kind words to try to calm her down. "Minnie, Please don't carry on so. Everything's going to be all right."

Minnie sat up abruptly. "How?"

Dixie flinched and Mr. Darcy lowered his front end to growl at Minnie.

"How can it possibly be all right? The town has lost everything… because… of… me."

"My goodness." Dixie puckered her lips. "You're as conceited as Helen."

Minnie stilled. Did Dixie just tell her she was acting like Helen? "What?"

Dixie blushed and pulled Mr. Darcy back into her arms. "You honestly think those two men robbed our bank just to get back at you? For what? Because they couldn't find your poppa's gold." She patted Mr. Darcy's back and he instantly flipped over to have his belly rubbed. "Honey, think about it. Why would Graves and Grey come to Gunther City to seek revenge on you? And if they did such a thing, just because of you, wouldn't they… I don't know… burn down the blacksmith shop… god forbid… or something a little more directly affecting you?"

Minnie stared at nothing across the room. Dixie made sense. Something must have happened for Graves and Gray to leave Portland and Butterfield to travel halfway across America… and rob a bank.

"Wait." Minnie jumped up and hurried to her tall boy dresser. She lifted the official looking letter from the Waterfront lawyers. "Mary Etta gave me this today. You don't suppose…"

"Well," Dixie exclaimed. "For heaven's sake. Open it."

Minnie sniffed and pulled out her letter opener. She sliced through the flap and pulled out several folded pages of parchment.

Chapter Twenty-Three

The top piece of parchment was an ink and quill scripted letter referencing her father's property, home and shop by a legal description she'd never seen before. Then it addressed her by her full Christian name.

Dear Miss Minnie Geneanne Smith,

It has been brought to our attention that due to the events of Mr. Jet C. Butterfield's attempt to claim the afore mentioned property titled heretofore to a Mr. Eugene Smith, your legal parent and guardian, you have changed your legal residence to Gunther City, Oklahoma and plan to seek a marriage arrangement.

Due to the illegality of Mr. Butterfield's claim on said property, we hereby inform you the afore mentioned property is entitled to you as Mr. Smith's only living relative.

However, because of the needs of the community, the town council has no choice but to inform you: if you do not claim said property in person within

sixty days of the date of this letter, we will be forced to sell said property to the highest bidder. Portland, Maine has a great need of a blacksmith. Therefore, if you have no desire to return to take possession of said property, it shall be placed on the auction block within ninety days and the proceeds from that sale will be placed in a trust in Portland National Bank in your name, minus any incurrence of legal fees.
With warmest regards,
Mister Lawrence Howell, Esquire
Weech, Eatum, and Howell, Attorneys at Law

Minnie yanked the top letter aside and read the second. It was from Pastor Robertson. He or Mrs. Robertson had typed it on one of those fancy machines.

My Dearest Minnie,
We hope this finds you well and happy. God knows you deserve it. Please excuse the impersonal correspondence, but Mr. Robertson insists I utilize his new machine called a typewriter.
It is with great blessings that we let you know Mr. Jet Butterfield has received the Lord's return for his sins. It seems he not

only sinned against you and God, but the place of business in which he was associated has filed charges against him for embezzlement and fraud. The case against him won on five accounts in a court of law and he is now sentenced to twenty years in the Maine State Prison down state.

As such, his claim on your father's property has been revoked and we anxiously await your arrival to reclaim it as your own.

We hope this blesses you and look forward to seeing you soon. We are asking the waterfront law firm who is handling your property in your stead to include this letter so that you receive both post haste.

I believe they are giving you a limited amount of time to take care of this matter and therefore encourage you to return as soon as possible. Perhaps, if you have any of your benefactor's funds, you will be able to arrange transportation by the same train which took you from us.

Looking forward to seeing you soon,

Pastor and Mrs. Robertson

Minnie dropped both letters in her lap and smiled at Dixie.

"Well?" Dixie scooted closer to Minnie. "What does it say?"

"I—" Minnie leapt to her feet. "I've gotta tell Sam!"

"What?" Dixie gathered Mr. Darcy in her arms and chased after Minnie.

"Butterfield's in prison… and I can get my poppa's home back! But, I've gotta hurry!" She flew down the stairs and out on the boardwalk.

Widow Drummond ran out from her room in her bed gown and nightcap. "What's going on?"

Dixie stopped short of the door. "Oh, Widow Drummond, the most wonderful news!"

Dixie stayed behind to fill Widow Drummond in on Minnie's news from home.

Widow Drummond listened carefully, but when Dixie completed her tale, Mrs. Drummond clasped her throat with a trembling hand. "Oh, that will never do!"

She rushed to her room.

Dixie stood dumbfounded. "Why not?"

"SAM!" Minnie ran down the boardwalk and leapt to the dirt street. She continued to run, screaming his name.

"What?" He rushed out of the shadows, leaning heavily on his cane, wincing as his boots landed on the hard dirt. He caught her by the shoulders. "What is all this?"

Minnie panted, trying to catch her breath. "I've gotta go home! Butterfield's in prison. I've gotta go home and claim my poppa's property! I've only got a few days!"

"Minnie, what are you saying?" Sam led her to the boardwalk.

She gasped for air and told him about the two letters. She needed to buy a train ticket and get back home as soon as she could.

"That's great news," Sam said. "So, I s'pose Graves and Gray were acting on their own, coming out west and robbing a bank?"

She stared at him a moment. The joy waned from her face. "I-I have no idea." She scanned the street. "Why here? Do you suppose they heard about the mail order brides coming here?"

"Minnie, the success of the Land Run is known across the nation. Anybody could have learned of our prosperity here." Sam pulled her into his chest and held her tight. "Listen. The train don't head back east 'til Saturday. We'll go buy our tickets tomorrow and —"

"We?" Minnie leaned back from him. "Will you go with me?"

"Of course I'm going with you. I would never let you go alone. Besides, you're going to need help going through your poppa's shop and sorting out your belongings."

"What are you saying?"

"You're going to sell your home in Portland, and your poppa's shop, aren't you?"

Minnie's jaw dropped. "I… don't know. I haven't thought that far ahead."

"Well." Samuel stepped back from her. "You're coming back here, aren't you? You agreed to let me court you. We're betrothed. Aren't you coming back to Gunther City."

Minnie stared at him. She hadn't calculated what this letter really meant. She didn't want to leave Samuel or her new life here. But she didn't want her poppa's home and shop to be auctioned off to the highest bidder. Her mind spun in a frenzy of confusion. She didn't know what to do.

"Minnie! I forbid you to leave here and never come back!" Samuel's brow wrinkled over the bridge of his nose.

She gasped. "You forbid—" She stepped back another step. Her cheeks filled with angry heat. "Now, just a minute Samuel Knight. We may be betrothed, but we are not married, and you do not forbid me to do anything I think is right for me to do."

"No. Minnie, I didn't mean—I just— Please, Minnie, I love you. I want you to marry me. I don't want to lose you! Please, let me go with you, help you sort this whole thing out and then bring you back to marry me."

She stood statue still, gawking at him. Did he just propose?

She couldn't think. She stepped another step back and turned to run to the Bride House, but Widow Drummond screamed, "You hold it right there, Miss Smith."

The widow held her spoon high in the air and waddled out into the street.

"Widow Drummond! What are you—"

"You cannot go traipsing around this country on a train, no less, unescorted, and unmarried! It ain't proper!" She caught up to Minnie and looped her arm into her elbow, as if to escort her. She held her spoon up toward Sam's face. "You! What's wrong with you giving Miss Smith a proper proposal?"

Samuel stammered, "Well, I... I was waitin' till I got my strength—"

"Strength, schmength." Mrs. Drummond shook her spoon at him. "Do you or do you not love this woman who has worked by your side for nearly a good month now?"

Samuel's eyes darted to Minnie and back to Mrs. Drummond. "I... love her with all my heart."

"Fine. Then what's the problem?"

"I—"

"Widow Drummond." Minnie tried to interrupt.

"Hush child." Drummond swiped the spoon at Minnie and turned it back on Samuel. "Well?"

"Widow Drummond." Minnie tried again.

"What!" she turned breathlessly to Minnie.

"I believe he *just did* ask me to marry him."

Her eyes rounded. She looked from Minnie to Samuel. Katherine Turner stepped out on the boardwalk. "It's the truth, Widow Drummond. Half my customers heard him say it." She chuckled.

Widow Drummond's mouth gaped and she turned from Katherine, to Minnie, to Samuel. "Well, good then. This wedding's gonna have to take place before the two of you go gallivanting off on a train. Otherwise, I'm gonna have to go with you to witness her virtue."

Samuel's eyes widened. "Oh, no. That won't be necessary, Widow Drummond, I assure you. We can talk to Preacher William Gunther tomorrow and get this squared away before Saturday's train."

Minnie gaped at the widow and Samuel. "Wait a minute!"

"Fine," the widow said. "You go talk to Preacher William in the morning and then come by the Bride House for breakfast. We'll start sorting out the plans and figure out what we need to do to have ourselves a weddin' by Friday."

"Wait. A. Minute!" Minnie shouted.

Samuel and Widow Drummond slowly turned to her. Startled eyes stared at her, waiting to hear what she was shouting about.

"I haven't even said yes."

"Well, why wouldn't you say yes, dear?" Mrs. Drummond glanced at Samuel and back to Minnie.

"I'm not saying I wouldn't. I'm just saying… I haven't." Minnie flushed pink.

"Oh." Widow Drummond stepped back and gestured for Samuel to step closer to Minnie. "By all means, Mr. Knight. Let's do this proper."

He stared at the widow. Not sure what she meant. Then he realized what she wanted of him. He stepped closer to Minnie and reached out to take her hand. She let him have her hand, while he used his cane to brace himself and went down on one knee with a wince and grimace.

"Minnie Geneanne Smith, you are an angel sent to me from heaven. I love you for your skills, your intelligence, and your heart. Please do me the honor of becoming my wife by Friday, so we can go together to reclaim your property in Portland Maine and figure out what to do from there. I'll do whatever you want. If you want to stay in Portland, I'll stay in Portland. If you want to come back here, I'll come back here. Whatever you want, my love. Just say you'll become Mrs. Knight and continue to live our lives together until I breathe my last breath."

Tears streamed down Minnie's face. Widow Drummond sniffed.

Katherine pulled out a hanky and blew her nose. "Must be the stables, my hay fever is horrible tonight."

Minnie pulled Samuel to his feet. He winced but stood. She continued to hold his hands. "Samuel Knight, I have loved you since the day I saw you in that wheeled chair at the train depot. The fact that you're willing to go to Portland with me, and to stay there, if that be what I want, makes me love you all the more. I don't know what I want to do about my poppa's house and shop, but I do know this…"

She glanced over at Widow Drummond and back to Samuel. "Yes, I will marry you, before Friday. I will become Mrs. Samuel Knight." She threw herself against him and he squeezed her tight against himself.

"Thank you," He whispered against her ear.

Widow Drummond cleared her throat. "We best be getting home now. We've got a lot of planning to do tomorrow, if we're gonna get you two hitched by Friday."

Minnie giggled and wiped her eyes. "Yes, Widow Drummond, let's go home."

The widow shook her spoon at Samuel one last time. "You come for breakfast and let me know what Preacher William said."

"Yes, ma'am." Samuel smiled and watch his future wife walk arm in arm with the orneriest woman in town.

Chapter Twenty-Four

The roosters at Claude's stables crowed. An answer to their call came from behind the blacksmith shop. Samuel Knight's roosters were awake, too. He'd not slept most of the night, anticipating his talk with Preacher Gunther. He wanted to marry Minnie Smith by Friday. The Preacher had to agree, because they had to board the Saturday Eastbound train for Portland, Maine. He held up his mug of coffee to cheer the cockerels in their morning tribute to the sun.

Samuel washed in his bedroom pitcher and bowl, and slipped on his only Sunday-go-to-meetin' suit. As he looped his string tie, he stood at his apartment window that overlooked Broad Street. The Sun crested behind his apartment, casting a golden yellow glow across the stables and other shops leading to the Bride House where his Minnie slept. Did she sleep? Or was she as anxious about everything as he was? How could she not be? He knew how important the news from the waterfront lawyers had been. She'd have hitched up a wagon and headed north-east last night if anybody would have let her.

The bank robbery changed a lot of things for Gunther City. People would have to adjust, maybe even suffer a little, unless they had some gold coin or nuggets stashed somewhere, like he did. A God-Only-Knows fund, his mother had called it. Hers had been a mason jar buried in the root cellar, his was in the forge.

Samuel knew this hardy stock of people he had come to know since the land run would survive. Somehow they all would regain what they lost and be back on their feet in no time. Look how far they had come just since the April's land grab. Gunther City would survive.

Except Eddie's hellcat. Samuel chuckled. She didn't look like she was from hardy stock or had a clue how to survive with nothing. She walked around as if in a trance, smiling as if she were having her portrait painted. It would be an interesting demonstration of personal growth to watch that one adjust and make do. Poor Eddie. The other brides seemed sad, but not despondent. Obviously, they had dealt with hard times before and were not terrified to do it again.

Sam considered the morning light. Could it be too early to seek out the preacher? He hung his head, knowing it was. For whatever reason, Sampson Cherry had not delivered firewood this morning. Folks depended on his daily delivery to supply their kitchen needs. Few had enough stored up to get by for more than two days. Cherry was regular like clockwork and his absence was noticeable.

Samuel turned to look down the road toward Sampson and Emma's sod dugout. It couldn't be seen from town, but far off in the distance there was a cloud of dust. The Cherry's had gotten a late start, like everybody else.

Sam shrugged it off and prepared his breakfast of fried potatoes and salt pork. After he washed the skillet and set it on the stove to dry, he walked to the front window. Smoke rose from chimney's, Claude's stable doors had been flung open, and horses were saddled and readied for riders who boarded their steeds with him. A few men walked the length of Board Street, gathering outside the Town Hall. Citizens wanted to know what to do now that the bank had been robbed. Even Mr. Hutton made his way toward the impromptu meeting. Sheriff GW waved his hands to quiet the men. Samuel nodded to himself. He needed to go down and hear what was being said. Preacher William would be officiating if they had an official town meeting anyway. Sam could catch him and talk to him about their wedding. Samuel glanced in the silvered glass before leaving his apartment. He'd make a sorrowful groom, but his Minnie would be an angelic bride. He knew it for a fact.

People were getting rowdy by the time Sam made it to the Town Hall. Even the sister brides and Widow Drummond were among the crowd. Samuel and Minnie's eyes met and a smile warmed both their faces. She stood near him while the Sheriff continued to calm those who were angry and vocally expressing their fear.

"Now, good people. Let's calm down and talk this through. Come on in and have a seat. Preacher William and most of the town council are already seated and have been discussing our options since the break of day. Calm down. Come on in."

He gestured for the people to walk through the door. "Don't crowd. We don't want no one hurt. That's it. Come on in." The Sheriff spoke slowly, softly.

Minnie and Samuel followed the funnel of people and found two chairs to sit with each other. Preacher Gunther stood and the people quieted. He cleared his throat. "Now, folks. I know this may seem like a desperate situation."

Some men started murmuring, but Preacher William gestured for them to be quiet. "I know, Frank. It is a desperate situation, but nothing we can't overcome. Now, first of all, Sheriff GW is sending out a likeness that Wilma drew of the two robbers. Thanks to Minnie Smith," he nodded toward her. "We know their names. Now, all we gotta do is find them and bring them to the Judge."

Murmuring rose again and William, once again stood and gestured for them to settle down.

"The longer we have to sit in here and calm all you down, the longer it's going to take GW to get a posse together and look for these scoundrels."

That closed the murmurer's mouths and people sat down.

"Now." The sheriff stood. "If anybody notices anything suspicious, report it immediately, no matter how little it might seem. Every little clue could be just the thing that leads us to these guys."

Samuel nodded and squeezed Minnie's hand. She smiled at him, wishing she had any idea what those two were thinking when they robbed the bank, then perhaps she could help the sheriff figure out where they went.

Once everyone had asked every question imaginable about what would happen next, the meeting finally came to an end. Preacher William banged his gavel and Mary Etta cringed from the sound. Samuel stood quickly and pushed his way to the front. "Preacher Gunther!"

William shook Oliver Forrest's hand, greeted Dixie, and patted Mr. Darcy's head. He turned upon hearing his name. "Oh, Mr. Knight, you're looking well."

"Thank you, Preacher." Samuel pulled Minnie up closer to him and wrapped an arm around her. "Miss Smith and I need to discuss something of urgency with you."

"Well." Preacher Gunther smiled but concern filled his eyes. "Then let's retire to my den at our home."

"Thank you." Samuel said and led Minnie out onto the boardwalk. Mary Etta and Preacher William walked with them to Division and around to the back street. The Gunther's home was just up the back street a short walk.

Sampson was alone at his wagon full of firewood. He slung the pack toward the back door of Town Hall and walked Bessy to the next. Samuel watched Sampson's odd behavior.

"Will you excuse me for a minute." He patted Minnie arm. The Gunthers and Minnie waited while Samuel walked over to Mr. Cherry.

"Sampson, everything all right?" Samuel approached his friend as he slung a bundle of firewood toward the back door of the Drummond's Bride House.

"What's it to chu?" Cherry said and walked Bessy further down the backstreet.

"Sampson!" Samuel hurried to catch up. "Where's Emma? What's wrong?"

Sampson turned wide eyed to Samuel. "Whatchu asking 'bout my wife fo. Ain't none yo business how my wife be."

Samuel stood in stunned silence.

"And 'nother thing, Mr. Knight. I gotta charge more fo yo har'wood. With this bank robbery, we can't get along on just your shoein' Bessy here. Me and Emma, we gotta take care a our own, now a days."
Samuel stared at Sampson. "What are you saying?"
Sampson blew out an exasperated sigh. "Emma be increasing's all."
"Sampson! Congratulations!" Samuel grinned.
"Shh!" Sampson frowned. "Ain't nobody's business! Not like we're friends or nothin'"
"Well…" Samuel watch him walk away leading his mule to the next drop off and slinging another bundle of firewood at their back door. This was so odd. Sampson always stacked the wood bundles carefully next to the steps, took the time to visit with folks, and what was this business about charging more and them not being friends. Maybe with Emma being in a family way, Sampson was worried. Men get like that with the pressures of having a family.
Samuel scratched his beard thoughtfully and walked over to where he had left Minnie and the Gunthers.

William spoke as they walked. "You know, we are considering naming this street First. Our house could be number one." He leaned his head back and laughed heartily. "One First Street. That sounds grand, doesn't it?"

"Sounds like a good idea." Samuel chuckled. "Since the big central street is so commonly known as Broad Street, we can start branching out to the North with First, Second and Third and to the South with… I don't know, president's name?"

William stopped and touched Samuel's arm. "Say! That's not a bad idea, either. We could start with Washington and then Adams, Jefferson, Madison and so on."

Samuel looked out across the prairie. "It's hard to imagine we'll ever need so many streets."

Once the town recovered from this major setback, and more settlers come in to build up the town, it would be amazing to watch all these things happen. Samuel led Minnie into the Gunther's home, following Preacher William to his sitting room. Mary Etta continued to the back of the house to bring coffee and biscuits.

"Now." Preacher William sat at his desk and gestured for Samuel and Minnie to be seated. Samuel looked at Minnie. It was her story, really, but Widow Drummond had ordered *him* to set up the wedding for no later than Friday. "My Minnie and I wish to be married, but circumstances have made it necessary for us to do so by Friday."

"Friday!" the preacher leaned back in his leather chair. "Why so quick, are you needing to protect her reputation, son?"

"Oh no, no." Minnie spoke up. She blushed. "You see, I got a letter from home… and… my poppa was murdered" —Minnie had to swallow and compose herself— "The men who came here and robbed our bank are the same men who murdered my poppa… they said they had a debt my poppa owed and took possession of our home and Poppa's blacksmith shop."

Preacher William's bushy eyebrows rose high on his forehead. "That explains a lot, little lady."

Minnie glared at the preacher.

"Did I hear you want a Friday wedding?" Mary Etta entered the room with a tray of coffee and cups with saucers. "Oh my, my. You know what is said? 'Marry on Monday for health, Tuesday for wealth, Wednesday the best day of all, Thursday for crosses, Friday for losses, and Saturday for no luck at all.'"

She looked at Minnie sternly. "Are you sure you wish to marry on a Friday, Dear?"

Samuel cleared his throat. "Well, you see she needs to get back to Portland to claim her father's property by the end of the month or it'll be auctioned off to the highest bidder, and I can't let her go by herself. We need to be married by Friday so we can take the Saturday train."

Samuel drew in a breath he had been needing several words ago.

"I see." The preacher pulled his glasses from his nose and wiped them with his handkerchief. "So we need a weddin' by Friday."

"Yes!" Minnie and Samuel said at the same time.

Mary Etta tsked her tongue. "Oh my. It won't take nothing to have a wedding by then. If you're certain that's still what you want to do." She smiled awkwardly. "So long as you don't want nothing fancy."

Minnie's shoulders rounded. She had had a plan. Mrs. Tanner had ordered the material. Minnie had described the dress from her memory and Mrs. Tanner had drawn out a pattern. She drew in a ragged breath. "I wanted to wear a replica of my momma's wedding dress." She sniffed. "Mrs. Tanner is working on it, but it's not ready."

"Well." Mary Etta patted Minnie's hand. "Circumstances have changed and as long as you have a clean dress, you can stand before the Lord and take Mr. Knight's hand, can't you?"

Minnie sighed. "Yes. Of course. It's just—" She lifted sad eyes to meet Samuel. Her heart beat increased two times its normal speed. Her breath caught in her lungs. He was so handsome in his Sunday suit. The yellow gown Jane Anne had made her was beautiful. She could gather some wild flowers from the prairie, and get Dixie to fix her hair the way the girls did for the First Dance. Sure, it would be fine. The important thing would be that she and Samuel were married so they could travel together.

"Of course. I have a clean dress, a new one in fact. And there's nothing stopping us from marrying Friday. If that day works for you, Mr. Gunther."

"Oh, my dear, Mr. Gunther could marry you two this minute if you wanted."

Samuel looked to Minnie hopeful. She met his enthusiastic expression with a frown. His stupid grin melted. "No, I think we need until Friday to get completely prepared."

Minnie nodded and Sam knew he'd responded correctly to please his bride. Besides, he did have something special he wanted to do before they stood to say their vows.

"Friday it is, then." William clapped his hands. "Now, what time."

Mary Etta filled the coffee cups and passed them to everyone. She turned to Minnie. "The two hands must be moving up on the face of a clock for a wedding to be happily ever after."

The preacher admonished his wife. "You and your superstitions, Dear."

"It's not superstitions, Mr. Gunther. It's just how things are." Mary Etta smiled at Minnie.

"So." Samuel looked confused. "After six thirty in the morning?"

"No way!" Minnie nearly stood. "There are more opportunities for the two hands moving up than just six thirty in the morning, Sam!"

Mary Etta chuckled. "Yes, many other times will be good. We just need to decide which of them is perfect for you."

"Yes, ma'am." Minnie considered Mrs. Gunther's words. "I think six-forty-five would be perfect for us."

Mr. Gunther stepped around his desk and sidled next to Samuel. "And don't worry about paying for the services, Sam. Just send a donation to the church when you get caught up after this bank heist is straightened out."

Sam nodded.

Chapter Twenty-Five

Samuel led Minnie out of the preacher's house. His stride was long and she had to broaden hers to keep up. "Slow down."

She lifted her skirts slightly so she could lengthen her gait.

"Come here, I've got something to show you." He sounded excited, almost breathless.

Curiosity wrinkled her brow. "Where are we going? The widow is expecting us for breakfast."

Samuel looked up at the sky. "It's too late for breakfast, besides I'm not hungry."

Minnie pressed her heels into the hard dirt and forced Samuel to stop. "This breakfast is not about hunger, Samuel Knight. Widow Drummond has prepared a special meal to celebrate our wedding plans. We have to go!"

Sam stared at her with disbelief in his eyes. "But I have something special, too."

She lifted one eyebrow and pursed her lips. "Samuel, whatever you have will have to wait. Widow Drummond has been up since before the sun. In fact all the brides have been. I'm not sure what they've been doing but there is a lot of excitement in our house. All I know is everyone is flittering around, whispering and giggling, and *we* will not disappoint them." Her jaw set firm and her chin rose as steely eyes bore into his.

Sam tilted his head back. His eyebrows slid up high on his forehead. So this is what it is to be married. He considered demanding they go to the forge instead, but the tenacity in her eyes told him it would be a bad idea. If he wanted peace in their lives, it would be a very bad idea.

"Of course," he finally agreed. She led him to the Drummond House with her arm in the crook of his elbow. When they crossed the threshold, Widow Drummond stood alone in the parlor, wringing her hands. "Well, did you talk to the preacher?"

"Ayah, ma'am." Minnie smiled.

"And… is he gonna marry ya on Friday?"

"Ayah, we will be married on Friday. In fact we've already set a time, six-forty-five."

Widow Drummond's worried face softened into glee. "Mary Etta talked you into having your wedding with the hands both moving up on the face of the clock, for good luck."

Minnie sighed with a smile. "For a happy ever after," she said. Apparently, it's bad enough that we are doing this on a Friday." Minnie shrugged, "Why tempt fate?"

Mrs. Drummond laughed. "Why, indeed."

She turned with an open arm gesture of invitation for Samuel and Minnie to enter the dining area. "Well, come on in and let's tell the girls we've got ourselves our first wedding. Ironic, isn't it."

Minnie stopped in her step. "Oh, I hadn't thought about that. Is Helen alright with this?"

The widow turned back to Minnie with a taut smile. "She's fine with it."

Minnie giggled. Helen had the spoon shaken at her and was told to be happy for their seventh bride. Minnie took Samuel's arm and led him into the dining room.

All of her sister brides were dressed and each smiled when she and Samuel entered the dining room. A banquet was spread out on the long table of sausage, bacon, ham, biscuits, cream gravy and red-eye gravy, scrambled eggs, hard cheese, jellies, and fried potatoes. The good Sunday dishes were set with silverware, water glasses and cups with saucers for coffee or hot tea. At one end, there were packages wrapped in various cloths, burlap, flour sacks, and whatever the girls had to cover the contents. Beautiful ribbons were tied on them to keep the material together.

Minnie's mouth gaped in surprise. "Oh my goodness. How did you—" tears clotted her words?

"Come." Widow Drummond pulled them in. "Sit, eat."

Dixie, who's face lit up with joy, stood and tapped a water glass with her spoon. She cleared her throat. "Minnie Smith, we couldn't let you go off and get married without giving you a few things to help you start your marriage on the right foot. So, please accept these gifts that most of us made with our own two hands. Some of us worked on them late into the night last night." She batted her eyes as if she were so sleepy she couldn't keep her eyes open.

Minnie laughed. She looked around the table. Even Helen had a pleasant look on her face. Widow Drummond must have made a good threat with that spoon for Helen to be this congenial.

"Thank you." Minnie stood next to Samuel, still clinging to his arm. "All of you. You… make my heart… so full."

"Open your gifts!" Martha shouted and then shrunk back. It wasn't like her to be so loud. The girls turned in surprise and laughed. Martha's face flushed.

"All right." Minnie said as Samuel pulled out her chair and the couple sat. Dishes were passed around and plates filled. Then Dixie handed Minnie a gingham wrapped gift. Slowly she pulled the ribbon so she could save it for her hair. "Oh Dixie, did you embroider these?"

Dixie blushed. "Yes, my momma used to embroider all her tea towels like that so you know which one to use on which day."

Minnie lifted the sack cloth one by one. Dixie had stitched the days of the week and a simple drawing of chores that belong to that day. A wash tub on Monday, an iron on Tuesday, a loaf of bread on Wednesday, chopped wood on Thursday, a rug and whip on Friday, a bunch of vegetables on Saturday, and praying hands on Sunday. "Oh Dixie, they're beautiful!"

"Open mine next." Helen cried out.

Minnie lifted surprised eyes to meet Helen's. "All right." She grinned. What could it be that Helen would be so excited about? The package was small and wrapped in butcher paper and twine. Minnie pulled the twine and set it aside. Inside were hankies. Each cross-stitched with a different single flower. A red rose, a blue cornflower, a yellow sunflower, a white daisy, and a purple iris. "Helen," Minnie breathed her name. A tear pooled in her eye. "How'd you— when— I didn't know you knew how to cross stitch?"

"Well, Dixie taught me." Helen glanced at Dixie, who nodded approval.

"She was a good student. We sat up together at night getting them done."

"Oh, ladies. I'm... I'm so honored. These are lovely."

Minnie continued to unwrap the gifts the girls presented. Even Widow Drummond had a gift of wooden spoons in various sizes and a cotton apron long enough to cover Minnie's tall stature. She lifted the apron and admired the stitching, and then realized the spoons were underneath. Everyone laughed and made comments about Minnie keeping

Mr. Knight in line. Samuel smiled and continued to eat his plate full of excellent food.

At last the presents were opened and Minnie had set the gifts aside on the buffet. She sat down and looked at her cold food. She was hungry and scooped cold eggs onto her fork. Jane Anne stood and cleared her throat.

"Minnie." Jane Anne had never spoken so meekly. It caused the entire table to look at her with interest. "I have one more thing to give you before your wedding Friday."

Minnie crossed her brow. "Oh my!" She took the tailor's box from Jane Anne. What on earth could this be? All the sister brides watched with excitement as Minnie lifted the lid. It clung to the bottom but eventually, she pulled the two apart. Tissue covered a soft creamy colored material. She could see a section of tatted lace and gasped. "NO! How—"

She gingerly lifted the tissue, revealing a gown of taffeta and hand tatted lace sleeves that flowed into the yoke across the bosom. She delicately lifted the gown and squeezed it against her chest. She buried her face in the material and wept.

All the girls stared in utter confusion. Even Samuel stood to comfort Minnie, although he had no idea why this dress had caused her so much anguish.

Jane Anne drew a ragged breath and sniffed. She wiped her nose with a hanky and folded her hands in front of her hips. "Do you like it?" she managed to say.

"What is it?" Alice asked. Lou Lou walked around the table and placed her hand on Minnie's shoulder. "I know what it is."

"What?" all the girls asked at once.

Minnie lifted her face. Her trembling lips smiled at her friend.

Lou Lou turned to the women. "It's a replica of her mother's wedding dress she ordered from Ruby Tanner. Minnie recalled every detail from memory, and Mrs. Tanner made the pattern."

Jane Anne cleared her throat. "The material had to be special ordered and the tatting we made ourselves. The thread had to be special ordered, too. Mrs. Tanner wanted to surprise you with it, and then she found out you were going back East and needed to speed up the weddin'. So we worked our fingers to the bone to get all that lace made so she could give it to me to give to you today."

Minnie drew in a deep breath. She reached out and touched Jane Anne's arm. "I'm sorry I kept it a secret from you."

"No." Jane Anne waved her comment off. "I'd have kept it a secret from me, too, if I were you."

The girls laughed and gathered around Minnie to admire the delicate dress.

"None of that!" Widow Drummond shouted and waved her spoon at Samuel. "Grooms are NOT allowed to see the bride's dress before the wedding. You divert your eyes or go in the parlor. I don't care which, just you don't look at that gown." Her voice cracked with emotion and she stepped between Minnie and Samuel, shoving her back side into him and forcing him to get to his feet and hobble from the dining room. The girls laughed at his indignant expression.

Mrs. Drummond approached Minnie to admire the dress, then sent her upstairs to put it away in her room. Minnie sighed and obeyed. Dixie gathered the other gifts and followed Minnie upstairs.

Chapter Twenty-Six

Finally, Minnie came back to the parlor. Her face was radiant with joy. Samuel smiled. He'd made the right decision to come to the special breakfast. He had had no idea it was a bridal shower, but was pleased to have been allowed to attend. Watching Minnie receive such heartfelt gifts from women he knew she had not been fond of prior to coming here, made his heart glad for her. It was his understanding that women needed women, for friendship, comfort, and solidarity. She had been so alone when she first stumbled off that train. Now she had several friends, locals included. Katherine Turner and Emma Cherry, especially, had grown fond of his bride-to-be.

The thought brought his mind back to Sampson and his odd behavior earlier.

"Widow Drummond?" He turned his attention to the elderly woman sitting as chaperone with him in the parlor, although she had dozed off in her chair.

She started when he spoke her name and smacked her lips. "Hmm."

"Did Mr. Cherry deliver wood this morning?"

She rolled her eyes to one side. "Yes, but he tossed the bundle and took off. We had to gather it back together into a neat pile. I can't imagine what was his hurry."

"Hum." Samuel recalled the sheriff telling everyone to report anything suspicious, no matter how small. But surely the man was out of sorts because of Emma being… in a family way. Besides, Sam had a very special gift for Minnie, and he wanted to get on with showing it to her. "Maybe I'll ride out and check on him before we leave Saturday."

"You best leave that to someone else, Sam." Minnie said as she entered the parlor. "We've got more important things to attend to before we board that train." She smiled coyly at her betrothed and his eyes rounded. Her boldness shocked and excited him at the same time.

"True," he muttered. "You have a point."

He bid Widow Drummond good day and escorted Minnie down to their Blacksmith shop. Once the doors were unlocked and spread wide open, he stood next to the forge. She moved to empty the charcoal into the bin, but he stopped her with a gentle hand. "Come here. I have something very special I've been saving to show you."

She looked at him curiously. "All right."

"A blacksmith's forge is very important part of who he is."

She nodded. "Of course, how else could he work the iron?"

Sam closed his eyes and smiled, but it was a tense smile. She stopped talking.

"If a smithy ever finds himself in a predicament where he has a need, his forge is everything he'll ever need." His gaze bore into her, seeking understanding.

Shock slackened her jaw as he spoke. He wanted to make an important impression on her, but he didn't mean to frighten her. "I'm just telling you this because there's something very important that only you can know about with this forge."

He stepped over to the front doors and pulled them together a little, just enough that the forge could not be seen from the street, but open enough not to alarm Claude across the way. He returned to the rock forge and knelt down. Working his fingers into the crack around a stone at the very bottom, he wedged and wiggled until he was able to pull the bed stone free. He reached into the hole and pulled out a bundle of double weave cloth, similar to their ember-proof aprons. Gingerly, he turned the bundle over and unfolded the cloth, exposing a thick and stiff leather bag.

Putting his hand on the forge's edge, he stood with some effort and pulled the sinew strap to open the bag. He shook it slightly and the sound of rocks hitting against one another could be heard.

Minnie stared in amazement, slack jawed, but silent. "You see, my love. When the bank was robbed, sure I was concerned, but not devastated. We have a way to start over. A blacksmith knows to keep valuable metal on hand just in case."

He poured the content into his palm and Minnie gasped. "Where — where'd you get this?"

"Now, that's an interesting story." Samuel leaned against the cold forge, running his thumb across the granules of gold. "Right after the land run, an interesting couple came through here on the train. Well, not ON the train. They had their own fancy Pullman private car which was hitched in with the westbound train. Now that I think about it, it was a lot like the one you brides came in on. They had their own livestock car, too. Seems they brought their own horses and a really nice buggy with them everywhere they went. He was an odd feller, too, wore nothing but buckskin and his wife was dressed as fancy as a lady could be. They were a mix-match from heaven and so in love, it was to be admired. I was just setting up shop, same as everyone else. You know we had a tent city in twenty-four hours that day and wooden structures by the end of the week."

Samuel looked into Minnie's stunned eyes. "Oh, don't worry. I didn't steal it. The man gave this sack to me and told me something I thought was asylum worthy at the time."

"What — what did he say?"

"He told me he had a callin' and it told him that I should keep this safe, and there'd come a day when I knew the time was right to take it out and use it. I kept it hid in here ever since, thinking he'd come back for it, but he never has. I built a special, separate fire-safe divider at the bottom of the forge just so it wouldn't get burnt from the heat."

Minnie gasped and covered a trembling hand over her mouth. She stumbled back against the charcoal bin. Shaking her head with disbelief. "That's incredible."

"Well, I figured there weren't no better time than now. And with your nimble fingers I want you to help me fashion you and me wedding rings."

Color drained from her face. "Sam, I-I gotta tell you something…"

Concern wrinkled his brow. He poured the gold nuggets back into the bag and gathered her into his arms. "What is it, my sweetheart?"

"I-I." She swallowed hard. "I think I know where that gold is that Butterfield killed my poppa over."

Sam turned his head but not his eyes. "In his forge?"

She could only nod her head vigorously. Tears spilled down her cheeks and she buried her face into his shoulder. "Oh Sam!"

"Sweetheart, it's all right. We'll be there in two weeks and can check it out ourselves."

Her eyes widened even more and he worried why she reacted this way. "Minnie? You okay?"

"Sam, if my poppa hid gold in his forge, like you done, we could save the bank, anonymously, in case Graves and Gray aren't caught."

Sam considered that. "Well, let's get to Portland and see where we stand, then we'll worry about saving the bank." He chuckled. "I love your generous spirit, though."

She tried to smile but pressed into his taut chest and sobbed. "I love you, Samuel Knight."

He held her as long as she needed him. Once she had cried it all out, she leaned back from him and wiped her face with one of her new hankies Helen had cross stitched for her. "So. You want me to make us weddin' rings?"

"I'll help." He grinned.

Minnie nodded and took the leather bag. She poured just enough gold into a melting pot and looked at it very closely. "Okay, I have an idea. Have you ever heard of blue gold?"

Sam turned his head. "Can't say I have."

She smiled. "Fire up the forge and watch this." She rummaged through the iron rods and selected one. Once the forge was hot enough, she went to work and blended the iron and the gold like a chemist would mix liquids. "Seventy-five to twenty-five is about right." She muttered to herself. Then she worked the alloy and shaped it. "I want to make us something representative of our lives as blacksmiths, is that all right with you?"

He nodded. Not sure what she had in mind, but he didn't care either. Whatever made her happy, and gave them a ring to show they were married, was fine with him.

She worked and cooled the metal. Shaped and worked it, then cooled it again. Finally she had two rings resting inside a cast iron bowl. Their colors slowly changed as they cooled. Samuel watched as they gradually became touchable. Then he lifted the rings and held them in his palm. "This is amazing. I love it."

Minnie smiled. "I'm so happy you like them."

"It's a golden wedge nail, and yet it's looks like fine jewelry. Not too thick where it would catch on things, but obviously shaped like a masonry or farrier nail. You amaze me, Minnie Geneanne Smith." He kissed her cheek.

She cupped his face with one hand and kissed his cheek as well.

The very first wedding since the seven brides arrived in Gunther City brought a flurry of activities to the little town. The bank robbery was not forgotten, but waned in comparison to the excitement of nuptial preparations. The few days they had left were consumed with packing, fittings, adjustings, cooking, hair styling, and finally learning to apply the rouge and a modest lip color, a gift sent over by Miss Turner.

The sister brides prepared their Sunday-best dresses and helped fix each other's hair. Dixie and Claude had agreed to stand with Minnie and Samuel. He had wanted Sampson Cherry, but no one had seen him for several days. Emma must be really suffering in her condition. Samuel didn't mention what he knew. It wasn't his to tell.

The sheriff and his posse had been out riding, but weren't coming up with any hint of where Graves and Grey might have gotten off to. The Rocking F's Mustangs they had stolen showed up on their own at the ranch's stables. They were hungry and run hard, but not really harmed.

Dixie had gone out to the prairie and gathered wild flowers for a bouquet just like Minnie had imagined herself carrying. They placed them in a pitcher to keep them fresh. Minnie used a pale yellow ribbon from her gifts to tie them together. The Bride House kitchen was busy, too, preparing and receiving dishes from the other ladies in town for the wedding dinner afterwards.

By six o'clock people were gathering at the Town Hall because, as of now, it doubled as the church, too. All Minnie and Dixie had to do was slip out the front door and in the next one over. GW waited in the parlor, wearing a nicely cleaned and pressed Sheriff's uniform. He'd even polished his boots after being out searching for the bank robbers. He'd told Widow Drummond that he'd greeted Miss Smith at the train when she surprised them as the seventh bride, and he felt responsible for giving her away to a husband.

He leapt to his feet when Minnie and Dixie descended the stairs. Mr. Darcy had a bow and some wildflowers tied around his neck. The Sheriff fidgeted with his Stetson as he cleared his throat.

"My! Miss Smith. May I say you sure make a purdy bride?"

She blushed and thanked him. Dixie took her hand and walked her into the parlor. "Are they ready next door, Sheriff?"

"You know, I'll go check."

He hurried out.

Silence filled the house. Minnie turned to Dixie and squeezed her hands. "Oh, Dixie, thank you. Thank you for everything. Being my friend, helping put this wedding together, letting me love on Mr. Darcy." They laughed. "I hope you and Oliver will be as happy as Sam and me."

Dixie pursed a smile. "Oliver is a wonderful man. Once he got over being mad at Mr. Darcy for showing up his prized cow dog."

They laughed again and wiped tears from their eyes. Dixie whispered, "Best of luck. Today and back home. Give everybody my love and tell them how happy we all are here in Gunther City."

Minnie sniffed. "I will."

The Sheriff stuck his head in the screen door. "Ladies, they're ready for us."

Minnie squeezed Dixie's hand one more time, patted Mr. Darcy's head, and nodded to the Sheriff. He stuck out his elbow and she took hold.

"This dress is a replica of my momma's wedding dress," she told him as they walked across the threshold. "Mrs. Tanner and Jane Anne made it for me."

"Well, it sure is purdy on you, Miss Smith. Sam's a lucky man."

Chapter Twenty-Seven

Dixie hurried to get ahead of Minnie and the Sheriff. Wilma Gunther sat at the organ and played a lovely tune. Dixie lifted Mr. Darcy and slowly walked toward the altar and stood to the left of the pulpit. Samuel and Claude stood to the right and Preacher Gunther stood in the middle.

Wilma looked up and saw the Sheriff and Minnie poised at the door. She began playing the Bridal Chorus. Everyone stood with the first four notes and the Sheriff stepped out on the fifth. Minnie looked toward the end of the aisle and caught sight of Sam in his only Sunday suit. He was so big and strong. His chiseled features made him so handsome and rugged. The hearth fire bronzed his skin. He had seen Phil at the barber shop and had a neat trimming of his dark beard. His hair was pulled back with a black ribbon and he stood with his hands behind his back. The music and the people all faded away, and all she could see was the love in his eyes as she made her way toward him.

She floated down the aisle and took his hand. The preacher said something and the sheriff kissed her cheek. She turned to Sam. His golden brown eyes drew her in and she basked in the love and desire that shone there. They repeated vows and exchanged rings. Preacher Gunther came into focus when he said, "I now pronounce you man and wife. Sam, you may kiss your bride."

Samuel let go of Minnie's hands, and placing his hands on her waist, he pulled her into him and caressed her lips with his. Their passion exploded like fireworks on the fourth of July and they pressed into one another longingly.

Preacher Gunther cleared his throat and the two of them forced themselves to pull back. The people laughed, and someone said something rude, to which everyone laughed again. Minnie turned to Dixie. She blushed and held Mr. Darcy's face so he couldn't see their amorous display. Minnie giggled and took Sam's hand. They hurried down the aisle, he leaning on his cane for support, and out onto the boardwalk. They had one more event, the wedding dinner, and then they could explore this passionate desire for one another again in their wedding bed.

After the wedding dinner, Samuel had one more surprise for Minnie. In the street waited a delicate buggy with Cole, a handsome solid black horse. Behind the buggy had been tied old shoes and tin cans. Minnie laughed when she saw what their friends had done. Another superstition instigated by Mary Etta, she mused.

Sam helped Minnie in and then he took the reins. She snuggled against his arms and laid her head on his shoulder. He turned the horse north and flipped the leather against Cole's rump. Minnie gazed at her new husband. "Where—"

He just smiled. "You'll see."

He pulled up to the Gunther City Hotel and eased down to help her. Her eyes were wide with excitement. "Samuel! I had no idea you planned all this. I assumed we'd spend our weddin' night in your apartment. I-I don't have none of my clothes."

"You think I'd take my bride on her honeymoon and not plan for her trousseau to be delivered to the hotel room?" He kissed her hand and tucked it into his elbow as he escorted her through the doors. Claude would be along later to take Cole and the buggy back to the stables. It would be a short walk across Broad Street to the train depot tomorrow morning.

Her eyes rounded and she turned her head toward him. "Mr. Knight! You are full of surprises."

"Mrs. Knight, I hope to always surprise you with examples of my love. 'Til death do us part."

She giggled and let him lead her up the two flights of stairs. He opened their hotel room door and she gasped. "Samuel! You got us the suite!"

"It's called the honeymoon suite, sweetheart. And you deserve only the best Gunther City has to offer."

She rushed in and spun around. A silver bowl with a bottle of champagne sat on a round table. A bouquet of wildflowers adorned a low table behind the sofa. Another set of doors were only slightly opened. She glanced back at him and then walked to them. "What's behind here?"

She flung them open and turned back to Sam. "Oh, Sam, it's beautiful."

The huge king's bed had a golden brocade spread. The top had been turned down and two pristine pillows sat up against the wooden headboard. "It's too beautiful to mess up."

He smiled and closed the distance between them.
"It'll be all right. They have staff to straighten it all back up tomorrow after we leave."
Her heart doubled its beat and she met his love-filled gaze with passion of her own. She bit her lip as he wrapped her in his strong arms and pulled her against his taut body. He reached up into her hair and pulled pins. She winced and helped him loosen her hair. Dixie had fixed it too well. They laughed as her dark locks finally fell, covering the tatted lace over her shoulders.
Samuel caressed the lace and lowered his lips onto hers. His passion grew as their lips possessed each other. His hands gently slid the lace from her shoulders and she returned his passion with her own desire as her dress fell to the rug. He stepped back and smiled.
"You're the most beautiful woman." He growled and scooped her up into his arms and laid her gently on the lovely bed.
Their night was filled with love and passion and the two became one just like the preacher had said during the wedding.
They woke the next morning to a tap on their door. Samuel rose from their bed of desire and wrapped

himself in a robe provided in the wardrobe. It was room service with a complimentary breakfast. He let the bellman wheel the little table into their room and thanked him with a generous nugget of gold. The man's eyes widened as he stared at the nugget in his gloved palm.

"Breakfast, my sweetheart." He called. She gathered the other robe in the wardrobe and joined him at the little round table. Sam poured her coffee and she buttered his biscuit. They fed each other and drank their coffee. Then she pulled him into the king's bed room and demonstrated again how much she loved him and how grateful she was to have him as her husband.

Minnie stood between the double doors to gaze upon the honeymoon suite one last time. Their marriage had been forged here and it would forever have a special place molded in her heart. Slowly she closed the doors with a wistful sigh and turned to take Samuel's arm. Their traveling cases had been taken down by the bellboy. Only two things remained: tell everyone goodbye at the depot, and board the train to Portland, Maine.

She had dressed in a light cotton dress because the weather in Oklahoma was still very warm for autumn, but she'd brought her wool garments, knowing it would likely be pre-winter temperatures in Maine.

Portland in autumn! Her skin prickled thinking of the cool salty air blowing off the sea, the fishermen switching gear for crabbing in the colder ocean waters, cranberry harvests and festivals, whale migrations, and God's canvas turning yellow, orange, and red. Like her father's forge, the colors dance in the woods for a month before they turn stark brown, then white with snow.

To be home thrilled her and terrified her at the same time. Remembering the last two days in Portland were her most desperate and fearful. A shiver traversed her spine as she and Samuel entered the train and handed the porter their tickets. "Very good," he said. "Please follow me. And may I say, Mr. Knight, congratulations."

Sam thanked him and turned to his bride. "Are you all right?" He squeezed her hand.

How could she put into words all the things she was feeling right now? "I'm all right. It's hard to say good bye."

He chuckled. "You women."

He followed the porter through the narrow aisle to their private Pullman sleeper.

They settled into their plush seats and looked out the window at the dear friends who waved and hollered, wishing them safe travel and hurry back home. They had all become such good friends. Her heart was so full, she just couldn't believe how things had turned out for her here in Gunther City. She scanned the faces as she waved her gloved hand at them. So much different from the day she arrived.

Nearly everyone they knew had come to see them off. All but the Cherry's. Sadness filled her heart suddenly. Why hadn't Sampson and Emma come to town for the wedding? She didn't expect them to be here today, but yesterday…

"Where do you suppose Emma and Sampson are?"

Samuel grinned but said nothing.

"Sam?" She turned to look him in the eyes and giggled. "What?"

"Oh, I suppose everyone will know by the time we get back." He looked out the window and waved to

Widow Drummond who shook her spoon at him. Probably telling him to take care of her girl.

Minnie tsked her tongue. "Sam! Tell me."

"Oh." An impish smile crossed his mouth. "It seems Mr. and Mrs. Cherry are going to be parents."

"WHAT!" Minnie nearly stood.

The momentum of the train tossed her back into her seat. "That's not possible!"

Sam turned from the window to see why she was reacting so strongly to such good news. "Why?"

"SAM!" Minnie did stand this time. "Emma can't have children! Remember? What exactly did he say?"

Sam thought. Sampson's behavior had been very odd. He told her quickly what Sampson had said.

"He was trying to tell you he was in trouble!" She skipped sideways toward the cut platform. "I know its Graves and Gray. They're hiding out at the Cherry's home!"

Samuel stood with her. Together they ran to the door. "I knew Sampson was acting weird! I should have known something was wrong! GOD! What have I done?"

"It'll be all right, but we gotta let the Sheriff know!"

"Right." Samuel slipped past her to open the car door. He hung off the cut platform and screamed, "Sheriff Gunther!"

GW's head whipped around at the sound of his name. He saw Samuel hanging off the train. What was wrong? He ran to hear what Samuel was shouting.

"It's the bank robbers! They're holed up at Sampson Cherry's!"

The sheriff put his hand to his ear. "WHAT?"

"THE BANK ROBBERS ARE AT SAMPSON CHERRY'S HOME!" Samuel shouted as loud as he could.

"CHERRY'S? THE BANK ROBBERS ARE AT CHERRY'S?" Sheriff Gunther repeated.

Samuel nodded vigorously.

Sheriff GW held up a thumb and turned to find his deputy. They'd gather the men from the posse and head out there immediately. If this was a fact, it explained why Cherry hadn't been delivering firewood and why they hadn't been able to find hide nor hair of those boys who robbed the bank.

He turned to wave one last time at the fading train. How did Samuel figure this one out? It'd be the first question he'd ask the man when they got back to Gunther City.

Chapter Twenty-Eight

The next ten days dragged by with Minnie worrying over whether the sheriff found Alford Graves and Hayden Gray, and if Emma and Sampson were all right. Samuel reassured his wife as often as he needed that they were right about the men being holed up at Sampson's place. His behavior that day was so off normal, he had to be giving Samuel clues that something was powerfully wrong. They were probably holding Emma the whole time and that was why Sampson couldn't say anything. That was why he hadn't been back in town either. They didn't want to risk him letting it slip where they were.

It did make Samuel curious as to what Graves and Gray had in mind. They couldn't keep Sampson and Emma hostage forever, for no other reason than they'd run out of food. Surely they had some plan to lay low and eventually take off to where ever and—

"A penny for your thoughts." Minnie laid her head on Samuel's shoulder. He loved her nearness. Now that they were married, he no longer had to bind his passion. He kissed the top of her head. "I don't want to upset you."

"It won't upset me. I'm sure you're thinking the same things I've been thinking."

"Really?" Samuel leaned back to look his wife in the eyes. "What have you been thinking?"

She sighed. "I've been thinking what on earth Gray and Graves thought they would accomplish by holding Emma and Sampson in their own home. It would only add to their charges once they got caught."

Samuel clenched his jaw. "Yeah, I s'pose they didn't think they'd get caught. Most bank robbers figure they'll get away with it. I don't know how a man like that thinks."

Minnie sighed again. "Well, I s'pose we'll just have to wait 'til we get home to find out."

Samuel wrapped her in his arm. "You just called Gunther City home, not Portland."

She smiled up into his face. "That's what it is. Only reason we're going to Portland is to claim my poppa's property and square away whatever may be left."

He pulled her in tight and held her for a while. "You think there'll be anything left of his place?"

This time her sigh was longer and deeper. "I have no idea."

At last the porter called, "Portland, Maine, next stop!"

Minnie's heart sped up. She didn't know if she was excited or afraid. But she knew one thing, she hoped to see Pastor and Mrs. Robertson before they went back home. She wanted to thank them and pay them back for her passage. When the train finally stopped and the porters opened the doors, she and Samuel stepped out on the platform together. She inhaled the salty air and sighed. She'd missed that smell. Then she heard her name.

"Minnie! Minnie Smith!" Mrs. Robertson waved through the steam that rolled along the platform. Minnie gasped and waved back. She pulled Samuel down the steps and ran to her dear friend. Pastor Robertson stood beside his wife grinning like a fool. They each hugged Minnie warmly. She wiped a tear and stepped back to introduce Samuel.

"Pastor and Mrs. Robertson, I want you to meet my husband, Samuel Knight. He's a blacksmith in Gunther City."

"Do tell." Mrs. Robertson laughed and shook Samuel's hand, then pulled him in for a big hug. Pastor Robertson shook his hand and congratulated him. "You'll have to tell us all about your time in Gunther City on our way to the Waterfront lawyers office."

Minnie stumbled. "Do we have to go there right away?"

"Yes, dear, the sooner the better." Mrs. Robertson placed her arm around Minnie's back and led her and Samuel to their carriage.

"I was hoping we could… settle in a bit, first." Minnie hated the whine in her voice. Facing those lawyers terrified her for some reason. It was ridiculous, she knew. All she had to do was claim her father's property and then go take possession of it. Maybe that was what terrified her to most. It was like going to view a dead corpse. She had no idea what she would find there, or if she'd find anything at all.

She pursed her lips, and then forced a smile for Samuel. She could do this. Samuel was here. She didn't have to do it alone. Not anymore. She nodded to herself and let the Robertson's lead them to the Barouche Carriage. They had a lovely dapple grey pair she knew well, from shoeing them over the years.

Minnie chuckled. "I see Jake still has the inside heel at his hind hoof. Who have you been taking him to?"

Pastor Robertson assisted his wife and then Minnie into the carriage. "Nothing gets past you, does it?" He smiled at her but it didn't reach his eyes. "There's not been no farrier as good as your Poppa, since his passing."

Minnie closed her eyes. The fury roiled in her gut. "My Poppa didn't just pass, Pastor Robertson. He was murdered."

Pastor signaled the driver to go and turned back to Minnie. "Oh, I know, my child. And Jet Butterfield is paying for that sin as we speak."

"Maybe, but his two cohorts are running around this country free, and robbin' banks, and holding good people hostage." Her words dissolved into tears.

Samuel held his wife and explained what had happened the week before they boarded the train to come east.

The Robertsons were shocked and sorrowful. "Minnie." Mrs. Robertson reached over to touch her glove. "We didn't know. We just assumed they had moved on since their 'boss' had been imprisoned. I'm so sorry."

Minnie sniffed and wiped her eyes. It wasn't these people's fault. She needed to get control of her outbursts. She had lawyers to speak to and she couldn't be addressing them as a blubbering idiot who couldn't control her own emotions.

Before long, they pulled up to the Waterfront District and stopped in front of a prestigious building with the names, Weech, Eatum, and Howell, Attorneys at Law. Minnie swallowed and squeezed Samuel's hand so tight, he flinched, but remained silent. He, more than anyone, knew how nervous she felt. They walked in and were ushered immediately into Mr. Howell's office. He scowled at them over his extremely large nose and extremely small glasses, and simply presented papers for her to sign, then handed her two skeleton keys tagged "house" and "shop." He suggested she contact them again should she decide to sell the property as they had already been solicited by interested parties, although no one had stepped foot on the property.

She promised she would make her decision by the end of the month. Not that she wanted to stay in Portland that long, but it felt good to wield the same power over them as they had her. They left after shaking Mr. Howell's cold moist hand and reentered the Robertson's carriage. Minnie held the papers close to her bosom and tried not to cry. No one had been in the property since Butterfield's arrest. What would she find?

Mr. Robertson directed the driver to her home. Within a few silent minutes, they pulled up to the clapboard house of her childhood. It had been a nice home and a good shop. Samuel and Minnie promised to see the Robertsons again before they left, and waved good bye as the carriage pulled away.

"Look." Samuel took her arm to stop her from approaching the house. "If this is… if we need to, we can check into a hotel."

She nodded. They walked together to the stoop. A harsh odor assaulted their noses.

Samuel turned his head slightly, but didn't say anything.

"Probably the root cellar. All this time, food's gone bad." Minnie explained his unasked question.

Sam nodded.

Her hand trembled as she attempted to insert the skeleton key. He gently took the key from her and unlocked the door. He let her open it. She turned the knob and shoved the door open.

"Poppa," she breathed the word and then wavered a bit before crumbling toward the wooden porch.

Samuel barely had time to catch Minnie in his arms. He eased her down to the stoop and glanced up from his wife's pale face to look inside the home. He swallowed hard to fight the nausea, and scrambled to get a handkerchief from his inside coat pocket to cover his nose and mouth. The residual stench had faded from what it obviously had been, but still remained sickening. There was evidence of someone, neighbors perhaps, sprinkling lye around the foundation, probably trying to relieve their own discomfort from the decay.

Eugene Smith, or at least what was left of his decayed body, laid on a rug in the center of the room. Nothing more than a dark imprint in the rug and some bones were left. His size persuaded Sam this had to be Minnie's father.

Curtains, furniture, clothes, kitchen ware were strewn across the house as if they had just yanked it down or out, searching everywhere and anywhere for the man's gold. Even some floorboards were pulled up where they had searched.

Was the shop in this bad of shape as well? Minnie had said he was murdered in the shop. They must have dragged his body in here and then abandoned him and the house after they could not find the gold.

The Robertsons had waited just a short distance from the house to be sure they got into the house. They saw Minnie swoon and hurried back to help. They gasped and stepped back because of the sweet rancid odor. "Dear Lord!" Mr. Robertson exclaimed.

Mrs. Robertson knelt beside Minnie, patting her face gently and trying to revive her. Samuel still held her in his arms.

"She can't stay here." Mrs. Robertson lifted her eyes to meet Sam's.

He nodded. "I know." His voice was husky with emotion. "Can you take us to a Hotel?"

"Of course."

Minnie opened her eyes and tried to look around Sam, but he blocked her and lifted her to her feet, with her back to the interior, "No, Sweetheart. We are going to the hotel and summon an undertaker to have your poppa's body taken care of proper."

Minnie's knees buckled. Sam and Mrs. Robertson supported her as they led her back to their carriage. Mr. Robertson closed the door and joined his wife. He mumbled a prayer as he joined them in the carriage.

In the hotel room, Minnie sat on a small sofa and stared at the floor. Sam summoned the proper authorities and explained the situation. Russell, the concierge, was very helpful and offered the name of some women who could go clean the home.

"They're very good and reliable," Russell assured Sam. "The Constable uses their services often after a devastating crime much like this, donchaknow? But," he admitted. "Never has there been…" he glanced around quickly. "… a corpse left for two months, Mr. Knight."

Sam sighed. "I realize these are extenuating circumstances, but they are what they are and we need to have Mr. Smith's body given a proper burial. My wife's mother was laid to rest in the Waterfront

Cemetery, I think she will want her poppa laid next to her."

"Very good, sir." The concierge agreed.

Samuel returned to their room and sat with Minnie. She told him about her life, her mother's death, living as an only child but being loved beyond compare. Learning to work iron under her poppa's apprenticeship. The pride he showed when she outdid him in detail and designs. She drew in a long breath and told her husband about the day Jet Butterfield turned all her happiness upside down and she boarded the train for the West.

"But." She lifted sad eyes to look into his. She moved a lock of hair from his eyes and pushed it tenderly back from his temple. "I have you and I have happiness I never knew could be possible. I love you, Samuel Knight, Blacksmith of Gunther City."

He smiled. "I love you, Minnie Geneanne Knight, Blacksmith of Gunther City."

That made her chuckle and she laid her head on his shoulder. He sat beside her a long time, just holding her and listening to more tales of her life in Portland, Maine. They laughed at antics that Helen. Jane Anne, and Alice had done as children. Martha, Dixie, and

Lou Lou, too. She had known them all her life. No one could imagine how rough and tumble they had been.

Samuel enjoyed hearing her laugh and reminisce about her childhood. These ladies turned on her when they became young women, yet she considered them all dear friends now.

Samuel's desired flared. He wanted to lift his wife in his arms and carry her to the bed. He wanted to love away her sorrow. To show her, again, how much he adored her and appreciated her becoming his wife, but he suppressed his passions. His wife needed this time and his needs were secondary right now.

In the back of his mind, he wondered about her poppa's forge and whether he had hidden the gold like Samuel had. That, too, could wait. Eugene Smith's service was in two days. After Minnie had that closure, then they could go back and face the house and the shop again. Hopefully the women he had hired would do as excellent of a job as the concierge had said they would, and all he and his wife would need to do is sort through what she wanted to keep and what she wanted to give away. And find the gold.

It was hers now, and Samuel would make sure every ounce of it was safe in Minnie's name. He hoped Emma and Sampson were safe, Graves and Gray had been caught along with the money they stole, and it had been returned to the bank. If not, he knew Minnie would anonymously give her gold to the town and restore everyone's economy.

Chapter Twenty-Nine

Two days later, Minnie stood in a downpour. Autumn in Maine meant rain and lots of it. She used to love the fall and the frequent rains. Today she watched as Poppa's beautiful brass coffin was lowered into the ground. Two men she knew since she was a child, Noah and Matthew held the ropes with leather gloved hands and gently let her poppa's casket sink into the hole they had dug earlier with two shovels. She appreciated all their hard work.

Pastor Robertson spoke kind and admirable words about her poppa's integrity and excellent craftsmanship. She barely heard a word he said. The rain expressed the tears in her heart. Samuel held the big black umbrella over her, but she didn't care how wet she got. The sky was crying with her and she wanted to feel its reciprocal sorrow in every drop that fell on her face.

The Robertsons led the people back to the church where there was more food than Minnie had ever seen. People from the entire Waterfront had attended her poppa's funeral and brought dishes for the meal afterwards. Their efforts and their demonstration of respect for her poppa was kind. He certainly deserved it.

They greeted her with sorrow and accolades for what a good man he had been and how tragic his death was. She nodded and accepted their thoughtfulness, although this was the first time she'd heard such warm hearted words from any of them.

She had been the freak who worked at a man's job and didn't belong in polite society. They had watched her run for her life to the church without offering any help or concern.

Today, she was admired for her strength and good fortune to have found such a handsome and caring husband.

Did her marriage wash away their outlandish view of her behavior, and make her suitable for society again? She hadn't changed. In fact, none of them realized she was still working in a smithy's shop, doing the same strenuous work she'd always done. But now she was married and that made her a decent person.

Her eyes met Samuel's and she tried to smile. He returned her morose façade, shook hands, and accepted condolences just like he had lived here his whole life. Finally the people trickled away and it was just Samuel, Minnie and the Robertsons. Minnie approached them in the church's kitchen.

"I want to thank you for everything."

Mrs. Robertson waved her off and made an odd noise with her mouth. "We're just doing what we do."

"No." Minnie touched Mrs. Robertson's arm. "You saved my life and paid for me to go west. I-I want to repay you for those expenses."

Mrs. Robertson glanced up as she wiped her hands on the blue apron tied around her waist. "My child, didn't we tell you?"

"Tell me what?"

"We didn't pay for you to go out west."

Minnie's eyes rounded and she tilted her head. "Then… who did."

"I'm not sure who he was." Mr. Robertson said. "A benefactor, I guess you'd say. A man came through here ten or so yeahs ago, round about the time your momma passed, I believe it was.

"He was a mountain man from Kentucky and made a generous donation to a fund we kept in secret, just like he said to. He told us he had a callin' and it told

him there'd be a day when we'd know it were right to use that money to help a poor soul get a new life."
Samuel stepped up closer to Minnie. "Did he wear buckskin and his wife was dressed to the nines?"
"Yes!" Mrs. Robertson's eyes widened. "How'd you know?"
"Because that same man came through Gunther City, right after we got settled. He talked about his callin' and gave me some pure gold nuggets to keep until, as he put it, the good Lord told me it was right to use."
The four looked at each other in amazement. "You don't suppose—?"
Samuel tilted his head. "It sure sounds like it."
"Well, don't the Lord work in mysterious ways."
They laughed and even Minnie chuckled. "So I s'pose I don't need to pay you back, but I will make a donation to the widows and orphans fund. It's the least I can do for the divine and mysterious help I did receive."
Mr. Robertson smiled and puffed out his chest. "I think that's a fine idea, my child."

The moment Minnie had dreaded the most, it was time to go to her poppa's house and see what they could salvage from their belongings. She took a deep breath and let Samuel lead her to the carriage. The Robertson's had told them to take it and return it when they were done.

Once again, Minnie found herself facing that same door and trying to push the skeleton key into the knob. Her hands trembled too much. She handed the key to Samuel and he unlocked the door. As it swung open, the aroma of burning sage from a smudge pot greeted their noses.

The house was no longer ransacked, and the rug where her poppa had laid was gone. Their belongings were sorted by item and folded in various places around the house. Her clothes had been washed and pressed and were hanging in her wardrobe. Same with her poppa's clothes. The curtains were clean and folded in a tall stack on the dining buffet. Everything in the kitchen had been washed and returned to the cupboards as best as one could without having lived there.

Minnie turned to Samuel with tears in her eyes. "How'd you do this?"

"The concierge at our hotel was very accommodating."

She chuckled. "I hope you tipped him generously."

Sam just pursed his lips and smiled. He had also arranged for trunks and crates to be delivered so that Minnie could pack what she wanted. She set to doing that while he slipped around to the forge to check it out. The shop had been cleaned too. While the women didn't know where the tools went, exactly, they had gathered them and placed them together as best they could, on nails and along the lip of the hearth. Sam examined the forge and knew he needed to go get his wife.

"Minnie." He spoke softly as he entered her childhood bedroom. "I think you need to see this."

Surprise and fear washed over her eyes.

"It's all right. Trust me." He held out his hand to her and she took it. He led her around to the back of the house and into the shop. They approached the forge and stood on either side. "I do believe your poppa is a man after my own heart."

"What do you mean?"

"Look here." He knelt down and wedged his fingers between the stones where there was no mortar. Little by little he wiggled the stone out of its place and stood.

As Minnie watched him pull the stone, her breath quickened. She knelt where he had been and reached inside. She felt a leather pouch and pulled it out. Then she reached in and pulled another. Her eyes got bigger and bigger as she kept pulling leather pouches full of gold coins and raw nuggets. There was no telling how much all this was worth.

"My God, Sam," she breathed. "My poppa was rich, but he lived as a common man. You don't suppose he kept all this just for me?"

"Well." Sam scratched his head. "If it were me, and all I had left in the world was a beautiful daughter like you, then some feller come along and gave me a windfall such as this, I'd have hid it just for her, too."

"Oh, Sam." Minnie collapsed into his arms. "I love you so." Then she lifted her head with a gasp. "We can save the town, now! And... whatever else the town needs!"

"Well, now, hold up." Samuel held her shoulders. "We can't just go back into Gunther City and wave this stuff around. It wouldn't be proper or polite.

Think about it. People'd think we were acting like high falutin'-brag-a-bouts."

Minnie smiled and then she giggled. "Like Helen."

He pulled her closer into his embrace. "Yes, like Eddie's hellcat."

"Oh, don't call her that!" Minnie giggled.

Samuel laughed. "Okay. You go gather and sort the things you want to take back home and I'll get this shop squared away. If you want, I'll make arrangements for all of this to be put on the market."

Minnie looked around. So many memories. But she and Samuel were building new memories back in Gunther City. "Yes, I want to sell this property, and perhaps we can build our own house on First Street next to the Gunthers."

Sam smiled. "That's a great idea! We could be Number Two, First Street." He chuckled. "But let's not do it right away. Let's give the town time to settle down after the bank robbery and build it next spring."

She nodded. "You make a good point, Mr. Knight. That must be why I love you so much."

He grinned and pulled her into his arms. He caressed her lips with his until their passion blazed and they pulled apart breathless and dazed. "We better get this done so we can go back to the hotel," Sam panted. Minnie nodded and rushed back to the house.

It took Minnie and Sam a week to get everything packed, sorted, given to charity, and readied for transportation. Mr. Howell had a buyer for the place and had given them papers to sign before they left town. Minnie contacted Mrs. Tucker and had her measure Samuel for four new suits. She promised they would be ready by the time they boarded the train heading west. It was amazing the change in attitude toward her by everyone now that she was a married woman.

Sam and Minnie had returned to the Waterfront Lawyers' office to secure the gold that had been found and have it placed under protective armor with a sub-constable who would accompany the armored boxes back to Gunther City and then return to Portland. He was sent ahead of them on an earlier train so that the delivery would not be associated with them. Sam wrote Eddie a letter to be delivered by the sub-constable explaining the circumstances and the discretion needed.

Now they wouldn't have to worry about the train being robbed during the ten days it would take it to get back home. The townsmen would figure it had something to do with returning the stolen funds from Graves and Gray.

Minnie's heart was glad to be going home, but sad to say goodbye again to the people who had become so dear to her heart. She promised to write often and hugged them soundly at the train depot.

Once they were seated in their private Pullman sleeper, her heart lifted and her mind settled on unanswered questions about home. She couldn't wait to find out if Emma and Sampson were all right? Did Graves and Gray get caught? Did Eddie keep his betrothal with Helen after her disgruntled behavior when the bank got robbed? Did Dixie persuade Oliver to let Mr. Darcy herd the smaller livestock? And most of all, how much iron work was stacked outside the Blacksmith's shop?

She smiled and snuggled in close to her husband. He looked deep into her eyes and she knew he had held his desires at bay for her to resolve all these issues in Portland. Now there was nothing holding them back from sharing their love. She took his hand and pulled him down to the sleeper. As the train jolted forward, the Blacksmith's daughter gave herself to the Blacksmith of Gunther City, mind, body, and soul.

Epilogue

Minnie stood at the forge hammering out a set of new shoes for a chestnut mare Eddie Hutton had bought from Gunther's stable. She was an anniversary surprise for Helen. The mare was skittish about fire and smoke, but Minnie knew exactly how to fit her and form her shoes without traumatizing the beast. Minnie chuckled to herself. The poor mare had enough to deal with being Helen's horse.

A wagon rumbled to a stop outside their shop and Minnie put down her hammer to see what they wanted. Was someone bringing wagons full of iron work that needed repair? It had taken her and Samuel an entire month to get caught up from when they traveled to her hometown in Maine to settle her poppa's estate. She swore to Samuel they'd never get that far behind again.

Samuel leapt from the buckboard with a huge smile. Behind him were two more wagons. They were covered in canvas and apparently had come across the country thus. She gave her husband an inquisitive look.

"I have a surprise for you, my Sweetheart." Sam said as he started pulling the canvas off the hooped frame. Minnie peeked over the wagon side and saw what looked like stones and metal plates, rods and an assortment of tools. Her poppa's tools! "What is this?"

He lifted the ice tongs her poppa had refigured for his more delicate work. "While we were in Portland, I arranged for your father's entire forge, tools, and all, to be sent here. These three men brought it with a wagon train headed this way. They just arrived today along with some more soon-to-be citizens of Gunther City."

Minnie stood with her jaw slack. "I can't believe you did this… for me."

"Of course I'd do this for you. You are my heart and soul. Now we can really work side by side. You at your forge and me at mine." He threw his head back and laughed.

"Why so many wagons?" Minnie looked the other wagons over. They didn't seem to be all that full.

"My Sweetheart," Sam smiled sweetly. "The stone is very heavy and the horses can only pull so much tonnage. It had to be split up among three wagons."

"I see… Well," Minnie mustered her most serious voice. "I don't know…"

Sam sobered and looked at his wife. "Why not?"

"I'm not sure how much longer I'll be working the forge?"

"Minnie! What are you telling me?"

She smiled coyly. "Because Mr. Knight, I'm just not sure if I'll be able to tie my calf-skin apron after a few more months."

Sam's mouth dropped open. He stared at her a moment and then ran his hands through his long hair. "You mean… We… You're in a family way?"

She smiled and walked back to her horseshoe, placed it in the fire, and lifted her hammer. "Yes, that's what I mean."

About that time, Emma walked into the shop carrying her little bundle of joy. "What are you two standing around fer? There's three wagons out here to unload and my Sampson ain't got all day to help you lazy people." She giggled. "So you best be getting this done."

Samuel's eyes darted from Emma to Minnie. He smiled like a fool and skipped sideways to run out to the wagons. "Yes, ma'am, Mrs. Cherry." He touched the babe's cheek with the backside of a crooked finger as he hurried past her to meet Sampson at the back of the wagon.

Emma laughed. "I take it you told him."

Minnie smiled and nodded. "I don't think it's sunk in yet, but it will."

The two women laughed.

Minnie peeked into Emma's bundle. "How's our little Miracle this morning?"

"She be wonderful, beautiful, and needing a change."

They laughed again. "What a beautiful outcome to such a terrifying thing." Emma gazed into her daughter's dark brown eyes. "Lordy, what would Sampson and me done if your Sam hadn't figured out Sampson's clues."

Minnie chuckled. "Well, he nearly didn't, poor man. If he hadn't told me that Sampson said you were... increasing, we'd have left town and never told the Sheriff Graves and Gray were holed up at your house."

"Aw, I miss that little sod dugout." Emma's eyes looked dreamy.

"Really?" Minnie turned from her forge to see if Emma was serious.

Emma laughed. "No, nothing beats a wooden structure for a house. But home is where your heart is." She bounced her daughter slightly. "And this little girl makes any place feel like home."

"I know what you mean." Minnie smiled and rested her hand on her rounding belly.

Emma sighed contently as she laid Miracle Geneanne Cherry on a table and changed her diaper. "Ain't God been good to us?"

Minnie lifted the hot metal shoe from the forge and placed it on the anvil. She brought the hammer down hard and lifted it again. "Yes ma'am. He sure has."

The End

Love the Story?
Leave a review, please.
Next book in this series is Dixie's Dachshund

About the Author

Lynn Donovan is an author, playwright, and director who spends her days chasing after her muses trying to get them to behave long enough to write their stories. The results are numerous novels, multi-author series, anthologies, dramatizations, and short stories.

Lynn enjoys reading and writing all kinds of fiction, historical western romance, paranormal, speculative, contemporary romance, and time travel. But you never know what her muses will come up with for a story, so you could see a novel under any given genre. All that can be said is keep your eyes open, because these muses are not sitting still for long! Oops, there they go again…

Want more?

You can learn more about Lynn when you follow her on her Facebook Author Page at https://www.facebook.com/LynnDonovanAuthor, join her reading group on FB at Books by Author Lynn Donovan @ https://www.facebook.com/groups/BooksbyAuthorLynnDonovan/, her website LynnDonovanAuthor.com and Twitter @MLynnDonovan,

For more publications by Lynn Donovan go to: Amazon.com/author/ldonovan

Appreciation

Thank you to everybody in my life who has contributed in one way or another to the writing of this book. My husband, my children, my children-in-law, and my grandchildren. You all are my unconditional fans. My BETA reader and grammar guru who make me look gooder than I am. [Bad grammar intended.] My fellow author friends who chat with me daily to exchange ideas, encourage, maintain sanity, and keep me from being a total recluse/hermit.

Mostly I thank God for the talent he has given me. I hope to hear you say, "Well done, my good and faithful servant," when I cross the Jordan and run into your arms—Many, many years from now. :).

Newsletter and a Free Gift for You

Hey! Thank you for purchasing and reading this book. I'd like to give you a parting gift to show my appreciation. Sign up for my newsletter at lynndonovanauthor.com/newsletter. I will send you an e-copy of a collection of short stories I wrote purely for your entertainment. I will happily send you this e-copy for FREE, if you ask. I will also add you to my NEWSLETTER list and you will receive up-to-date information on new release before anyone else.

This book will **not** be sold anywhere, at any time, I am keeping it exclusively for you, my readers, and only if you ask for it.

Thank you again, and God Bless.

~Lynn Donovan

Printed in the USA
CPSIA information can be obtained
at www.ICGtesting.com
LVHW011745060624
782520LV00008B/171